No. 2
Whitehall
Court

No. 2
Whitehall
Court

ALAN JUDD

SIMON &
SCHUSTER

London · New York · Amsterdam/Antwerp · Sydney · Toronto · New Delhi

First published in Great Britain by Simon & Schuster UK Ltd, 2025

1 3 5 7 9 10 8 6 4 2

Simon & Schuster UK Ltd
1st Floor
222 Gray's Inn Road
London WC1X 8HB

Simon & Schuster Australia, Sydney
Simon & Schuster India, New Delhi

www.simonandschuster.co.uk
www.simonandschuster.com.au
www.simonandschuster.co.in

The authorised representative in the EEA is Simon & Schuster Netherlands BV,
Herculesplein 96, 3584 AA Utrecht, Netherlands. info@simonandschuster.nl

A CIP catalogue record for this book
is available from the British Library

Hardback ISBN: 978-1-3985-2059-2
eBook ISBN: 978-1-3985-2060-8
eAudio ISBN: 978-1-3985-2066-0

Typeset in Palatino by M Rules
Printed and Bound in the UK using 100% Renewable
Electricity at CPI Group (UK) Ltd

To the secretaries of MI6,
seldom publicly acknowledged.

CHAPTER ONE

In later life Emily Grey strove to recall every detail of that summer, the summer of 1914, the last summer, as she always thought of it. After that everything changed. It had been hot – though others, before and since, had been hotter. Fine too – though others, before and since, had been finer.

It was people that changed. People were different after 1914. Not just in manners, which became broader and looser, less respectful. Nor just the pace of life, which became faster and harder, more grabbing. What changed was how people saw themselves, how they were with each other, the allowances made for difference and distance. There was, in retrospect, an innocence about those long warm days leading up to August 4th, days of finely mowed lawns and ample blossom in which the sense of an ending, already somehow apparent, engendered premature nostalgia.

Especially if you were in love, as Emily had been, and especially if you were in Heidelberg with Hans, gentle Hans, a philosopher who wanted to be a poet and whose grey eyes,

1

long lashes and soft fair skin had melted her, temporarily robbing her of all ambition for herself. Their last afternoon in July was so vivid that the days and weeks before it paled in recollection. They had climbed up to the ruined castle above the town and were sitting on a bank below one of the crumbling towers, gazing in silence at the wooded slope below.

The day before he had shown her the letter from his father in Munich, urging him to enlist. Every day now there were recruiting parades in the town and bands playing. It was exciting and cheerful, many of his fellow students had already signed on. He had avoided it so far by claiming that his family's tradition was naval and his father would never forgive him if he joined the army. But the pressure grew, daily.

'You must go back to England,' he said, still gazing down at the treetops. It was not clear whether it was a statement or a question.

'And you must join the navy?'

'Only if you go back.'

'And if I don't?'

She sat with her hands clasped on her knees. He rested his hand on hers. 'We will marry and for a short time we shall be very happy. But then our life will be miserable.'

It was too obvious to need saying. He had already asked her to marry, formally, nervously, on bended knee as they walked in the dusk by the river. 'Of course, of course,' she had smilingly replied, amused that he could have been in any doubt. For the weeks that followed they inhabited a blissful present sustained by an imaginary – but essentially unimagined – future. They had no money, neither of their families knew, they had nowhere to live, no profession awaited him. Unable to afford a ring, he had paid a blacksmith to fashion a plain band from a silver spoon. Their engagement being secret, she had only ever worn it when they were alone. But she never lost it and, years later, would occasionally take it from the little black box she had found for it, smiling by then at the magical suspension of disbelief that that had kept them hovering above other realities until war came.

'If I go back will I be permitted to return when it's over?' she asked.

'They must do, if it's peace. Or I could come to England. We could marry there. If your parents will accept a German poet without poems.' He smiled.

'How long do you think the war will last?'

'Not long. It cannot be long before France surrenders.'

She smiled. 'I would surrender immediately.'

'I know.' He kissed her.

It was late evening before they parted. He walked her back to her hostel through streets thronged with student revellers, drunk on beer and the prospect of war. Their parting was truncated by the reappearance of one of Hans's friends, an engineer called Karl Krueger who had left the term before to join the Imperial German Navy. He was reeling from side to side of the cobbled street, arm-in-arm with half a dozen others, all singing lustily. He had returned to recruit for the navy, he breathlessly explained. Hans must join, everyone must join, Emily too even though she was English. Laughing and swaying, he kissed her hand, promising they would celebrate victory over France together in London. Her farewell to Hans, then embraced by Karl and another man, was reduced to a lingering look and a half-raised hand.

Back in her hostel she found a telegram from her father, folded into a sealed brown envelope. WAR IMMINENT, it said. RETURN IMMEDIATELY.

CHAPTER TWO

A year later Emily sat in a crowded lecture room in the Admiralty. It was a sultry London afternoon and the lecturer, a civil servant, was drawing yet another diagram on the blackboard. 'Wiring diagrams,' he called them, designed to display Admiralty hierarchies and the links between departments. The AIC – Admiralty Induction Course – comprised a mixture of civilians and naval personnel, with one army officer. All were being transferred or seconded to shore-based Admiralty posts and had to spend three days learning Admiralty structures and procedures. The unstated message was that the Admiralty differed from all other earthly organisations, necessarily and beneficially. There were right ways of doing things, wrong ways and Admiralty ways. The latter differed especially from the War Office which looked after the army and seemed to be regarded as no less a threat than the Imperial German Navy.

Emily again glanced around at her fellow students in the stuffy lecture room. Most were still copying the wiring diagram with their Admiralty-issue pencils. There were thirty-one, including her as the last-minute addition, one of only four women. She was also, so far as she knew, the only one from outside government. The three other women were dockyard secretaries who had been transferred to London, most of the men were naval officers who had been brought ashore, as they put it, and the civilians were civil servants from other government departments. The army officer and she were anomalies, he especially as he had a Germanic name – Hueffer – and looked to be in his forties, which was unusually old for an army lieutenant. Overweight and florid, he had fair hair, a soft sibilant voice and very blue eyes. Like others who had asked which department she was from, he had accepted her explanation that she had been a student at Cambridge – she did not mention going to Heidelberg afterwards – and because she had studied German, assumed that she was to be employed as an interpreter or translator.

In truth, she did not know what she would be doing. For months after returning from Germany she had lived with her parents either at Slivericks, their country house in Sussex, or at their town house in Barnes. They were months that felt like bereavement. She had had a single postcard from Hans – a picture of Heidelberg castle – posted a few days before war was declared. He was joining the navy as his father wished, but she could write to him at his parents' address 'as if she was just a friend'. He hoped he would be able to write to her when he reached somewhere abroad. Meanwhile, his love for her was undying. She had hesitated long over her reply, torn between wanting to express her love and not wanting to say too much, in view of his warning. Too long; war came and post to Germany was suspended.

Those months at home were difficult. She loved her parents but was reluctant to slip back into adolescent dependency, which they seemed only too happy to resume. It might have been different if her younger brother, George, had been at home, but he was still undergoing medical training in Bristol and was already talking of signing on. Her mother, sensing an unexpressed sadness, asked tentative questions to which Emily responded at first with affected nonchalance. She would have loved to talk about Hans but feared to open up. After a while she conceded she had had a particular friend in Germany and even mentioned his name, trying to make it sound as if he was just one among a group of friends. That was indeed how she had got to know him.

Her mother was not fooled. Emily had never before mentioned a particular male friend and seemed uncharacteristically listless and indifferent. It wasn't like her daughter to mope around the house, as she put it to her husband. A busy sort of woman herself, she assumed that busy-ness was what people needed, especially when they seemed inclined not to be busy. During weekends at Slivericks she organised teas and dinners for Sussex neighbours, invited ladies for lawn tennis and determinedly hunted down anyone with sons or daughters of Emily's generation. When they were in Barnes she organised a knitting and sewing group of ladies who made warm clothing to be sent to soldiers in Flanders or donated to homeless Belgian refugees in London. Emily permitted herself to be corralled into all this, floating along with apparent equanimity but without enthusiasm.

'I thought you would relish the chance to do practical war work,' her mother said one day, 'after all that studying at Cambridge. Something that makes a difference to people's lives. It does you good to feel you're making a contribution. Cheers you up.'

'I'd happily make a contribution,' said Emily. 'I'm sure I shall. I just have to work out what it should be.'

'You'd think there'd be great demand for German speakers now.'

'You would, yes. I'm sure there must be. I'll keep looking.' She left the room. Her mother had disapproved of her going to Cambridge, feeling that reading German was a waste of three years of a young girl's life that would have been better spent preparing for wifehood and motherhood. Discussions touching on Cambridge usually ended unsatisfactorily, if not with outright disagreement then with a lingering sense of suppressed resentment. Emily avoided them whenever she could.

It was her father who had encouraged her to continue her education and go to university. He nagged her to work hard at school, recounted his days as a Cambridge medical student before he had joined the navy as a ship's doctor, and over dinner would initiate discussions of world affairs or ideas he had read about in *The Times* at breakfast. 'Being a girl doesn't mean you can't widen your horizons,' he would say. 'The higher your arrow flies, the more chance it'll land somewhere worthwhile, somewhere you want to be. The money's there, we can afford it, so make the most of it.'

In fact, she needed little urging. She grew up with an increasing sense of a world above and beyond, a world she wanted to be part of. Her father's joy when her college accepted her was almost as gratifying as the acceptance itself. It had come as a shock when, on falling in love with Hans, she had felt she would give up everything to be with him. Part of the reason she drifted with apparent passivity through the months at home was her inability to decide whether she had lost something unique and wonderful, something that would never come again, or whether it had been an escape. It felt like both.

They were mostly in Barnes because her father, having left the navy, now practised in London. There, apart from more refugee and war work, her mother was anxious for her to pick up with her university friends. 'I know you were all that time Heidelberg but you can't have lost touch with everyone, surely?'

'I haven't, no. We write. I shall see them. Those that are not too busy.'

'There was that nice girl you used to talk about – what was her name? Laura? The one whose mother is the daughter of—'

'Laura is in Canada, visiting her brother. I'm in touch with lots of people, I'm not becoming a hermit.' She tried not to sound as exasperated as she felt. She was devoted to her mother, whose care for her and her brother was, she knew, unbounded. But the obverse of love without limit was smothering, not knowing when to stop showing it. 'I'm sure I shall soon be out and about more,' she said. 'I'm just waiting to hear back from one or two people.'

In fact, she had already arranged to meet Zara, her closest Cambridge friend, but had not yet told her parents. They had gotten to know Zara when she stayed a few days one summer at Slivericks and blamed her for turning Emily into a suffragette, which Emily felt she was not, quite. She argued that she was a suffragist, a supporter of women's suffrage who believed it should be achieved by parliamentary means, as the prime minister Mr Asquith seemed about to achieve until the war came. Zara, however, was a proud activist who had been arrested for chaining herself to railings in Whitehall, though she stopped short of throwing herself beneath horses or attacking people or buildings.

'I want to be able to vote, that's all. That's the big thing so far as I'm concerned,' she said, as if to excuse herself for not dying for the cause. 'Dead women don't vote.'

Emily had accompanied her on marches, more because she didn't want to disappoint her than because she believed marches would hasten the parliamentary process. She was very fond of Zara, her physical opposite. She was short, quick and vivid, with dark hair and almost black eyes inherited from her Armenian mother. 'You fizz like a match that's just been struck,' she once said to her. 'Only you're fizzing all the time.'

'And you're a sphinx,' said Zara. 'Watching and judging, always waiting to see. So self-controlled. No one ever knows what you're thinking.'

It wasn't only Zara's liveliness and energy that attracted Emily but her ready sympathy and loyalty; natural, spontaneous and enduring. They had met on their first day at Cambridge when Zara's father, a British diplomat, had delivered her to their hall. The visit to Sussex, however, had left Emily determined never again to mix friends and family. It had begun with an argument with her parents over dinner about women's rights in which Zara had tried hard to be restrained without compromising her beliefs. But the beliefs themselves were shocking enough for Emily's parents, with the result that discussion over the next three days involved an enervating avoidance of anything serious. Thereafter her father would refer jokingly to 'your revolutionary friend, the diplomat's undiplomatic daughter'. Her mother evidently found Zara too distressing to be mentioned.

Emily and Zara had arranged to meet in the Lyons teashop in Piccadilly, which Zara in her letter thought preferable to a hotel because it was 'more real'. When Emily told her mother they were meeting, she implied that it wasn't only with Zara but other friends as well. Her mother was plainly relieved that she was doing something on her own initiative again. 'But mind who you sit near on the train. There are some strange men about.'

'Mother, I travelled unaccompanied to Heidelberg and

back by train. I think I can manage Waterloo.' She was aware of sounding sharp again, so smiled to soften it. 'But I'll keep my wits about me.'

Zara wore a new red hat with matching gloves. 'Gift from my Ma," she said. 'Unexpected, unrequested, unwanted, to be honest. She was so fed up with my old green ones from Girton and now that I'm at home looking for a job she notices everything of course. So I'm on a campaign to age them as quickly as possible, wearing them all the time until they look like the others. How are you finding life back at home? Any jobs in prospect? Any men?' She laughed.

Emily didn't mention Hans. She wasn't ready to talk about him. Instead, they discussed the jobs problem. Zara wanted to do something that would help change society. She was attracted to journalism but there were so few openings for women and she didn't want to waste her time writing about fashion. 'Perhaps I should take up motor racing like that Dorothy Levitt woman who always seemed to be writing things or being written about. Before the war, anyway. We don't hear of her now, do we? The secret is to be famous for something, no matter what. Then you can do anything. What about you? Any chance of using your German? There should be now.'

'You'd think so but I haven't found anything yet. Socially at least, it seems to be regarded as a handicap, judging by my mother's set. Almost treasonous.' She didn't confess that she hadn't actually been looking. She knew she should, knew that she was becalmed, floating and listless, reluctant to awake from the dream of marriage to Hans or to acknowledge that he was now, so far as everyone else was concerned, the enemy. It would also be good to have money of her own rather than depend on the allowance from her father. He was generous to her and her brother George and didn't begrudge them a penny. But George was already on his way to earning while she merely drifted. If she could choose anything it would be to continue her studies, to go on learning. She liked learning but it didn't pay.

'Not to mention men,' said Zara, a smile in her dark eyes.

Emily smiled back. 'You've got one?'

'Yes – well, no, not ... but yes, you could say that, yes.' She laughed. 'A friend, put it that way. He's gorgeous, especially in his uniform. He's a sailor. Never thought I'd go for anyone military but ... well, you know. He's Irish, too. Lovely voice, warm and soft. Sean, he's called Sean. Only trouble is he's not one of us, not a suffragette. Yet, anyway. Give him time. I'm working on him.'

'Where did you meet?'

'In Golders Green at an Irish Home Rule meeting. I nearly didn't go, it's not my ... but I thought I ought to know more about it so I took a girlfriend along with me. Found out a bit more than I bargained for.' She laughed again.

Emily spent the following weekend at Slivericks with her mother. Her father was dining in London on the Friday and was not due down until the Saturday. The papers had been full of the inconclusive naval engagement in the North Sea near the Dogger Bank, from which it appeared that the

German flagship, *Blucher,* had been sunk. Her father arrived late on the Saturday morning, having dined the night before with her godfather, Admiral Hall.

'Seems we gave as good as we got at Dogger after all,' he said. 'Better, in fact, despite signal confusions. Beatty took a lot of casualties on *Lion* but the *Blucher* was sunk and lost many more. She had a complement of 847 and there were only 234 survivors. Reggie showed me the casualty list. He's going to try to get it into the papers if he can find a way of doing it without the Huns discovering how we got it.'

'How did we get it?' asked Emily. She winced inwardly whenever anyone referred to Germans as Huns but felt she couldn't object, given continuing stories about German atrocities in Belgium.

'I didn't ask and he wouldn't say, of course. Quite rightly, runs a tight ship, Reggie, always did. But he'll have got names and figures through whatever dark arts they practise in that Room 40 of his. If only we'd got our signalling right there'd have been many more. As it was, the rest of the fleet got away.'

On the Monday morning, when they were back in Barnes, she handed her father a note of half a dozen names before he left for the hospital. 'If you see Uncle Reggie again could you ask him to check whether any of these are on the German casualty list? They're all boys I knew in Heidelberg.'

Her father put on his glasses and glanced at the German names. 'Did they all join the navy, then?'

'One or two of them did, others might have. They were all

friends.' Aware of her mother looking at her, she hid her face in her teacup.

'You'd think most of them would have joined the army. Not exactly a seafaring city, Heidelberg.'

They remained in Barnes the following weekend. Her mother had invited neighbours for Sunday lunch and her father had arranged for a man from the Wolseley garage to come and do something to his car on the Saturday. The two men were bent beneath the bonnet, but as Emily and her mother passed through the garden on their way to the shops her father straightened and said, 'By the way, Emily, Reggie got back to me yesterday about your list of Huns. None of them listed as dead but one listed as missing presumed dead, or whatever the German phrase for it is. I made a note of the name, can't remember it now but his first name was Hans, I know that. He was the only Hans on the list.'

'Thank you.' For a moment Emily felt blank. She had turned away to join her mother when it came upon her, a sudden, choking spasm. She sobbed and gasped, her chest heaving. She had known it, she felt, known it for months. It was as if grief had been accumulating silently inside her in anticipation, and now that the wait was over it erupted, overwhelmingly. Her father, who had bent back to his engine, straightened as if electrocuted. The garage man looked embarrassed and continued working. Her mother stared open-mouthed, then came running.

Seated back at the dining room table, with water and strong tea provided by the cook, Nancy, who had discreetly withdrawn, and with a copious supply of handkerchiefs provided by her mother, she told them everything. They showed no surprise, nor even any concern that she had gotten engaged without telling them, clearly more worried about her present state. Gradually, attention, sympathy, talking, repetition and a bowl of Nancy's thin beef soup restored her to something approaching her usual self-possession. That afternoon, at her mother's urging, they went to the Army & Navy store in Victoria Street to choose curtain fabrics.

During the next few weeks she made herself busy, doing whatever she could find to do. She tried not to imagine Hans's death, whether by drowning or being blown apart by gunfire or burned alive by flaming oil on the sea, but no matter how busy she was, unwanted visions bubbled up in the cracks between tasks. She saw other friends from Cambridge and school, those who were not away or working. The war seemed to have made people so busy and many women were now working. She knew she should join them, that it was better to do something rather than trail after her mother doing charitable or voluntary works, useful though they were. She wanted to feel she was contributing to the national effort. All she could think of was teaching, but she disliked the prospect of going from school to college and back to school without something different in between.

Then one day her father said, 'I'm dining with Reggie again tonight, at his club. Would you like me to see if he can find a berth for you in the Admiralty?'

She was secretly reluctant to be helped by the man she

knew as Uncle Reggie, feeling he was partly responsible for Hans's death. He was, after all, an admiral and, unreasonable though she knew it to be, she couldn't help blaming him for being the bringer of bad news. But she nodded and shrugged. 'Well, yes, if he knows of anything I could usefully do.'

'Can't promise anything, of course. There'll be others around so I may not be able to say much. It's a reunion for some of us who served on *Fox*, bless her leaky old soul. But as he's an admiral now he ought to be able to pull a few strings.'

She was still up when he returned that night, obviously pleased. 'Reggie says you're to come aboard forthwith as some sort of general service civilian. No idea what that means but there's a course starting next week. He's fixing it. He says you should stand by for joining instructions by letter.'

The rattle of the tea trolley in the corridor aroused her fellow students. The speaker finished with the promise of a presentation on pay scales the next day. For the rest of the afternoon, after tea, they would work in their groups on a procurement exercise. There were six groups, Emily's comprising the army officer, Lieutenant Hueffer, a secretary from Chatham Dockyard called Marigold, a plump, bespectacled mathematician from Oxford called Edward, a naval officer, Lieutenant Commander Cooden, and Albert, a civilian architect recruited, he said, to 'do dockyards'. Cooden was already overseeing security at the port of Rosyth, home of the Grand Fleet, and Hueffer was being posted to join him. Although roughly of an age, around forty, they were not an obvious match; Hueffer, newly joined and much the junior, had a drawling, shambling, unmilitary, almost sleepy manner. He spoke as if he didn't always mean what he said, as if his words were in inverted commas, ironic and detached. His uniform was too tight in some places, too loose in others. Cooden was plump and balding, with a round moon of a face yet sharp-featured with a small nose and eyes and puckered lips. He was immaculately attired with mirror-like toecaps and had a prim, corrective manner, pouncing with relish on mistakes of fact or vocabulary. When Emily was introduced as the extra in their group he barked a mirthless laugh and called her the supernumerary, which he continued to do. He called Marigold, a quiet, conscientious girl who was to work for the Admiralty Board, the poppet. Only Edward and Emily did not know where they were to be posted.

Edward did not appear at all for the final day of the course and Emily was summoned away during the morning coffee break. She was standing talking to Cooden and Hueffer, and had just learned that Hueffer's father, a German married to an Englishwoman, had been music critic of *The Times* and that Hueffer himself was an author in civilian life who had only recently volunteered. An Admiralty messenger approached and handed her a note in a small brown envelope like the one that had contained her father's telegram summoning her home. She was to open it upon receipt, the messenger said. Inside was a folded white paper with two typed sentences instructing her to report forthwith to Admiral Hall, Room 40.

She was to bring the note with her and should not discuss it with anyone.

As she made her excuses and collected her handbag, coat, gloves and hat, Hueffer said, 'Not bad news, I hope?'

'No, thank goodness. I think it must be in connection with whatever job they want me to do.'

'And what's that?' asked Cooden. 'Who wants you?'

'No idea, I'm afraid. Just a room number.' She slipped away before he could ask which.

The messenger led her through a maze of corridors painted brown and cream. Room 40 turned out to be a set of rooms behind an unremarkable door in Old Admiralty Building. The messenger knocked and waited. It was answered by a tall woman with coiffured red hair, a long gown and a triple-looped pearl necklace. She was smoking a cigar.

'Miss Grey, presumably?' she asked in a carrying voice. 'He'll see you now. You've got two minutes.' She led the way through an anteroom into a large office filled with the clatter of typing from about a dozen women and three or four men, then along another corridor. She walked swiftly without waiting to see if Emily was keeping up, her gown billowing behind her and cigar smoke trailing. One of the typists put up her hand and started to ask a question, addressing her as Lady Hambro. 'Not now, Margaret,' she said, briskly. They passed several offices opening off the corridor until, at the end, was one freshly painted in the universal brown but with a skull and crossbones added in white. She gave a perfunctory knock and entered without waiting.

Emily's godfather, the Admiral Hall she knew as Uncle Reggie, sat writing at a desk. 'Not now, I'm busy,' he said, without looking up.

'Miss Grey. You sent for her. Two minutes, no more. Then you've got the Board.' Lady Hambro swept from the room.

Uncle Reggie looked up and smiled. 'Emily, good. How are you liking the AIC? Bored till your teeth drop out, I should think. Don't worry, I've got something for you. Bit of sport, if you're up for it. Sit down, let me just finish this.'

She sat and he resumed writing rapidly. She hadn't seen him since leaving Cambridge and was struck anew by how his hooked nose pointed down to his jutting chin. A *Punch* cartoonist would have them joining, she thought. He still had the occasional facial twitch that had fascinated her as a child.

He finished writing, blotted the page, placed it face down in his wooden in-tray, screwed the top back on his pen and stood. He was uniformed, which made him look decisive. Not that, from all that she had ever known of her godfather, he ever needed to look it.

'MI1c, sometimes known as MI6, is the Secret Service. Run by us and the War Office, reluctantly paid for by the Foreign Office. Cat's cradle of an organisation, typical of Whitehall. They're based in Whitehall Court and C – that's Cumming, you don't know him, do you? Mansfield Cumming, splendid fellow, most ingenious. Needs a German speaker with working knowledge of Danish for something he's doing with our help. You speak a bit of Danish, don't you – family on your

Ma's side? It's a one-off but there's a chance he might keep you on if you're any good. Fancy it?'

Emily nodded. 'Yes, please, anything. Only I don't know what the Secret Service is.'

'Don't worry about that, it's all good sport, you'll love it. Cut along and see them now, they're expecting you. Don't bother going back to the AIC. The goddess Hambro will tell you where to go.' He took his cap from the hatstand and stood holding it by the brim. 'One other thing. I understand from your parents that you had bad news a while ago. I was sorry to hear it but don't let it – the fact that he was German – worry you now that you're working for us. Nothing to be ashamed of. There are some very fine Germans, we all know that. But personal loss is still personal. Don't feel you have to hide it. They're used to all sorts over there. Pretty rum characters, some of them.' He grinned.

The door opened and Lady Hambro bellowed, 'Two minutes are up!' The admiral put on his cap and left the room, saying over his shoulder, 'Fair winds to your Ma and Pa.'

Lady Hambro held the door open, her cigar still smouldering in her other hand. 'Didn't mean to alarm you, Miss Grey,' she said in a gravelly voice, this time not so very far above normal. 'It's just that in a department like this with all sorts of funny people from all over the place you have to crack the whip a bit, even with the admiral. Herding cats, organising this lot.'

'What is it you do here?' asked Emily.

'Well, if your godfather hasn't told you, I'd better not. Ask

Commander Cumming, the man you're going to see next. He knows as much as anyone. Number two Whitehall Court, they should be expecting you. Go straight in. You're on their list.'

In one of the offices opening off the corridor she glimpsed the Oxford mathematician who had disappeared from the course.

CHAPTER THREE

It was only a few minutes' walk from the Admiralty to Whitehall Court, a modern mansion block facing the Thames. She had read that it comprised prestigious apartments as well as housing a hotel, the National Liberal Club and the West Indian Club. Mr Gladstone had lived there, she believed, as had the playwright, Mr George Bernard Shaw.

On Whitehall she had to pass the War Office main door which was guarded by two soldiers with rifles and bayonets. An officer with a bulky briefcase under his arm was paying off a hansom cab. They saluted him as he bounded up the steps. When she turned down towards the Embankment she saw that the hem of her coat was smudged with sooty smuts., probably from the train she had taken from Barnes that morning. It was bad enough that she had turned up to the AIC with her coat in such a state, mortifying to think that Lady Hambro was bound to have noticed. She paused by a gas lamp to try to brush them away.

As she straightened, she noticed that a man had stopped

some twenty yards behind her. He wore a dark raincoat with a brown bowler hat pulled down over his forehead. He took a newspaper and began reading it. That and his stillness caused her to notice him. Everyone else on the street was moving, apart from the horse guards opposite, although even their horses tossed their necks occasionally. This man, however, was as still as the gas lamp, seemingly engrossed in his paper and taking no interest in anything around him. Emily was used to being noticed, an unwanted but inevitable part of street life in London. Some men – invariably men – stared blatantly and sometimes she was whistled at from building sites. She was aware of women noticing her too, but they were usually more circumspect. She was now sufficiently used to it to notice when she wasn't noticed.

She continued down Horse Guards Parade and turned left into Whitehall Court, pausing before the steps up to number two to take a couple of deep breaths. The man with the newspaper was now walking slowly along the other side of the road, parallel with but behind her. He seemed in no hurry and carried his paper folded under his arm.

Relieved to be leaving the street, she mounted the steps and, finding neither bell nor knocker nor nameplate, pushed open the door into a spacious lobby with wide carpeted stairs and a lift of polished wood and brass. To the left was a desk manned by an elderly man wearing a uniform that looked like a policeman's but wasn't. His chest was beribboned with medals and he had in front of him a notebook and a telephone.

'Good morning,' she said. 'I've an appointment with Commander Cumming.'

'Miss Grey, that would be, would it?' He ticked a list in his notebook. 'Fifth floor, miss. 'Fraid the lift's not working today. Just as well you're earlier than expected. Take your time.'

Breathless after only three floors, she paused, not wanting to begin the interview gasping. She was nervous enough anyway, not having been interviewed since before she went to the university.

She had resumed her climb when she heard wheezing and grunting as if someone was struggling with a heavy piece of furniture. When she reached the next landing she saw a short, thickset man of middle age wearing a heavy dark blue three-piece suit. He was descending slowly, supporting himself with two stout walking sticks. Before taking each step he leant his shoulder and rump against the wall, placed both sticks on the next step down and carefully lowered one foot between them, then stepped down with the other.

He stopped when he saw her, smiling and breathing heavily 'Don't wait on me, madam. Come on up.' He pressed himself against the wall.

'No, please, you come down.' She stepped back onto the landing.

'Beauty before age.' He had a large head with thinning grey hair cut ruthlessly short and a nose almost as hooked as her godfather's. He was clean-shaven, his skin reddish and wrinkled, almost a farmer's face. His eyes were pale blue and his sprouting grey eyebrows had been allowed to run wild, unlike his head hair. He inclined his head. 'Come on, up you go.'

She squeezed past. He smelt of tobacco. It was different to the usual cigarette smell, richer, more exotic, a smell she associated with her godfather who smoked Turkish cigarettes called Balkan something.

'Hold hard,' he said, when she was past him.

She paused. From above he looked almost square, as if compressed on all sides by powerful forces until he could be compacted no further.

'Where are you going, if I may ask?'

'To the fifth floor. I've an appointment.'

'With?'

She hesitated. It was none of his business, surely. His expression at that moment was kindly, though it was easy to imagine it severe. 'With Commander Cumming.'

'Ah.' He nodded. 'You must be Blinker's Miss Grey.'

'I am Miss Grey, yes, but Blinker I don't—'

'Go on up. The office is manned. Tell them you've come about a special job. They'll look after you. Shan't be long.' He turned, placed his sticks on the next step and shuffled down.

Beyond the lift on each of the floors two polished doors opened off at angles, presumably to separate apartments. On the fifth floor, however, the stairs ended with a wall and a single door facing the stairs. Suspended beside it was a ship's bell engraved with? *HMS Modeste*, with a rope pull. Finding no alternative, she pulled it gingerly. There was a loud clang and after a few seconds the door slowly opened.

Inside was a large panelled office lit by tall windows over-looking the Embankment and the river. Two desks faced the door, a typist at each. To the left the next flight of carpeted stairs continued. On the wall to the right were portraits of the King and Queen. A third desk was before the windows, occupied by a man in the uniform of a naval sub-lieutenant. Emily couldn't remember ever having learned naval ranks; she had grown up knowing them.

The door appeared to have opened without human agency and was now closing slowly behind her. Both typists smiled. 'Don't worry, it's meant to do that,' said the nearer one, a fair-haired older woman, wearing glasses. 'We operate it from here by electricity. Come in, it'll close itself.'

Emily stepped in. The door closed with a click.

'One of C's beloved gadgets,' the woman continued, stand-ing to shake hands. 'You must be Miss Grey. I'm Dorothy, Miss May, this is Miriam, Miss Godson, and that's Frank, Sub-Lieutenant Stagg. You've just missed him, I'm afraid. C, I mean. He had an urgent summons to the War Office, left his apologies and said you were to wait until he gets back. In fact, I'm surprised you didn't see him getting out of the lift. He's only just gone.'

'The lift isn't working. I met someone on the stairs, a man on sticks.'

'That's him. Is it still not working? That's awful. He should insist the War Office comes to him. It's ridiculous, going down all those stairs with one leg. He will keep doing it but he shouldn't.'

'And up again,' called out the sub-lieutenant from his distant desk before the windows. 'He does it deliberately. Reckons the exercise is good for him.'

'Is C Commander Cumming? That's who I was told to ask for.'

'C does indeed stand for Commander Cumming. Could only have been him. He didn't introduce himself? That proves it.' They laughed.

Dorothy indicated a chair beside her desk. 'Do sit down. Would you like tea?'

'Tea would be very nice, thank you.'

Miriam, a dark-haired girl of about her own age, got up. 'I'll get it. Anyone else?' They all wanted tea. She went to the stairs and paused. 'Milk and sugar?'

'Yes, please.'

Miriam disappeared through a door at the top of the stairs. The sub-lieutenant came around his desk, proffering his hand. 'Frank. How d'you do?' He had light brown hair, freckles and a friendly, open expression. 'Blinker sent you over, then?'

'Blinker?'

'Hall, Blinker Hall, Admiral Hall. Room 40. So called because he ... you know ... does this.' He blinked several times and then winked exaggeratedly. 'Always has, apparently. He's famous for it.'

She had no idea her godfather was named after his facial tick. 'Yes, he did send me. He said I was to come here and see Commander Cumming who might have a job for me.'

'He didn't say what kind of job?'

'No. But on the stairs just now he – Commander Cumming – C – seemed to know who I was and said I was to say he had a special job for me. I've no idea what, though. I'm afraid I don't know what you do here. It's secret service – Admiral Hall – said.' She had almost said Uncle Reggie.

Dorothy laughed. 'It's certainly service. Anything from cleaning up after each other to climbing telegraph poles and doing things to wires to . . . well, anything else you can think of. And lots you can't. All jobs here are special so far as the Chief's concerned. What have you been doing?'

'I was at university.'

Frank stepped back in mock horror. 'Lord, not another intellectual. The Old Man keeps finding them. As fast as he finds them we send them over to Blinker in Room 40. That's where they need all the clever clogs. But Blinker sent you to us? Must be getting his own back.'

Emily was conscious of Dorothy's gaze, now unsmiling. 'Apparently he has no room at the moment. So my father said.' She wasn't sure she should have said that. 'My father knows him.'

'What did you study?'

'Classics, Greek and Latin. And German. I spent a year at a German university before the war.'

Frank held up his hands. 'Even worse, you'll show us all up, won't she, Dorothy? We're mostly monoglots here.'

Dorothy opened the Walker's Desk Diary she had closed

as Emily entered. 'There's a note about you in C's diary from a briefing by the admiral. It says you speak Danish too.'

'My mother is – was – Danish.'

'What does your father do?' asked Frank.

'A doctor, a naval doctor. Or was. He's in civilian practice now.'

Emily noticed now that all three had covered or turned over the papers on their desks so that she could not read them. Dorothy leafed slowly through the diary, keeping it on the other side of the typewriter. Emily glimpsed densely written pages in green ink. 'Yes – I see it's ... you were mentioned in C's meeting with the admiral last week. We were expecting you today as you know, but he hadn't told us why.'

Frank laughed. 'Are we surprised?'

'Not greatly.' Her manner was crisp. She read a few lines more, then closed the diary and looked up. 'You've had a recent sad loss, he says.' Her manner was still crisp. 'Sorry to hear it.'

'Thank you, yes. Like many others, I'm afraid.' She was reluctant to talk about, it but their respectful silence made her feel it would be churlish to say nothing more. 'My fiancé. Former fiancé. He was a – a naval officer.'

'Killed at sea?' asked Frank.

'At the Battle of Dogger Bank, yes.'

Frank nodded. 'Well, if it's any comfort – which it can't be, of course, not really – you're not alone here in that respect.'

'I'm sorry. Have you—?'

'Not me, no. Nor Dorothy. But a couple of people upstairs

have lost family, Miriam her brother. And the Old Man, of course. Lost his son very early on.'

Miriam came down the stairs with a tray, china clinking in the silence. Frank returned to his desk. Miriam handed them their teas. Emily thought she had got away with it until Frank asked, 'Which ship was he on?'

'He was . . . he was on the *Blucher*.'

Miriam paused in the act of passing Dorothy her tea. They all stared. 'You mean, as a prisoner?' asked Frank. 'Or—?'

'Not a prisoner, no. He was German. An officer of the German Navy.' She slipped easily into her explanation, having given it dozens of times to friends and relatives, but she still felt – and was sure she sounded – nervous and defensive. 'We met in Heidelberg where I was studying after Cambridge, improving my German. Before the war, of course. He was a fellow student, he was going to be a . . . a lawyer, probably – and we became engaged. Not formally, not quite – our parents hadn't met, but we were planning that for later in the summer. We didn't think there was really going to be war until I had a telegram from my father telling me to come home. I took the night train, leaving some of my things there because I assumed – somehow – that it would all be all right, that it wouldn't really happen and that I would be back. So did Hans. And then of course it did happen. I assumed we would write to each other but of course we couldn't. He sent one postcard before war was actually declared, saying he was going to join the navy and that he would not be able to write anymore. There wasn't time for me to reply and I heard nothing more until . . . until the *Blucher.'*

In the silence that followed she felt her lower lip tremble. She hoped it wasn't visible. Dorothy reached for the cup and saucer proffered by Miriam, saying, 'C noted that he was German. The admiral told him but said it should be of no account because so many people have German connections.' Her manner softened slightly.

'A near miss for you both,' said Frank. 'It would have been awkward if you had married. How did you hear he had been killed?'

'My . . . Admiral Hall told my father. He was listed as missing presumed dead on a German list. I don't know how Admiral Hall knew.'

No one offered an explanation. 'It might be best if you wait in the Chief's office,' Dorothy said. 'Leave us to get on with all our boring stuff here. You'll find bits and pieces to read in there.' She smiled. 'Stuff you're allowed to read, so don't worry about it. Miriam, would you—?'

Miriam led her through a door the other side of the stairs to another panelled office overlooking the river. 'Some of these War Office meetings go on and on but I'm sure he'll be as quick as he can now he knows you're here. Help yourself to his magazines. Though there's probably not much in them for you.'

The office smelt of Turkish tobacco. There were a dozen or so magazines on a low table set between two brown leather armchairs. The armchairs looked inviting but Emily felt awkward about making herself comfortable in someone else's office. She took the top three magazines and sat on the upright chair by the desk. The desk was leather-topped and had no papers on it, only a large glass ashtray marked GR, an ink bottle and blotter and three empty wooden trays marked In, Undecided and Good Riddance. The magazines were old copies of *Autocar* which had no interest for her apart from an article about the pre-war racing driver woman Zara had mentioned, another Dorothy, Dorothy Levitt. She was pictured climbing out of a car wearing overalls and a leather helmet. Emily took up more magazines, this time from the bottom of the pile.

The first was a 1905 copy of the *Fish Trades Gazette and Poultry Game and Rabbit Trades Chronicle*. A page corner was turned down to mark a long report on the provision of engines to sail-driven fishing boats. It was by Lieutenant Mansfield Cumming, Royal Navy, retired. The next magazine up was a 1903 copy of *Autocar* with an account of an accident in the Paris–Madrid race in which Lieutenant Cumming's Wolseley hit a wall. Emily read both, but all she could glean of the author was that he must be very persistent and had an enthusiasm for mechanical detail. She put them down and simply sat, her empty teacup on the desk beside her. Whatever the job was, there seemed little chance that her languages would be much use. Perhaps she should have learned shorthand and typing after all, as her mother had urged. There was plenty of work for women secretaries.

She started at the clanging of the ship's bell. There were

voices in the outer office. She thought of opening the door but that might seem presumptuous, as if it were her office. Anyway it might be another visitor. Then the door opened to reveal Miriam cradling papers and files in both arms, followed by the short, square figure of Commander Cumming with his two thick sticks. Emily stood.

'Be seated, my dear, be seated. Bad of me to keep a young lady waiting but the War Office is short on manners. Along with everything else. Yes please, tea, Miriam, thank you. And another cup for Miss Grey, yes?' Miriam stacked the papers in the In tray while the commander shuffled stiffly behind the desk. Emily, embarrassed, handed her empty cup to Miriam and had begun to thank her when the commander's voice cut across her. 'Shut the door, Miriam, and do be seated, Miss Grey, you make me feel uncomfortable.'

Emily sat. He pulled open a draw. 'Doesn't bother you if I smoke, does it? Good. Do you? No? You should. Settles the mind. Not that anything around here is ever settled for long.' He shook a cigarette from a Balkan Sobranie carton and lit it with an unusually large lighter which spurted flame. He sat back and exhaled. 'Did your godfather tell you anything about us, what we are, what we do? No? Nothing at all? Better start from the beginning, then. Open the window, if you wouldn't mind. Stops the girls complaining.'

She struggled with the sash window but eventually forced the bottom half open by about a foot. The inrush of air brought with it sounds of engines, hooves and carriage wheels from the Embankment below.

'Leave it there, that'll do. It's getting worse, that one. I'll get our carpenter to have a look at it.' He waited until she was seated. 'Now, we are' – he took another pull on his cigarette – 'the Secret Service. His Majesty's Secret Service. But we don't tell anyone. No one's supposed to know we exist apart from His Majesty and our Whitehall masters who use the secrets we produce for them. The War Office likes to call us MI1(c) which is their section dealing with spies. We often use that name because no one knows what it stands for and it sounds boring – section 1(c) of Military Intelligence. Its disadvantage is that it encourages the War Office to think they own us, which they don't, despite their best efforts. We also sometimes call ourselves MI6 – Military Intelligence Department 6, which provides interpreters for interviewing foreigners, refugees and so on. That's useful because people don't query it and it means we can poke our noses into pretty much anything. You speak German and Danish, I'm told?'

'And French, though not as well.'

'Most of the time, if anyone asks where you work, just say the War Office. If they ask which bit, say War Office Intelligence Department and you can't talk about it. They'll assume you spend your time mapping enemy positions and counting ships and guns and working out where they get cotton for their socks and all that sort of thing. All clear so far?'

'Yes, thank you.'

'No questions?'

'Well, I'm afraid I still don't … don't quite understand what the Secret Service does. Does it mean I have to wear a disguise and follow people and that sort of thing?'

'It can, we do a bit of that. Done it myself. Good sport, lots of fun.' He leant forward, elbows on the desk and hands clasped before him, the cigarette pointing at her. 'What we do,' he said with careful deliberation, 'is persuade people to betray other people.'

He was waiting for a reaction but she wasn't sure what to think about that, so simply nodded.

'We do it for King and country, to learn things the enemy doesn't want us to know. We lie, in other words. But we lie for truth, to discover the enemy's secrets. We then report to our masters so that they can counter whatever the enemy's doing. We call the people we deal with, the people who tell us things, agents. Some are rogues and scoundrels, some are honourable men – and women. Women play this game too.' He sat back, his pale eyes searching hers. 'If you think you wouldn't like this kind of work, or feel awkward about it, just say. Don't worry. There are plenty of other jobs you could do, some of them in this very building.'

It didn't sound very nice, was her first thought. Yet the people she'd met so far seemed nice enough. Or at least normal. Also, she'd be doing something, however small, to contribute to the war effort. She couldn't fight in the normal way but this was, perhaps, a different way of fighting. And it didn't sound as if it involved doing anything that might have harmed Hans, had he lived.

She nodded again. 'No, I ... I'd be happy – honoured – to help if I can. Though I'm not sure what I could—'

'Don't worry, there's a job already lined up for you. You've come at just the right time. Like Miriam with our tea.'

Miriam unloaded her tray onto the desk and poured the teas without making eye contact with Emily. This time there was a plate of ginger biscuits. 'Lieutenant Nisbet is here, sir,' she said. 'Shall I send him in?'

The commander held up two stubby fingers. 'Two minutes. I'll give you a shout.' He waited until Miriam had closed the door before pushing the biscuits across to Emily.

'No, thank you. I had a rather large breakfast.'

'Sure? I'd have thought your father and godfather would have impressed a bit of naval lore upon you: eat when you can, sleep when you can because you never know when you'll next do either.' He helped himself to two biscuits. 'Blinker – Admiral Hall – told me about your fiancé. I was sorry to hear it. Doesn't matter that he was German, makes no difference. He wasn't our enemy when you got engaged. I hope you'll find people here understanding. They should be, we deal with Germans, men and women. You must tell me if they do. It was a different world, before the war. Different country, almost. Dogger Bank, wasn't it, where he was killed?'

'Listed as missing presumed dead, yes.'

'On the *Blucher*?' He nodded. 'They stay with you, losses like that. You must let them, don't fight them. Try to absorb them through your skin, so that they become part of your-self. No good trying to wash them off or pretend they didn't happen. Live with them rather than despite them. Let him continue to be part of you. That way you both go on.'

'Yes, I ... I try to do that.' She paused. 'I understand you too have suffered loss? Sir.' She added 'sir' because she had heard Miriam do it.

'Indeed. Our son, Alastair. Very early on, in the first months. In an accident. I was with him.' He turned towards the door and shouted, 'Ready now!'

It was a shipboard shout, so loud and unexpected that Emily almost spilt her tea. The door opened and Miriam ushered in a young man. He was dark-haired, thin-faced and pale, with a neat dark moustache. He wore a thick dark blue suit that looked too warm for the time of year. The Chief waved his cigarette hand. 'Emily, this is Lieutenant Nigel Nisbet, Royal Marines. Nisbet – Miss Grey.'

'How d'you do, Miss Grey.' They shook hands. 'Good morning, sir.'

'Lieutenant Nisbet will be your guide and mentor – no, not mentor, your companion and facilitator – in this little business I want you to do for us,' said the commander. 'Draw up a chair, Nisbet.' He turned to Emily. 'He's also only recently come aboard. Not as recently as you, of course – what is it, Nisbet, two months? Thereabouts?'

'Three and a half, sir. All very enjoyable and worthwhile.'

'Afraid you'll find a lot of marines around here.' The commander grinned at Emily. 'A surfeit, a veritable surfeit. The Admiralty recruited too many, you see, so they keep farming them out to anyone who'll take the buggers. Excuse my French. Not so many as before the war, though. We take walking wounded from the army now too. No shortage of them, either, I'm afraid.'

Lieutenant Nisbet's laugh was abrupt, almost a bark.

The commander took a buff file from his In tray. 'Now, I'm going to tell you both a story, spin you a yarn. A good one, but true. Before I do you must promise me – on your honour, before God and on pain of death – that you will never, ever breathe a word of it to anyone with whom you are not authorised to discuss it.'

The lieutenant's expression had something of the concentrated solemnity of a spaniel expecting a biscuit. 'Absolutely, sir.'

Emily nodded. 'I promise.'

'If you do.' The commander opened one of his desk drawers and took out a black Webley & Scott revolver, laying it on the desk with a clunk. 'If you do I – personally – will shoot you dead. Understood?'

Emily was used to guns. Her father still had his service revolver and in their Sussex garden at Slivericks they had shooting competitions at targets staked into the bank behind the tennis court. Despite the commander's dramatic warning, she thought she glimpsed something – a wryness, a hint of mischief or complicity – in his eye. She resisted the temptation to smile.

Lieutenant Nisbet, however, was prompt and, if anything, yet more solemn. 'Absolutely, sir. Understood.'

The commander put the revolver away and took another

39

cigarette. He offered one to Lieutenant Nisbet, who accepted with profuse thanks which went unacknowledged. He then opened the file and read in silence. Emily sipped her tea, the lieutenant smoked. Eventually the commander looked up.

'This story began in November 1914 when the man we call TR/16, or the Dane, walked in to the British Legation in The Hague and asked to be put in touch with someone in our line of business. He said he had information about the German Navy which would be of great use to us. This is not uncommon. Since well before hostilities tricksters, vagabonds and ne'er-do-wells have walked into official premises all over Europe with promises of wonderful secrets which they are prepared to sell for wonderfully large sums of money, invariably demanding a substantial payment in advance as evidence of our good faith. Nine times out of ten, if we put money in their hands, they vanish. And good riddance too. I dealt with a number myself in the early days, before the war.' He chuckled. 'There was one who claimed to know the chief German agent in London whom he said we could identify because he had four rows of teeth. Another said he commanded an army in Mexico and had a poison tie-pin with which he could kill at ten paces. Another had drawings of what he claimed was a new German gun but which turned out to be a design we had originated ourselves and abandoned in the last century. And so on and so on. We call them walk-ins, these people.

'But someone has to listen to them because one time out of ten they might have something, or know someone who has something. An early example was a French lady I met, a lady of a certain age, but ... but a respectable well-dressed lady of the middling sort, not unprepossessing.' He broke off, smiling and nodding to himself. 'This lady knew no secrets herself but she had a sister with a German lover, an army officer who told her things – "for love", she said – which she and her sister were prepared to tell us, for money. And so they did until war came, when we passed her over to our French allies. Most of what they told us was of no interest but there were specks of gold dust among the dross. So you have to listen, you see.'

'Follow up everything,' said the lieutenant. 'In case you miss something.'

'But without leaving your judgement in port.' The commander paused again and leafed through the file. 'By great good luck the legation official who saw TR/16 that morning was a sensible sort of chap who got on well with Tinsley, our head of station in Rotterdam.'

'Heads of station have nothing to do with trains,' interjected the lieutenant, turning to Emily. 'It means whoever is in charge of our office in a particular place.'

The commander glanced at him but said nothing. 'He took TR/16's details, including examples of information he could get, and asked him to come back at the same time the next day. He did, and this time Tinsley was there to meet him. They swiftly agreed terms and set up future contact arrangements. The station already had these to hand because they had, to their credit, been preparing for just such an eventuality. TR/16 is a German naval engineer – a proper ship engineer, capable of designing, building and renovating ships, not an artificer or mechanic. He has full access to German dockyards and can travel where he pleases. He came over to us because he was court-martialled and downgraded in rank following a fight in a bar with a drunken officer. It turned out that the officer was a distant relative of the Kaiser, God bless his soul. By striking the officer – hitting him back, by his account – TR/16 was deemed to have insulted the Kaiser. The other officer went unpunished. TR/16 is understandably resentful and that, Tinsley reckons, is his prime motive for spying for us. His reports are invaluable, graded 100 per cent by your godfather, Miss Grey, and regularly read by the First Sea Lord himself. He is able to tell us which ships are in which dockyard, their state of readiness, the thickness of their armour, the quality of their guns, and which ships the Germans are building. He has less knowledge of what they're up to and where they're going when they put to sea but does pick up some useful hearsay. We pay him well.'

'Comes down to money in the end. Always does,' Lieutenant Nisbet said to Emily.

'Does not, always. Does not.'

'Sorry, sir. Apologies.'

The Chief maintained a basilisk stare at the lieutenant for a few moments before resuming. 'Meetings with TR/16 are monthly and in Holland. He is allowed to leave Germany in order to survey neutral ports and report on any allied shipping or activity. He is normally seen by Tinsley but if Tinsley can't make it his capable number two, Henry Landau, sees him. But such is the sensitivity of the case that Landau, capable though he is, does not know TR/16's real name. Neither shall you. Landau knows him either by his number or by his informal code-name, the Dane. He has no access to this file and thinks TR/16 is a Dane who is a naturalised German. TR/16 speaks Danish because he went to school in Copenhagen when his father was a trader there. They converse in German, though TR/16 has some English, too. The next meeting is at the beginning of next month, in Rotterdam. Tinsley can't do it because he'll still be recovering from his appendix operation. Landau did the last meeting and will do this. I want you to go to Rotterdam and see TR/16 with him.'

Nisbet nodded. 'Very good, sir.'

'Miss Grey, that is. Your role, Nisbet, is chaperone. You are to accompany her to The Netherlands, make sure everything works – transport and so on – and generally to be on hand and useful.'

'Very good, sir.'

The Chief stubbed out his cigarette and turned to Emily. 'Your godfather tells me that according to your father your Danish is fluent.'

'Conversational Danish, yes. My mother usually spoke to me in Danish at home when I was a child. My father and I have always spoken in English. But I don't know Denmark at all well, having been only a few times, visiting her family.'

'How good is your German?'

'My literary German is – good.' She had reason to claim it was very good but didn't like to. 'My colloquial German is also ... well, pretty good. Or was. I studied there for a year before the war but it's now some time since I used it.'

'There is a particular subject on which I want you to question TR/16 very carefully – something arising from what he reported at his last meeting. He reported as faithfully and accurately as he could, I'm sure, but Landau's German, though good enough, is far from perfect. I want you to interrogate TR/16 on the precise wording of what he reported, in German, Danish and English in order to remove any possible ambiguities. What he said, you see, was something that could have serious consequences for our entire naval deployment and the safety of the fleet. But it depends on interpretation and before we report it we must be absolutely sure we've got it right. Complete accuracy may be impossible, of course, because TR/16 is reporting what he heard someone else say and they may have got it slightly wrong, or been ambiguous. Not to mention his own interpretation. But we have to be able to assure our masters that our report is as accurate as can be. Are you happy to do this?'

'Very happy, yes. As long as someone can help me understand what it's about. '

'Don't worry, you'll be fully briefed on the subject. Frank Stagg will see to that. He'll also sort out your pay. We do pay people here, now and again.' He grinned. 'But it's essential you maintain the fiction with Landau that TR/16 is really Danish. Agents' identities must never be known beyond the very few people who really need to know them. We're very keen on that here. Are we not, Nisbet?'

'Very keen, sir.'

'Take Miss Grey upstairs and show her round. Find a desk for her and ask Frank to organise some introductory briefings. If this goes well there'll be plenty more work of this sort for you, Miss Grey.' He smiled and lit another cigarette with another great flare from his lighter.

Lieutenant Nisbet was on his feet before Emily moved. She was still savouring the mention of money, having never done any paid work. The prospect felt like an affirmation, acceptance into the fully adult world. Hitherto any money she possessed had come from her father. Now she would be able to pay her own way without feeling beholden.

Mistaking the reason for her stillness, the commander held up his lighter. It looked heavy, filling the palm of his hand. 'Didn't mean to alarm you. Made it myself from dockyard materials. Bit over-enthusiastic, needs refinement. Next model I should be able to make smaller. Almost a weapon of war, this one, eh?' He chuckled. 'Tell Frank and the girls you two are to be called the Special Projects team. They'll know what you're up to but no one else will. If you're asked, just say you can't say.'

Lieutenant Nisbet took it on himself to explain to Frank Stagg, ignoring Dorothy and Miriam who were busy typing and, Emily felt, determinedly showing no curiosity. She went to hand her empty cup and saucer to Miriam. 'Thank you for the tea, it was most welcome.'

45

'Just leave it with the tray.'

'I'll wash up if you tell me where.'

Miriam paused her typing. 'Oh, that's kind of you but ... no – don't worry, I'll show you another time. You've probably enough to be going on with at the moment.'

Lieutenant Nisbet walked over to Dorothy's desk. 'The Chief wants you to arrange pay for Miss Grey.'

Dorothy stopped and looked up. 'Oh, does he? Did he say how much and from when?' She did not look at Emily.

'I'm sure it's not urgent,' said Emily.

'I'll ask him,' called Frank. 'I've got other stuff to sort out with him.' He stood, gathering papers from his desk. 'Nisbet, could you take Miss Grey upstairs and show her round, introduce her, that sort of thing? I'll discuss training requirements with the Old Man.'

Dorothy resumed typing.

'This way, madam, if you please,' said Lieutenant Nisbet, half-bowing and waving theatrically towards the stairs. 'First time I've ever been upstairs with a university lady.' He laughed.

Emily was embarrassed and irritated but anxious not to appear churlish. She could sense hostility emanating from Dorothy's bowed head, whether because she had been to university and was accorded special treatment or because of Hans or because she was young and new, she had no idea. She strode swiftly to the stairs without acknowledging Nisbet's quip.

CHAPTER FOUR

At home in Barnes that evening, Emily had to give an account of her day to her parents, although unsure how much she should say. Not mentioning TR/16 was obvious, but she felt she had to tell them she was going abroad for a few days and could hardly not say where, if only to reassure them she was not being sent to the Western Front.

'Not on your own, surely?' said her mother. 'With a party? Or a chaperone?'

'A chaperone. I won't be travelling alone.'

'Who is she?'

'It's a he, an officer of the Royal Marines.' Her mother's concern was unabated. 'It's all right, he's quite old,' she lied.

'But why Holland? You'd think with your languages they'd send you to Denmark.'

'As I said, it's a conference about war trade and neutral countries and ... and that sort of thing. Perhaps there'll be Danes there. I don't know anything about it, only that it's happening and they want me to go.'

'Unusual for someone so newly joined to be sent abroad to an international conference, surely?' said her father.

'Apparently it is, yes. I'm told I should feel honoured.' She disliked lying to her parents in this way. She had never done it so systematically. Of her relationship with Hans she had merely withheld information, which didn't feel like lying. But Frank Stagg had advised it when she saw him on her way out after Nigel Nisbet had showed her round upstairs.

'Do as the Chief told you,' Frank had said. 'Telling people you work for the War Office is usually enough to forestall enquiry. If they persist you say War Office Intelligence Department and tell them you can't say any more about it. With family it's a bit different, though. They'll know you're in Intelligence anyway – having the Director of Naval Intelligence as your godfather and sponsor is a bit of a giveaway. They're bound to ask about it because they'll be so pleased to have found you a job. So with them you just make sure you never say what you're really doing, just make it sound boring and routine – helping out at conferences, checking old files, lists of aliens and foreign travellers, that sort of thing. Isn't that what you do, Dorothy?'

Dorothy looked up. 'It's easy for me. I tell everyone I spend my days typing. Which is what I do. No one asks what I type.' She went back to her Underwood, again without acknowledging Emily.

It was after six. Miriam had gone, her desk was clear and the Chief's door was closed. Emily supposed she was free to go but no one had said, and she had lingered by Frank's desk in order not to have to leave with Lieutenant Nisbet, who had said he was going to meet some fellows and wondered if she'd like to join them. She had pretended she was expected at home soon.

The tour upstairs would have been more interesting without Nigel Nisbet's interruptions. When people told her what they did he interrupted with his own interpretation, as if he thought her too young to understand. They toured two more floors of offices, including a workshop with drills and lathes, a room in which three men were barely visible among electric gadgets, and a small chemical laboratory. The offices spread laterally across other staircases, each with its own exit, and there were references to further rooms which included a canteen and the Chief's apartment – known as his cabin – somewhere in the roof. In the chemical lab a short, bald man in a brown coat demonstrated two methods of secret writing and techniques for rendering it legible. In the next room another man in a brown coat had a kettle and showed her how to steam open letters, lifting the flaps by rolling a pencil. In the workshop another brown coat showed how telephone calls could be intercepted by adding wiring in an exchange switchboard. She also learned that door hinges squeaked more at night and was shown a suitcase with a concealed compartment built into the base.

'But you might prefer to use one of these,' the man said, reaching beneath his bench for a smart black ladies' handbag.

'Looks like one of them from Harrods, doesn't it? Well, it was, that's where it come from, but it was got for us on loan as it were by the Universal Fixer. Mr Browning, that is. Freddie. Friend of the Chief's. Knows everyone, he does, gets hold of anything. Have you met him yet? You will. See if you can see what we done with this bag.'

He gave it to her. It felt and smelt brand new, an evening bag with the slimmest of straps and obviously expensive. She searched it thoroughly but found nothing. 'Put your finger underneath the catch on the inside,' he said. 'Pull it towards you. Bit stiff. Try again. There.'

The catch slid back and one side of the bag came apart. 'Wouldn't fit the crown jewels,' said the man with a smile, 'but you could get the Kaiser's moustache in there. Meant for documents, really. You know, young lady like you has dinner in the Savoy, sits next to some diplomat with a secret telegram in his pocket, you pick his pocket, slip it in there and Bob's your uncle.' He laughed.

In other offices people – nearly all men – were working on papers. They described what they were doing in general terms or by subject area – war trade, looking after the Scandinavian stations, Italian liaison, Russian liaison, French liaison, blockade breaking, recruiting neutrals who could travel to Germany, countering German propaganda in the US, Middle Eastern matters – but none mentioned anything specific. One of the empty offices had a Universal Fixer sign hung on it, with a smaller one beneath saying Out Fixing.

'Freddie Browning,' said Nigel. 'The man they mentioned in the workshop. Ran the War Trade Intelligence Department before he came here – you know, those huts where the lake used to be in St James's Park. Often wonder what happened to the ducks. Knows everyone. Got us a cook from the army who used to be at the Savoy so we have a proper canteen now, no more buns at your desk for lunch. Gets our supplies from the Savoy too. Maybe that's where the ducks went – we've eaten them. The Chief says he has no need for the usual channels since Freddie came, except in the mornings.' He began to laugh and stopped. 'Sorry, that was a bit vulgar. The Chief – he's quite broad sometimes.'

'Don't worry, I was brought up among sailors.'

His relish for explanation made him slightly less irritating, in so far as it was based on a desire to be helpful, but it was counterbalanced by his equal relish for implying to others that she was his new assistant, 'here to learn the ropes'. He several times mentioned her having been to university, describing her as the 'intellectual ornament' of the team and feigning a mocking respect for academic achievement, which she suspected was born of envy. Having explained the operational benefit of good relations with allied secret services, he would add, 'Of course, with your brain power you've probably worked all this out for yourself. You don't need clod-hopping marines like me to tell you.'

Emily was accustomed to such raillery from her father's former naval colleagues, until they realised that it was he who had urged her to try for the university. But the resentment she sensed from Dorothy and to a lesser extent Miriam was more troubling. She would have hoped for more support from her own sex. Lingering in the outer office before going home that evening after Nigel had at last gone and Frank had been summoned by a bellow from the Chief, she walked over Dorothy's desk. 'I'm sorry if I've come at an awkward time. You all seem to have enough to be going on with without having to look after an ignorant newcomer.'

Dorothy stopped typing and looked up. She was older than Emily had first thought, with more crow's feet around the eyes and less of the youthful freshness and elasticity of Miriam's complexion. Or her own, she reflected. Maybe that was a factor.

'Don't worry, not your fault. It's always pretty non-stop here. The Chief never stops working.'

'I rather had that impression. What time do you normally finish? When he finishes?'

'He never does, that's the point. We all have to go home some time, of course, but he doesn't. This is his home and his office. Even when he was ... when he had his foot amputated, he was sending messages from his hospital bed in France. I had to go over and take dictation once he had a room of his own.' She managed a smile. 'Are you ... where do you live?'

'In Barnes, with my parents. My father is a doctor there and my mother's people live nearby. But our main house – our real home – is in Sussex. And you? Do you have to travel far?'

'No, not far.' She looked at some notes beside the typewriter, handwritten in the Chief's green ink. 'Your – your mission – I'm just doing a letter about it to the Rotterdam station. You know you're going to have to leave pretty smartly? Maybe as early as tomorrow night?'

'No, I didn't know that. No one said anything about when.'

'The next meeting with TR/16 is on Thursday. Presumably they want you there for that.'

'Oh dear, I'd better get packing, then.'

'You better had.' Her tone was brisk again. She looked up again. 'Battersea. I live in Battersea. See you tomorrow.' She smiled.

It was only when she left Whitehall Court that Emily remembered the man with the raincoat and brown bowler. There was no sign of him, thankfully. Given that she was now part of the Secret Service, she assumed she would have to report anything suspicious. If it was suspicious, rather than coincidence. But at the station she glimpsed a brown bowler among the crowd coming in from the other entrance. She could see no more because of the crush around her and did not see it again. She was worried. She thought she would feel sick if someone was following her. But London was full brown bowlers, she told herself.

It was indeed the following night when they travelled. Packing for Emily was not straightforward. 'You'll probably be there for one night but prepare for two," Frank had said. No one could give her a weather report for Rotterdam, nor any indication of what the crossing might be like. 'You never know with the North Sea,' Frank said. 'Could be anything at any time. Hope for the best, plan for the worst. As in war.' And then of course her mother wanted to be helpful but her guiding principle – packing what might conceivably be useful rather than what could not be done without – would have meant travelling with her father's naval trunk that took two men to move. After many vacillations and some irritation on her mother's part, Emily chose the leather Gladstone bag with which she had returned from Germany, a long travelling coat to go over her full-length dress, a pair of short boots, two pairs of gloves, spare skirt and blouse, her mother's smart maroon hat – a conciliatory gesture – and – defiantly – her own favourite which she privately named Flopsy, an old brown hat which she had worn almost daily in Cambridge and Heidelberg.

Lieutenant Nisbet, she found when they met at Victoria Station, adhered to her mother's packing principle. She was twenty minutes early, which gave her time to count no fewer than five men in brown bowler hats. Happily, none appeared to be interested in following her, all rushing to or from trains. With seven minutes to go there was still no sign of Lieutenant Nisbet. She left the concourse and walked out to the cab rank where, struggling with a large suitcase, a bulging hold-all, a smaller bag and an umbrella, he was engaged in an altercation with the cab-man. She waited until it was settled, apparently to mutual dissatisfaction.

'We're going to miss our train,' she said. 'There's less than five minutes to go and there's a queue at the booking office. We won't have time to get our tickets.'

Lieutenant Nisbet waved at a porter with a barrow, who ignored him. 'Don't need them. We have War Office railway passes. Frank got them.' He waved and shouted at another porter.

Despite the clement weather he wore a three-piece suit of mottled green tweed with a matching hat and feather. At least Flopsy was disposable, Emily thought, unlike Nisbet's, which looked new. On their last trip to Denmark her mother had worn the predecessor of the smart maroon one, bought specially. It had disappeared into the North Sea the moment she came up on deck.

The train was crowded and the goodwill of their first-class compartment was tested by the manoeuvring of Nigel's heavy case and holdall up onto the rack. The porter stood waiting for his tip as whistles blew. Nigel struggled to find change in his trouser pocket and eventually, with obvious reluctance, handed over a ten shilling note. Two other travellers, plump young clergymen, had to sit with their cases on their laps, as did Emily.

There was no question of conversation in front of the others, although there was plenty Emily wanted to ask about: where were they to stay, where would they meet Henry Landau, which ferry line went from Channel ports up to Rotterdam – an unusual route – and what was the threat from German submarines. Her father had mentioned that out of her mother's hearing. She mentally rehearsed the questions she was to ask

TR/16. These were not to be discussed with Nigel, Frank Stagg had told her, because he was not to attend the meeting. TR/16 might be alarmed by a committee of interlocutors. The passing Kent countryside basked in late afternoon sun. She mentally rehearsed her questions in three of her four languages. Nigel sat with his hands folded on top of his bag. The carriage was stuffy and his head was nodding before they left London.

The two plump clergymen got off at Ashford. At Folkestone the other passengers hurried off before they could be expected to help Nigel retrieve his suitcase and holdall from the rack. Emily felt obliged to offer.

'Fine, thanks, don't worry. But if you could take this small one I'll join you on the platform.'

By the time he emerged, breathless and flustered, the last of the other passengers were leaving the platform for the wooden walkway to the ferry. A porter ambled along, shoving the doors closed with one hand. Nigel asked for a trolley. 'Gone, sir, all gone,' he said with unconcealed satisfaction. 'Passengers take them to the ferry, leave them at the gangplank. Pick one up if you want.' He moved on.

'Hadn't we better hurry?' said Emily.

Nigel looked along the platform, shading his eyes as if scanning the horizon. 'Don't worry, I think we'll make it.'

'I'll take your small bag.'

'No, no, you've got your own. I can manage them all.'

'It's all right, I'm balanced. Equal weight in each hand.'

Twice they had to stop for him to change hands. 'What have you got in them?' she asked.

'What have I got? In them, you mean?' He put them down again. 'Well, you know, stuff. Sort of stuff a chap needs. Might need. It's different for women, I know.'

'Is it?'

'Things that might come in handy. Have to be prepared for anything in this business. You'll learn that soon enough. And we're at war, don't forget. The Netherlands may be neutral but there are plenty of Boche in and out of the country all the time, up to all sorts of mischief. Have to be on our guard. May need disguises, that sort of thing. Not to mention protection.'

'Protection?'

'Against the Boche. In case they get ideas. If they knew what we're about they'd have no compunction about kidnapping us, none at all. Sort of thing they do. So I've packed my revolver and plenty of ammo. That all weighs a bit.'

'You've got a gun?'

'Yes. Well, you never know, do you? The Old Man charged me with your protection, remember. Bit awkward if I go back and tell him you'd been hoicked over the border. I'd be back on regimental duties in no time.'

She thought of the brown bowler again. 'Is that very likely?'

'Not really, no. But you never know.' He picked up his luggage again. 'On we go. Onwards and upwards.'

The ferry loomed high above the harbour wall. People crawled up the gangplanks like overburdened ants, but Nigel turned towards the other side of the wall where stone steps with no handrails led down to the water. Tied up below was a smart launch flying the Red Ensign.

'Aren't we going on the ferry?' asked Emily.

'Special dispensation. Courtesy of the navy. The Chief knows which ropes to pull. *HMS Vixen*, one of the new destroyers. Out there, look.'

Beyond the harbour wall, riding the swell, was a sleek grey warship.

'Just for us?'

'Wouldn't surprise me. But probably has other tasks as well.' Panting again, he put his suitcase down, then his holdall on top of it. 'Don't know how we're going to manage these. Will you be all right on those steps? I mean ... you know ... wearing a dress?'

'You're not suggesting I take it off?' She smiled. The remark seemed to embarrass him. 'Don't worry, I spent my childhood clambering in and out of boats and ships.'

While they were talking, two sailors skipped nimbly up the steps from the launch below. 'We'll take your bags, sir, ma'am. Bring them down after you.'

There was little breeze and Emily managed the descent without embarrassment. They left the harbour at speed, bouncing across waves that had looked like mere ripples from above. She took off her hat, but Nigel's left him at the third bounce. It was caught by the helmsman with a loud 'Howzat, sir?' Nigel got up to take it from him and sat heavily as the boat rocked.

'Are you ... are you a bit of a sailor, then?' He had to raise his voice. 'Not seasick?'

'Not usually, no. Are you?'

'Not bad, not bad.' He stared ahead, gripping the rail.

Boarding the destroyer involved climbing a ladder lowered over the ship's side. Fortunately the breeze dropped enough for Emily's dress not to billow uncontrollably, but Lieutenant Nisbet was less fortunate. The launch dipped into a trough as he reached for the ladder and his outstretched right foot caught the crest of the next wave. However, their luggage, about which he was more concerned than with his wet foot, followed them up on the shoulders of the launch's crew, who made it look easy. On deck they were greeted by a young midshipman, who saluted and addressed himself deferentially to Nigel. 'I'll show you to your cabin, sir, and then take you along to the wardroom. Take your bag, ma'am?'

He led them through hatches, along narrow steel passages lined with pipes and studded with rivets, up and down steps and past silent sailors who made way without appearing to notice them. Progress was slow. Emily had taken Nisbet's smallest bag while Nisbet struggled with his others, his wet foot squelching. Most of the ships on which she had visited her father were cruisers or battleships, self-contained towns. The *Vixen* was a cramped, crowded village by comparison, with far more packed into it than looked possible from without. Eventually the midshipman halted outside a narrow curtained doorway. Inside were two wooden bunks, two shallow cupboards, a small washbasin with a tiny shelf and just enough room for one person to stand or wash at a time.

Emily's unease, which had begun as soon as she realised they were to board a warship, was confirmed.

'Just the one cabin?' she said to the young mid.

The boy looked embarrassed. He turned to Nigel. 'We were told berths for two, sir. We thought two men. We didn't know there was a lady. Sorry, sir.'

'Don't worry, we'll sort something out,' said Nigel. 'We'll just dump our kit here and then we'll see about it.' He looked at Emily. 'Always possible to sort something out on ship.'

His luggage was stowed on the lower bunk, Emily's on the upper. There wasn't room for them both to be out of their bunks at the same time.

'Heads are here, ma'am,' said the midshipman, pointing to an even narrower entrance opposite their cabin. 'Toilets, that is.' He looked embarrassed as he pulled aside the curtain for her benefit, showing a small metal toilet bowl with no seat. Emily thanked him. 'First Lieutenant says I'm to take you along to the wardroom. He will meet you there.'

The ship was now under way. The hum from the engines deepened, there was a tilt to starboard and a slight wallowing.

The First Lieutenant joined them in the wardroom with two junior officers. He was sharp-featured and busy, like a terrier that has scented something, and spoke with naval briskness. 'Blowing up a bit but shouldn't be too bad, not enough to delay us. Treat for us to have a lady on board. Captain will be down shortly. Have you sailed before, ma'am?'

'Only to Denmark a few times and some short trips with my father when he was in the navy.'

'Naval family, eh? That'll help you find your sea legs.' He looked to Nigel. 'Everything shipshape with the cabin?'

'Yes, thank you, sir. I just wondered whether ... is there possibly another empty one?'

'Of course, you're in the same one. We expected two chaps. Typical of the Admiralty not to mention ladies. Just told us one VIP and a spare marine.' He laughed and turned back to Emily. 'No empty cabins, I'm afraid, we're over-complement as it is. But fear not, marines are resourceful types. I'm sure Lieutenant Nisbet here will find somewhere to bunk down, won't you, Nisbet? Now, if you'll excuse me, I'm due back on the bridge.'

The captain was a round-faced man with receding brown hair and small white ears compressed against his head as if clamped. He and two junior officers dined with them, while various other officers came and went for no obvious reason other than, Emily suspected, to have a look at her. Conversation was mainly about the war and the lack of variety in rations. The weather worsened and the troughs and swells deepened. Nigel ate little and was mostly silent. The captain assured them there was nothing like a storm in prospect. 'Just the North Sea, querulous as usual. You'll taste a bit of spray if you go up on deck but nothing to worry about and don't be alarmed when we start zig-zagging. In case of submarines. Unlikely to see any but if we do you'll know all about it. So will they.' He gave an estimated time of arrival and warned that they might have to heave to outside Rotterdam harbour pending clearance to enter. 'Neutral port, you see, so warships need special permission to enter, which is given only for approved reasons. We're there delivering diplomatic bags. So-called bags. Lots of heavy boxes our embassy in The Hague seems to require and can't trust to ferries. Expect you know all about that?' He raised his eyebrows at Emily.

Emily, knowing nothing about it, smiled. The captain nodded and winked. 'Thought so. Mum's the word, eh?'

Nigel excused himself, looking pale. After dinner Emily thought she would go up on deck, returning first to their cabin for her hat and coat. The mirror above the washbasin was so small she had to duck and weave to re-pin her hair. Nigel's luggage was still on the lower bunk but there was no sign of him. Reckoning that any way up had to lead eventually to the deck, she climbed several ladders and steps, directed by grinning sailors about her own age or younger, until feeling her way through an unlit hatch to a narrow wet gangway on deck. Spray broke over the railings, there were no stars or moon and not even much sea to be seen, just a great swelling of darkness studded with white streaks of foam. Above and behind loomed the bridge. She stood with her back against the steel structure, appreciating the freshness after the fug below.

'Is that you, Miss Grey?' Nigel's voice came faintly from the darkness to her right. He was crouching a few yards away, hard to see until he eased himself upright, leaning against the wet steel. 'Was going to come to find you but thought I'd take a break out here. Better out here than below. Below makes me feel queasy.'

'It's always worse below deck. I think everyone feels that.'

'Don't you?'

'Yes, but I can tolerate it up to a point. You get used to it. D'you often suffer from seasickness?'

'Not often, no. Well, I haven't sailed much, to be honest. My training was interrupted. Couldn't finish it – I had to ... look, I was going to say something.'

He paused. She feared he might be about to be sick. 'Would you be better off over by the railing?'

'No, I'm all right, thanks. All right.' There was another pause.

'You haven't found another cabin?' she asked. 'I mean, obviously, we can manage if we have to. So long as we agree who gets changed first, that sort of thing.' She almost smiled at the thought of what her mother would say, but then had another thought, which she didn't like to dwell on. 'Unless you think you're more likely to be sick down there?'

'No, no, don't worry, I'll find somewhere. Always somewhere on a ship, one thing I did learn at sea. No, it was just that ... the First Lieutenant and the other officers, even the Captain – important they don't know what we're doing.'

'Yes. There's no reason they should, is there?'

'No, but important we don't let on.'

'Of course.'

'Mustn't tell them anything.'

'Of course not.'

'That's all right, then.' He nodded to himself. 'Sorry, think I'm—'

He lurched over to the railing, vomiting. Fortunately, she was upwind. Her first reaction was relief that he had got rid of it here than in the cabin; her second that he was best left to himself while she took the opportunity to undress alone. 'I'll go and change while you're sorting yourself out,' she said, and ducked back through the hatch without waiting for a response.

Her night was undisturbed. The hum and roll of the ship and the narrowness of the bunk did nothing to delay sleep. At some point she heard voices beyond the curtain, but knew no more until daylight filtered around the edges of the cover of the tiny porthole above her. The ship had lost way but was still rolling. She peered over the edge of her bunk. Nigel's luggage was still there, unopened. There was no Nigel.

The heads were unoccupied and no one passed the curtain while she was in there. After hurriedly dressing and washing in the confined space, and arranging her hair before the inadequate mirror, she made her way back to the deck gangway where she and Nigel had talked the night before. She half-expected to find him still crouching there, wet and shivering, but there was only a huge herring gull on the railing. Its pitiless button eyes held hers before it spread its wings and was suddenly, silently and effortlessly, fifty feet above her. For a moment she imagined it having breakfasted on Lieutenant Nigel Nisbet, Royal Marines.

They were off Rotterdam's huge harbour, forested with distant cranes. The sea was surly and the weak sun struggled against scudding clouds. A merchantman flying the Dutch flag passed across their bow. She made her way back to the wardroom where she found Nigel standing with his tie untied and his tweed jacket over his arm. 'I feared you'd been eaten,' she said cheerfully. 'There was the grand-daddy of all gulls on deck.' There was no answering smile. She felt both grateful and guilty for having had the cabin to herself. 'You didn't spend the night on deck, did you – I hope?'

'No, no, snug as a bug in a rug down here.'

'Here?' The wardroom had a table and chairs, all bolted to the floor, but no bunks or couches.

'There.' He pointed to the floor space the other side of the table.

'You should have come to the cabin. At least there's a bunk.' She could say it now, and almost mean it.

He rubbed the stubble on his cheek. 'Didn't want to wake you. Floor was fine. Used to it. I'll cut down there now if you don't mind. Get shaved and so on.'

She regretted her flippancy. 'That was thoughtful of you, very kind. Thank you, Nigel.'

There were sounds and smells of breakfast and presently a steward emerged from the galley with teapot, cups and saucers. 'Cap'n'll be down soon, ma'am,' he said.

In fact it was the First Officer who appeared, as spruce and brisk as before. 'There's a Hun about to leave harbour. We'll be cleared to enter as soon as she's gone. They won't entertain us both at once, you see. She's only a minesweeper but we'll get a chance to have a close look at her and try to work out what she's been up to.'

Emily was finishing her toast when bells rang and orders were shouted. The First Officer and another who had joined them left in mid-sentence. Soon after the thrum of the engine deepened and ship heaved to port as she got under way again. The steward was hurriedly clearing away breakfast when Nigel reappeared, shaved and looking a little less jaded. 'Ah, breakfast. Think I could manage that now.'

'Breakfast finished, sir. About to dock.'

Henry Landau met them on the quayside. He was short, stocky and energetic, in his late twenties, Emily reckoned, with ginger hair, freckles, a thin moustache and green eyes that were never still. His handshake was brief and hard, his speech rapid, his accent South African.

'Good trip? No Hun trouble? Good, good. Thought I'd better use my diplomatic passport to meet down here, make sure you have no nonsense with immigration. We'll have to wait in the customs shed while they unload the diplomatic bags. Then we escort them to the legation. Unless that's them?' He nodded at Nigel's suitcase, hold-all and bag. 'Joking, don't worry. Thought you were only here two nights?'

'That's the plan,' said Nigel. 'But I – we – thought we'd better be prepared. You never know, do you?'

'Guess not. Follow me.'

The cavernous customs shed was crowded with motor vehicles, bits of machinery, wooden crates and, in one corner, stacks of hand luggage. Uniformed customs officials came and went, others in civilian clothes wandered about with clipboards and lists, occasionally coalescing like minnows and then dispersing at the approach of a traveller or uniformed official.

'Our stuff should be first off,' said Henry Landau. 'Wait here.'

He left them by a stand of black Humber bicycles, balanced precariously against each other. A unformed official approached and asked Nigel a question. Nigel looked to Emily.

'I'm afraid I don't speak Dutch,' she said. The official repeated his question, pointing at Nigel's suitcase and holding out his other hand.

'D'you think he wants money?' Nigel said.

'Probably papers, papers to show what's in your baggage.'

'I haven't any.'

Emily turned to the official. 'Sprechen sie Deutsch?'

'Ja.'

'What is your question?' she continued in German.

The official wanted to know what was in Nigel's large suitcase and where were the papers for it.

'There are no papers. It is personal luggage. We are part of the British diplomatic ... diplomatic bag.' She doubted that diplomatically protected deliveries were called a bag in German, but the man understood her sufficiently to ask for their diplomatic passports and papers. 'We don't have any. We are with someone from the British Legation who is ... who is over there somewhere – and he is looking after us.'

By this time two more officials had joined, anticipating a feeding frenzy. The first official pointed again at the suitcase. 'He must open it.'

Henry Landau was not in sight. Emily translated for Nigel. 'Do I have to?' he asked.

'Well, I suppose we could just stand here and argue until Mr Landau gets back.'

'It's not so much what's in there, it's the principle of the thing.'

'Then wait for him. I'll tell them he has the key, if you like.'

Everyone looked at Nigel. He shrugged, knelt, undid the two leather straps, felt in his trouser pocket for the key, unlocked the case, opened it and stood.

The suitcase was crammed full. The top item was a small pistol in a brown leather shoulder holster with a spare magazine and two boxes of ammunition. It nestled on a red silk dressing gown and matching pyjamas. Packed beneath were silk shirts and formal evening wear, with more below that Emily couldn't see. There was a volley of remarks in Dutch from all three officials. The first knelt and pushed the pistol aside, feeling beneath the dressing gown. He looked up at Emily.

'Where is this silk from?' he asked in German. 'Is there more underneath? Is he bringing it here to sell? He must unpack it all.'

Emily translated. 'They don't seem at all interested in your gun,' she added.

'Of course not. There's a war on. They must know that,

they're not fools. They're just after my silks. They want to confiscate them.'

'Are there many more silk items, then?'

'A few. Some. Yes. And some other stuff. In case we're ... you know ... invited to diplomatic functions or balls. Best be prepared for anything.' He looked anxious and his moustache twitched. 'But they're not for sale. They're just what I like to wear. Sometimes.'

The official held up a black silk shirt and said something to the others, who laughed.

At that moment Henry Landau bustled back with a sheaf of papers. 'What's going on?'

Emily explained. Henry spoke to the customs officials in rapid Dutch, haranguing them. One responded, pointing at Nigel's pile of silks. Henry looked at the silks, glanced at Nigel and responded with another torrent of Dutch. Then he turned to Nigel. 'Close it and lock it and follow me. You should never have opened it. They had no right.' He gestured to Emily. 'After you, Miss Grey.'

He soon overtook her and led them out of the customs shed onto the quayside where a small Ford lorry was parked, its engine on tick-over. Behind it were four or five wooden crates guarded by two British sailors with rifles. Two more sailors were loading crates into the lorry.

'Not our usual diplomatic bag,' said Henry, lowering his voice. 'Comms kit, newfangled communications stuff. We're testing it for deployment with agents in the field. Bit on the heavy side, from the look of it. Just as well that Hun ship left. They'd love to have had a decko at this little lot. Mind you, they've probably got spies here watching us at this very moment, secretly photographing from one of those windows. Lot of that sort of thing goes on here. Or they'll get someone to draw pictures, calculate the measurements and weight and add two and two to make a hundred and seven, with any luck. It's the Old Man, you see, loves new kit. Did you see him before you came out? How is he? How's his new leg?'

He clearly assumed she was as familiar with the Service as he was. 'He seems to manage very well. The day I joined he went all the way down the stairs by himself when the lift broke down. Extraordinary with a wooden leg. How did he—?'

'Cork, it's cork. Experimental one. More new kit, you see. Can't resist it. Hang on here a moment.' He walked briskly to a car parked beyond the lorry.

Nigel and she waited. Neither spoke. She had been schooling herself to resist the urge to fill silences ever since noticing that her mother could never resist it. It must come over as a weakness, she felt. But it was difficult. Nigel lit a cigarette and stood looking out across the harbour, unembarrassed by conversational silence. To any watching spies, she thought, we must look like a married couple who have had a row. Eventually, despite herself, she said, 'Have you been to Rotterdam before?'

'Not Rotterdam, no.'

'Amsterdam?'

'No.'

'The Hague?'

'No.'

'Nowhere in The Netherlands?'

'No.'

'Where have you been, then?'

He took the cigarette from his mouth, seemed about to speak, looked down at his highly polished shoes, then at her. 'Well, it's a bit difficult to explain. My training was interrupted so I never got very far. Never finished it, actually, still haven't. First it was a knee problem, then it was a kind of ... a kind of illness. Just came upon me. When I got better I was sent to Whitehall Court, instead of back to training. The Old Man said he'd take me on. So here I am.'

'Nisbet, hop in the lorry with the driver. My driver here will go in the back with the kit. That way we'll have two guarding it. Mustn't have fewer. Miss Grey will come with me in the car. Chop chop everyone.' Henry Landau clapped his hands. He was now with a small man wearing a dark suit and an oversized cap. He turned to the sailors. 'You men, make sure there's room in the back for this officer's luggage. And get a move on. We don't want to hang around here. Miss Grey, follow me. Your bag, please.'

The car was a Wolseley, like the Chief's. The journey from the quayside and through the extensive docklands was punctuated by jerky acceleration and braking, with frequent grating of gears. 'Keep an eye on the lorry behind us, will you?' Landau shouted. 'Mustn't get too far ahead.'

The docks eventually yielded to busy streets lined by tall, narrow shops and houses, all brick built. The traffic was a mixture of motor cars and horse-drawn carriages but with fewer buses and more cyclists than in London. Landau seemed to have an aversion to the kerb, driving almost down the middle of the road.

'A Wolseley!' he bellowed, pointing at the floor of the car. 'This is. The Old Man's choice. Insists on them. Used to race them before the war.' He swerved round an oncoming cyclist who shook his fist. 'Have you often been in cars?'

'Yes. My father has a Humber.'

'Don't suppose he's let you drive it, has he?'

'He has, yes. Before the war he had a Vauxhall as well. For racing, hill climbs, that sort of thing.' She didn't want to sound as if she was trying to impress. Yet it was the kind of thing that did impress men, so why not, she thought. 'I did a few of those too.'

Henry Landau swivelled towards her. 'You raced?'

'Only three or four times. Look out!' He swerved to miss a horse and cart emerging from a side road. When he had regained control, and after several attempts at double-declutching, he had the grace to smile. 'Perhaps you should be driving rather than me. Haven't done much, to be honest. One day I'll get a car myself and learn properly.'

She liked him for that. She smiled back. 'But we're getting there, aren't we? If I could just . . . my father was always saying this to me – when you double-declutch you need make sure the clutch is fully disengaged before you rev.'

'Good point, thanks. I keep getting the timing wrong.' He concentrated on driving for a few seconds. 'Your oppo – your assistant – Nisbet, that marine fellow. Queer cove. What's he here for?'

'For looking after me, I believe. The Chief said I had to have a chaperone to make sure everything works. I'm new, you see.'

'I'm not letting him loose on TR/16. Probably try to flog him some of those silk shirts. That's his game, is it, black-marketeering? Surprised the Old Man puts up with it.'

'I don't get the impression he sells them. I think he wears them. He's quite particular in how he dresses.'

'Maybe he has silk underwear too. We get all sorts in this business.' He guffawed.

The British Consulate General was stone rather than brick built, solid and four-square. There was a walled courtyard at the rear with high iron gates, opened by a uniformed marine.

'Don't mind if I don't introduce you both, do you?' said Henry as they watched the gates close behind the lorry. 'Saves inventing explanations. People are used to comings and goings in our office. They think we're tracking German imports and exports, blockade-running, that sort of thing. Consul General knows you're here but that's all. I've booked you into a nearby hotel, one we normally use. What's going on over there? Wait here.'

A single crate had been unloaded from the lorry. The driver, Henry's driver and three other men from within the consulate were crowded around the lowered tailgate. Nigel Nisbet was sitting on the ground. Henry Landau strode over, had a short energetic conversation, then strode back.

'They dropped the crate on his knee. Nisbet's. Says he can't stand. I've told him to get it strapped up and join us for the briefing. Or have it cut it off. Meanwhile, coffee. Better coffee here than any you'll find in London.'

CHAPTER FIVE

The coffee in Henry's top floor office was stronger than any Emily was used to. He made it himself on a gas stove planted incongruously on the landing at the top of the stairs, with a shallow stone sink with brass taps beneath the window behind. A locked door at the foot of the flight of stairs prevented access from below. His office opened off the landing.

'What a lovely view,' she said. 'All those rooftops.'

'It's the boss's. I grab it when he's away. Mine's across the landing, shared with everyone else plus with the safes and all the comms stuff. No room to swing a cat.'

Nigel joined them after a slow climb up the stairs. He sat with his right leg raised on an office chair and cushion. 'Not so bad when I don't put any weight on it.'

"Have it cut off like the Old Man and you could be the next Chief,' said Henry. 'Now, to business. TR/16. What do you know about him?'

Emily said she'd read the file in London. Nigel said he hadn't, adding, 'I suppose there are papers here I can read?'

'If you want. More than there are in London. We don't copy everything, though London think we do. Not that you need to read it since you won't be meeting him.'

' I won't? If Miss Grey is I should. To make sure she ... you know ... everything's all right. She's never met an agent before.'

'But you don't speak Danish, do you? Or German? No point in seeing him, then. He knows I'm just the stand-in for the boss, he's not expecting anyone else and we don't want him to feel he's in front of a jury. Also, we keep reassuring him that very few people apart from the Chief know about him, so it wouldn't look good. He knows I don't even know his real name, for example. It's not in the file but in a secret annex to which only the boss has access. Quite rightly, no need for me to know. All I know is he's Danish and a marine engineer. That's all I need to know, the boss says. Good enough for me, good enough for you, isn't it?'

'But my brief is to look after Miss Grey. The Chief himself—'

'I fancy Miss Grey can look after herself. Speaks the languages, drives racing cars and all that. Who knows what else?' He grinned at Emily.

Emily was a little embarrassed for Nigel but relieved he wasn't to be there. 'The Chief did say it should just be me and Mr Landau,' she said. 'It's only for the one meeting and it won't be long, I imagine.'

'Tell you what you can do, which would be very useful,' said Henry. 'Mount counter-surveillance. Check that no one follows TR/16 to the meeting. Or from it. So long as he doesn't spot you. He's very particular about his own security. You'll have to walk on two legs, though. Stand out a bit otherwise.' He turned to Emily. 'Meetings are in a safe house owned by a shipping company which owes us a few favours. Before every meeting we have a safety signal procedure which involves the boss or me sitting in the window of a particular bar at a particular time while TR/16 walks past. If he sees one of us, he knows it's safe to go ahead. One of the station – one of us from here, usually the clerk – watches him approach to check that he's not being followed. But you can do that this time, Nisbet, so long as you're up to it. If he is followed – which has never happened – you signal to the boss or me in the bar window and we remove ourselves pronto. When TR/16 sees that neither of us is there, the meeting is scrubbed and we try again an hour earlier a day later.

'TR/16 can scrub the meeting himself if he suspects he's being followed by simply not appearing or by walking the other way along the street. This time, of course, he doesn't know he's going to meet Miss Grey. I don't want to spring it on him – he's usually a bit on edge, even in neutral Holland, knows the Hun are as busy here as we are. So I propose Miss Grey joins us at the house twenty minutes after he arrives, giving me time to explain what you want and why.' He turned to Nigel. 'Problem is, where are we going to put you, Lieutenant Hopalong, so that you can spot any followers and scoot past the bar in time for me to disappear if he's being followed? How're you going to do that on one leg, eh?'

'I can use Miss Grey,' said Nigel. 'She's still got two good legs. She can scoot along and tell you.'

'But we need to know what he looks like,' said Emily.

'That's easy. Looks like an artist. You know, one of those arty types.'

'You mean he carries an easel?'

'Wears a wide black felt hat and brown corduroys and one of those shapeless jackets French peasants wear and carries a sketch pad. Only when he's here, that is, or on leave in Germany. Rest of the time he's in naval uniform. He really is a bit of an artist, you see. Bird-watcher, paints birds and landscapes. Very useful from our point of view because he can draw ships and ports from memory, aeroplanes too. The Admiralty say his drawings are very accurate, so the boss tells me. They don't know who he is, of course, or how we get them.'

'Wouldn't photographs be better?' asked Emily.

'Attract attention around ports and aerodromes. People are wary of cameras.'

At 9.45 the next morning Emily and Nigel sat outside a café in a narrow cobbled street leading off a square near the dock area. The bar where Henry Landau waited, which TR/16 was to walk past at 10.00, was farther up and round the corner. TR/16 was to enter the street after crossing the square so that any followers would have to close up rapidly in order to see where in the street he went. Nigel's knee was improved that morning but he walked with a limp. Emily was to act as his runner – if they saw that TR/16 was followed she was to slip round the corner and walk past the bar in time for Henry Landau to remove himself.

'Unlikely he'll be followed,' said Henry. 'No indications that his Hun masters suspect him. Quite the contrary, he's been reinstated, got his rank back. And the man who got him into trouble, distant cousin of the Kaiser, has been posted.'

Nigel lit a cigarette, his second since they'd finished their coffees. 'Find I smoke more when I'm on operations. You don't, I daresay? Don't smoke at all?'

'Rarely. Anyway, I've never been on an operation before. I suppose smoking calms the nerves, does it? Is that why soldiers smoke so much?'

'It's not nerves with me, not really. You get used to ops. No, for me it passes the time, that's all. Apart from the fact that I like it.' He contemplated the cigarette, holding it upright between his thumb and forefinger. 'But you mustn't worry about feeling nervous, mustn't let it get to you. You'll calm down when you're used to it.'

From Nigel's account of his career Emily doubted that he was any more familiar with what he called ops than she was. Nor did she feel she needed to calm down. She was enjoying watching the street and it was novel to think she was being paid for it.

Nigel fingered his moustache. 'Funny thing about doing something secret and getting away with it is that it gives one a bit of a ... a bit of a lift, a thrill. I daresay you'll find that when you're used to it and your nerves are steadier.'

She felt her nerves were quite steady enough but there wasn't time to display pique. 'I think that might be him.'

A slim man, his face largely obscured by a black hat, turned into the street from the square. He wore a faded blue jacket and brown corduroys and carried what looked like a sketch pad. He walked purposefully. Nigel turned in his chair. 'Where?'

'On the other side of the road, coming this way. Just passing the chemist's.' He looked slightly familiar but she couldn't place him. 'It must be him, surely.'

Nigel stared openly. 'Could be, yes.'

'Better not stare. He might notice and think we're Germans following him.'

'No.' He spoke under his breath as if to himself, but continued staring. 'Two naval officers, look, following him. Huns by their uniforms. Can't be coincidence. You'd better scoot up past the bar so Landau can see you and call it off.'

'But ... but they wouldn't be following him in uniform, would they?' It was true, there were two uniformed men, talking to each other as they walked and seemingly in no hurry. 'They'd want to disguise themselves, wouldn't they.'

'Double bluff. It's been known. You'd better get moving.'

'Look, they've gone into the chemist's. They're probably shopping.'

'I think you should go. We should call it off. It's too risky.'

She recalled the Chief's briefing. Nigel was not in charge of her; he was to escort her and help with arrangements. TR/16, assuming it was him, was closer now, walking briskly. If she delayed longer he would be level with them and it would be too late for her to get ahead and warn Henry Landau. But she still wasn't convinced. 'Let's see what they do.'

'Do it myself if it weren't for my rotten leg.' His petulance reminded her of her younger brother.

The two officers emerged from the chemist's and turned left, away from TR/16 and back towards the square. 'There,' she said, trying not to sound as triumphant as she felt. 'They're not following him. They're going away.'

'Could be another double bluff.'

'What do two double bluffs add up to? Could be no bluff at all, couldn't it? Like double negatives.'

'All very well for you, coming out with this university stuff. This man's life could be at stake.'

'I know that, I know that very well.' She knew she sounded petulant herself now but didn't mind. 'I really don't think there's anything to worry about. We haven't noticed anything at all suspicious, have we? Apart from the two officers and they've gone.'

'Even so.' He lit another cigarette. TR/16 was level with them. The brim of his hat was low and he appeared to be looking straight ahead. 'Too late now anyway.' Nigel proffered his cigarette packet. 'Sure you won't? Try one. Senior Service. Settles the nerves.'

She almost retorted that it wasn't her nerves that needed settling but felt that might be seen as evidence of what it sought to deny. Anyway, perhaps he'd intended the cigarette as a peace offering. She hadn't yet seen any Dutch women smoking in public. 'Not just now, thanks. Another time, if I may.'

Twenty minutes later she knocked on the door of the red-brick terrace house two streets away. It was not a wealthy area but the houses were in good order with clean white doorsteps and window ledges. The front windows of all were uncurtained and the rooms within furnished for display, with polished sideboards showing off china wear, armchairs with pumped-up cushions and tables with cloths as thick and heavy as carpets. Most sported a vase of flowers and every room looked spotless and unlived-in. As she walked the length of the street, she at first tried to peep discreetly at each window, as she would have in London, but by the time she reached number 55 she realised they were intended for display and so stared without embarrassment. Number 55 was like all the others except that the table in the window, carpeted in rich orange, red and black squares, had instead of flowers a model of a Dutch sailing barge, painted blue and white. There was no carpet on the polished floor.

The door was answered by Henry Landau. 'Welcome,' he said in German, louder than necessary. 'Enter, please.' He shepherded her down the narrow hall and past the stairs to a back room. There, seated at another table covered by a thick green cloth, was a young, fair man, no taller than Henry but more slightly built. His sketch pad was on the table before him and his black hat hung on the back of his chair. He wore gold-rimmed spectacles, which made him look studious, but there was no doubt that he was Hans's naval friend, Karl Krueger. There was no doubt, either, that he recognised Emily. Consternation froze his features for a moment, but when he stood to shake hands he smiled with apparent confidence.

'No names no pack drill,' said Henry in English. 'We don't use names here, do we?' His attempt to render the army phrase into colloquial German resembled the slow foundering of a ship on rocks, until he gave up and they all laughed.

It gave time for Emily to recover herself. She was sure she, too, had betrayed surprise and shock, but Henry was too intent on his tangled translation to notice. She held out her hand. 'I am pleased to meet you,' she said in German.

'And I you,' said Karl Krueger, bowing his head and clicking his heels.

She had last seen him with his arm around Hans, drunkenly urging him to join the navy. They both sat.

Henry turned to Emily. 'I've already explained that you've come all the way from London to discuss with our friend in his native Danish the exact meaning of a phrase in his last report. I will make coffees while you two talk.'

He disappeared into the kitchen at the back before Emily could protest that she didn't want more coffee. 'Thank you for agreeing to see me,' she said in Danish. 'My Danish may not be up to date but I hope it is sufficient for our purposes.'

'You are fluent. I am less so, as you perhaps you can tell. But it is enough for Henry to think I am Danish. He told me someone was coming from London. He didn't tell me it would be a lady. Still less that it would be you.'

'He wouldn't know we had any connection.'

'It is better he does not?'

'Probably, yes.' She paused. 'You heard about Hans?'

'Hans? No ... is he—?'

'He was killed. Well, missing presumed dead is the phrase. On the *Blucher.*'

He bowed his head again. 'I did not know he was on the *Blucher.* I am sorry. He was ... he was a good man. Yes, a good man.' He nodded several times. 'I am sorry for you, too, Emily.'

Then why are you doing what you are doing? she wanted to ask. *What do you think Hans would think?* For a few seconds her image of Hans was so vivid that she almost felt he was sitting at the table with them, listening, watching, questions and puzzlement in his quiet grey eyes. And what would he say to her, to what she was doing?

TR/16 dissolved her reverie. 'Henry still believes I am Danish. Is that correct?'

'Yes. It is for your security. Henry is completely trustworthy but our policy is for the names of people who help us to be known to as few as possible. But in London it is known that you are German.' She suspected she sounded more assured than she had any right to be. *You persuaded Hans to join the navy,* was what she wanted to say – *the navy you are now betraying.*

With the tips of his fingers he carefully aligned his unopened sketch pad with the edge of the table. A precise man now, she thought, not at all the drunken student roisterer she remembered. She wondered if all agents were careful or whether he was an exception. Most were risk takers, Frank Stagg had said. Whichever he was, the Chief said he was exceptional. 'Please tell me the phrase you wish to discuss,' he said.

Frank had told her to carry nothing in writing but to memorise the phrase. In fact, she had memorised the entire paragraph. She explained this, adding, 'I can repeat it all for you if it would help. The report I read in London is in English, presumably translated by Henry from German?'

'It would have been in German, of course. Henry took notes while I talked. I have not seen what he wrote. Please repeat the paragraph, if you can.'

'You were describing a conversation you had over lunch in Bremen with the harbour master and the commander of a flotilla of fast torpedo boats. There was also a senior officer from Berlin whose name you were not told but whom the others referred to as Herr Kommandant. You gathered he was from an intelligence service but you did not know which. You guessed that sabotage was one of its functions because the others referred to another naval officer you had met, a Captain Franz von Rintelen, whose speciality was sabotage. The Kommandant said that he would like to have involved him in the operation, which he called *Hermes*. But von Rintelen was doing such good work in America that he could not be recalled.' She had rehearsed both this preliminary and what she was about to quote so often that she no longer had any feel for it. 'I hope I've got that right? Do you remember it?'

'I remember. All is correct.'

'Good, thank you.' She took her pocket book and pencil from her handbag. 'Don't worry, I haven't written it down and I'm not about to take notes. It's just that I think better and remember better with a pen or pencil in my hand.'

'You are a philosopher. Hans used to say you were. He said you have ink instead of blood in your veins.'

She hadn't known that. 'It's true that I am accustomed to writing.'

'Then I hope your handwriting is better than Henry's.' He switched from Danish to German and smiled as Henry reappeared with a loaded tray. 'Henry writes like a drunken spider that has fallen into the ink.'

'Good for security,' said Henry. 'Only I can read it. Coffee won't be long.' He put down the tray and left the room.

Emily waited until he was out of earshot before resuming in Danish. 'You told Henry that the paragraph I'm about to quote was based on notes you had written in Danish after the lunch.'

'I wrote my notes in Danish, yes, for security. Then I burnt them in this fireplace, here, after I had reported to Henry.'

'I'll quote the paragraph in Danish, since it was based on your Danish notes. But of course you then translated it into German for Henry and he translated it into English for London. But the conversation you heard must have been in German. So it goes from German to Danish then back into German and into Henry's English and now back into Danish. Many opportunities for mis-translation, so what I am about to say may vary from what you put in your notes. Unless you'd prefer I did it in German?'

'Danish first. We can do German afterwards if necessary.'

'The conversation was already in progress when you arrived but this is what you remembered.' She paused again, concentrating, her pencil poised over her pocket book as if she were about to write.

The flotilla commander said to the Herr Kommandant, 'Will six be enough?' And the Herr Kommandant said, 'Three to deliver and recover, three to act as guards or distraction in the event of discovery.' Then the flotilla commander said, 'But the defences are formidable. It is after all their home base. We will of course do our best but shouldn't we assume we will take losses? In which case if we could have a couple of destroyers to take on their gun positions—' But the Herr Kommandant interrupted him, saying, 'You have surprise, speed and surprise, they are the key, speed and surprise. By the time the English know something is happening they will think it is a skirmish, not a serious raid, almost a bit of play, you know, just to test the defences. And by the time they see what it really is and what we've done it will be too late. Of course it is their home base and of course it is well protected, but when all their big capital ships are there what do they feel? They feel safe. And because they feel safe they are not looking for something as unorthodox as this. They will guard against the expected, only the expected, just as we do.

Emily looked up. 'Is that accurate, so far as you remember? Would it be easier if I wrote it out for you?'

He was staring with unseeing eyes, his focus inward. 'I think so, yes.' He spoke slowly. 'Yes, I think so.'

'Are you sure they didn't name a place?'

'If they had I would have said.'

'In London it is assumed that by "home base" and "big capital ships" they meant Rosyth, the home of the Grand Fleet. You never heard anyone mention Rosyth at any point during the lunch?'

He shook his head.

'And they said nothing more about what the plan is?'

'Maybe before, before I arrived. After this they talked about promotions, gossip, you know. Which I also reported.'

'And you have no idea what kind of thing – of attack – they plan? Except that they will use six torpedo boats?'

He shook his head again, but then said, 'I wish I had my Danish notes. I think – it was my impression, anyway – that they were using torpedo boats but not for their torpedoes. For their speed. They are fast boats and when the Herr Kommandant talked about surprise and speed he emphasised speed. He said it heavily.'

'But no indication as to what is to be delivered and recovered? Could it be mines? Were they planning to lay mines in the harbour?'

'Possibly, but why would you want to recover them?' He smiled.

'Of course, sorry, stupid of me.' She scribbled a cross in

her pocket book as if to cancel what she'd said. She hoped he wouldn't tell Henry, imagining them laughing at this stupid impractical woman and her questions.

He held up his right forefinger. 'But you remind me of one thing. You used the word "deliver"? You say I said, "Three to deliver and recover"?'

'Yes. Why – did you not?'

'If that is what Henry wrote then, yes, almost certainly I said it. But I think my Danish notes probably said land – to land, you know, to put on land? To land being the same as to deliver in this context. I assumed "deliver" is what the Herr Kommandant meant, but now I hear you say it I am not sure it is what he actually said.' He reverted to German. 'I think he said "to land".'

'Which suggests it was people – men – who are to be landed and recovered. You would only recover men, wouldn't you?'

'Yes, men.' He smiled again. 'Not mines.'

'Saboteurs,' said Henry, returning with the coffee pot. 'They're planning to land groups of saboteurs to blow up our ships while they're in port. That's what I took it to mean, anyway.' He poured a cup for Emily. 'Except that how do they think they're going to get all the way up the Forth into Rosyth without being seen, then out to the anchored ships with half a ton of explosive, then climb aboard or dive beneath each ship, place the charges, then get far enough away to detonate them and then get picked up by German torpedo boats which have been hanging around unnoticed in the Forth for half a day or night? It would be hard enough in peacetime but in

89

wartime ... well, it's just fairyland.' He sat. 'So if not saboteurs, what are they planning on landing and recovering?
And to what end?'

They kicked the subject around for five or ten minutes,
Henry facetiously suggesting increasingly fantastical sce-
narios. Emily, having nothing more serious to suggest
herself, kept quiet and feigned amusement. TR/16 sipped his
coffee, nodding and smiling but saying little. She wondered
what he thought of her, now that he knew what she did. He
might think she had always done this, that she was a spy in
Heidelberg. He might even think that Hans had been a spy
too. Eventually, after Henry had posited a German plot to
sail up the Thames and blow up the Houses of Parliament,
which he maintained would be wildly popular and lead to
the election of the Kaiser as prime minister, Karl Krueger put
down his cup.

'There is something else,' he said. 'Something mentioned
at the end, not in my report because it didn't seem to connect
to anything. I still don't understand it but now I think it must
connect because it meant something to them, at least to the
Herr Kommandant and the flotilla commander, perhaps not
the harbour master.' He paused while Henry poured more
coffee. 'Please, no milk. Why do you English ruin your coffee
with milk? I do not understand.'

'To keep our farmers in business,' said Henry.

TR/16 smiled. 'I think you are psychic, yes? Perhaps a
little? The word I am going to tell you, the word that was
mentioned, has to do with farming. An English word. Heifer.'

90

'You mean a cow?'

'A young female cow who has not yet had a calf. That is correct, I think?'

'Why were they talking about cows?'

'They were not, that is the point. It was when we were leaving. We were talking about football by then and all stood and the harbour master was telling me about a house he would build himself after the war, when I overheard the Herr Kommandant say: *Of course we have to wait to hear from Heifer that they're all in. It should not be long and your teams must be ready when he gives the word.* I assumed they were still talking about the naval football championship but now I think maybe they were, maybe they weren't. Maybe they had gone back to what they had been talking about before.'

'You have no idea who Heifer could be?'

'I have never heard of anyone named after a young cow.'

Henry sighed. 'You know what this means for me? If I report it – as I shall have to because Miss Grey will if I don't – London will want me to go through the list of players of every damn German football team known to man.' They laughed.

CHAPTER SIX

Emily walked back to the legation without, as she had half-feared, getting lost. Half-feared, because she would have loved to explore the bustling city. Henry had said there was no need for her to stay while he and TR/16 got down to what he called the normal business of their meeting, the state of ships and shipyards. Also, he added, she should get someone in the legation to look into whether there was a chance of a Dutch ferry booking to take them back to Felixstowe or Hull that night.

'Ferries? Are there still ferries?'

'A few and so long as they're flying the Dutch flag you're safe enough. We don't interfere with Dutch trade with Germany nor they with Dutch trade with us. Not sure how long that will last, though. Get the gallant Nisbet to find out about it. Give him something to do.'

Karl Krueger stood and held out his hand. 'It has been a pleasure to meet you again, Emily,' he said in Danish. 'And a surprise. I did not know your Intelligence Service employed ladies. Henry had kept that a secret. What would Hans have thought?'

'What indeed?' The flippancy of his remark surprised her into responding in the same tone. It seemed incongruous that this polite, well-mannered man was a spy, betraying his country and his colleagues at risk of his own life for reasons she would have loved to ask about. Both he and Henry made spying seemed normal, a routine collaboration, like she imagined a business meeting. Yet he had given details of the armour of every German capital ship, she had learned in London, with the result that shells were now being designed to penetrate it. Perhaps his information had helped kill Hans.

'I hope we meet again,' he said, with another half-bow and a smile.

When she gave her name at the front desk of the legation she was asked to wait. 'Lieutenant Nisbet will be down for you.'

She made to go to the side room where visitors waited, but the man at the desk prevented her. 'Sorry, madam, it's in use. Lieutenant Nisbet said you were to wait here for him.' She saw now that the door was closed.

It was not long before she heard Nigel's halting step on the stairs. He had a stick now and hobbled across the floor, putting his face uncomfortably close to hers. 'We've got a walk-in,' he whispered. 'Can't talk here, come outside.' He ushered her back out onto the steps, where they stood facing the street.

'A what?' she asked. 'We've got a what?' He whispered

again, but the noise of wheels, hooves and engines was overwhelming.

'A walk-in!' he said loudly. 'A volunteer.'

'A volunteer for what?' All she could think of was Kitchener and his volunteer army.

He came close enough for her to feel the warmth of his breath on her ear. 'Information. Someone with information. A possible spy for us. In the anteroom, wants to talk to someone. He hasn't got long. Foreign Office people don't want anything to do with him. Passed him on to us. But Landau's not back and I can't speak to him.'

'Why not?'

'He's Belgian, speaks French. No English. Can you see him? Hold the fort till Landau gets back.'

'I suppose so, yes.' She moved her head away. 'Who is he? What do you want me to say?'

'Didn't give his name. You'll have to ask. But don't say anything, don't volunteer anything yourself. Just ask him what he wants, what he can offer. Make no commitments but get his contact details, say you'll have to refer and ask if he can come back tomorrow. That's the drill, the walk-in drill.' He turned away and looked at the traffic. 'So I was told when I joined, anyway.'

The man in the anteroom was probably in his thirties or forties, with neat dark hair and moustache. He wore a well-cut suit and sat in one of four chairs around a table on which were Dutch newspapers. He looked surprised to see Emily when Nigel ushered her in. His hat was on his knee and he took it up as he stood. She greeted him in French, hoping she wouldn't inadvertently revert to German or Danish. 'I understand, monsieur, that you wish to see someone from the Intelligence Service?'

'That is correct, madame.' He waited for her to sit.

Nigel, whom Emily had assumed would leave her to it, took a chair to the side.

'The officer in charge is not here at present but will return shortly. May I ask to whom I am speaking?'

'You are with the Intelligence Service?'

'I am.' She felt at once proud and fraudulent.

'In that case, permit me to explain myself—'

Nigel's stick fell loudly onto the parquet floor. The Belgian and Emily got half out of their chairs to reach it at the same time he bent to do it himself. One of his feet caught the table, shoving it noisily sideways. When he had recovered his stick, the Belgian and Emily repositioned the table. Emily took out her pocket book and pencil.

'Do you mind if I take notes, monsieur?'

He waved assent. She noticed he had a substantial gold ring on each hand. He gave his name and then began what sounded like a prepared speech. He was a lawyer, he said, and had come as the representative of a small group of friends, reliable, respectable people – a doctor, a priest, a banker, a teacher – who felt as he did about the criminal German invasion of their country. They wished to do something about it, to fight back. They all had contacts, God-fearing, patriotic Belgian men and women whom they trusted and who felt as they did. These people also wished to fight for their country. They could not fight as soldiers but they could contribute as civilians by providing information about the dispositions of German forces in Belgium, their movements, their equipment, their use of the railways for transporting provisions and reinforcements.

'You mean, you – they – wish to spy for us?' asked Emily.

He shook his head. 'We would not be spies. We would be soldiers fighting for our country in the only way we can fight. We cannot join the Belgian Army but we can join yours if you will have us. We would be soldiers of your army fighting in Belgium but in secrecy and without uniforms. We wish to be recognised as soldiers, not as spies.'

'What's he saying?' asked Nigel.

Irritated, Emily nevertheless summarised. Nigel leaned forward on his stick, clasping it in both hands and shaking his head like an old man. 'Won't do, it's been tried. Army's always trying it, running networks of agents on the other side of the line. But they all get penetrated by the Hun, networks rolled up, everyone imprisoned or shot. The other problem is getting their reports out. They can't get them across the Front, of course – through the trenches – so they have to get them across the border to here, to The Netherlands. But the Huns have closed the border with machine guns and electrified fences and all that except for official crossing points. You probably know nothing about that.'

This time she did not suppress her irritation. 'I did know, as a matter of fact. I read it in the newspaper. I also know people serving at the Front.' And likely to stay there, she almost added. She turned back to the Belgian. 'How would you communicate your reports? How would you get your information to us?'

'That would be for you to devise, madame. We can get the information your Intelligence Service requires but you must provide the means of transmission. We know nothing about such things. We are not spies.'

'And, if I may ask, how were you able to come here today? Did the Germans allow you out?'

He patted a slim briefcase propped up against his chair. 'Fortunately, I have official business – legal business – to transact. I represent a company that makes parts for telephones and is part-Belgian, part-Dutch and part-German. The Germans wish to buy out the Dutch now that they control the Belgian part. I was permitted to cross the border to negotiate but I doubt I shall be allowed to cross again. That is why we must rely on you, the Intelligence Service, for communications. You have experience of this, I hope?'

Emily nodded, although she too could only hope.

'Emily,' said Nigel in a low voice. 'Miss Grey, I mean.'

'Yes?'

'Are we sure he's genuine?'

'Well, he seems it, sounds it. How would we know?'

'Precisely. Could be a Boche deception. They're clever like that. Done it before.'

'What do you suggest I do?'

'Proceed with care. Don't give anything away.'

'I am and I'm not.' She spoke sharply, no longer trying to soften her tone. 'And how do we know he doesn't speak English, come to that?'

'Didn't seem to know what I was talking about. Couldn't explain himself to me. Seemed pretty convincing.'

'Seemed?'

There was a knock and the door was opened by the man from the reception desk. 'Visitor for Miss Grey.'

Henry Landau looked perplexed and annoyed. 'What's going on? Who's in there?' As she explained, his perplexity and irritation mutated into eagerness. 'Just what we want, what we've been looking for. No end of people willing to spy for us over there but the problem is contacting them. As for getting their stuff out, your marine's right for once, that's where all these networks have fallen down. But we've been working on it and we reckon we've got several routes that might do. Just no one to use them. Until now. Unless he's too good to be true.'

'He might be, mightn't he? That's what Nigel kept inter-rupting me to say. How would we know?'

'Proof of the pudding. You go upstairs to the station, make yourself at home. Well done on this, by the way. And this morning. You made your mark with our friend.' He grinned and opened the anteroom door.

As she turned the corner to the second flight of stairs, she heard Nigel hobble across the hall below and say to the man at the desk that he'd been sent out for coffees but didn't know where to find them.

Henry, clutching an armful of papers, joined her later in his office. He was brimming with good humour now. The meeting had gone well, arrangements were made for a trial run and for two-way communications and the man had produced from his briefcase detailed notes of German dispositions only two days old. 'If these people can do half of what they promise we're in business. I have a good feeling about them. They're all professionals, mainly Catholic, and unlike many I talk to they're not after money. They've got a banker on board who's prepared to bankroll them. All they want in return is recognition.'

'That's not compatible with secrecy, surely?'

'Afterwards, when the war's over. When we've won. They want to be accredited with British Army ranks, pay and pensions. Medals too, if appropriate. Very keen that they're not seen as spies. They want to be honoured as patriots fighting a cause. He's coming back tomorrow for an answer.'

'Can we – you – promise that?'

'Not without War Office agreement, no.'

'How many of them are there?'

'About a dozen at present. He gave me the names of the organisers of whom there are five plus him, but if it goes nationwide as they intend it could be in the hundreds. And we won't know who they are, most of them. War Office will never agree, of course. He's coming back tomorrow for an answer. Before he goes home.'

'What will you do?'

'Tell him the War Office has agreed.'

He dumped the papers on his desk. 'I know, I know. But look at it this way. I could report in full to London and the Old Man, being the Old Man he is, would move heaven and earth to get War Office agreement to ranks, pay and pensions for an unknown number of unidentified foreigners. But they wouldn't do it. Even if they did, it would take years of negotiation and we've got twenty-four hours. This is our one chance. If I tell him London agrees and he goes away and it all works and it helps us win the war – wonderful. I'll tell the Old Man then, cross that bridge when we come to it. They can sack me if they want, but we'll have won, that's the thing. But if we lose, it won't matter anyway, there'll be no British Army to pay their back pay or pensions. And if – which is sadly more likely – it all works for a while until someone betrays them and the Boche round them up and shoot them, then at least they'll die thinking of themselves as soldiers.'

Nothing in Emily's life had prepared her for such rule breaking; the few rules she had knowingly broken – at home, at school, at Cambridge – were minor and breached only after cautious deliberation and protracted consideration of consequence. Hans used to tease her about her caution.

'I'm only telling you this because you were in at the start of it,' Henry continued, 'and because you handled our Dane so well I trust your judgement and discretion. I'll write it up for London now in time for the diplomatic bag which leaves tonight on the same ship as you – the legation people have secured berths for you, by the way – but I won't of course mention anything about agreeing to their conditions. I hope you won't, either, will you?'

Emily hesitated, despite knowing she would agree; it worried her slightly that the practice of deception was becoming remarkably easy, almost routine. 'Well, it's really nothing to do with me, is it? It's just chance that I was here and saw him. I can say hand on heart that I didn't hear anything of what you said to him or he to you. So I suppose I can plausibly know nothing about it so far as London is concerned. But Nigel—'

'Sat through it all and didn't understand a word of it. Gone back to your hotel to pack now. Seems to think it will take him half a day, must be all those silk shirts. He hasn't sold them, has he? We'll be in trouble with the Dutch if they find out that's what he's up to.'

'I'm sure he hasn't, no. He hasn't had time even if he wanted to. I think he brought them just in case he needed them. In case we were staying for longer.'

Henry Landau looked down at his papers again, as if he had forgotten she was there. He looked up when she got up to go. 'Hope you don't mind my asking, but you're not engaged or anything, are you? To be married, I mean.'

'No, I'm not.' She paused. She didn't want to tell the whole story, but it was perhaps better that he heard the bones of it from her. 'I was, before the war, but my fiancé, who was German, is missing presumed dead. At sea.'

'Oh. Very sorry to hear that.' He glanced at his papers again, then back to her. 'Well, if you don't mind my saying – it's a pity you're not staying longer. But as it is, perhaps we could … you know … make the most of it.'

He smiled as he came around his desk towards her. She backed away until she felt the door handle pressing into her spine. She hadn't anticipated anything like this but, as it was happening, wasn't surprised. It was as if she had known it without admitting it to herself. Still smiling, he put his hands on her upper arms, pinning her gently – but still pinning her – against the door. As his face neared hers and the bristles of his ginger moustache became individually identifiable, she turned her head away and pushed with both hands against his shoulders. 'No, go away, get off. Leave me alone.'

He ceased closing on her but didn't let go. 'Are you sure? Not just a little … just one kiss until we meet again? You might—'

'No! Leave me alone!' She raised her voice and pushed him again. Her handbag, hanging from the crook of her elbow, swung first against her and then against him.

He let go and stepped back, holding up his hands. 'Sorry, Miss Grey, I just thought … I didn't mean to upset you – just a farewell kiss, that's all.' He looked surprised.

She moved aside from the door and opened it. 'I'm sorry, I'm not … I'm not ready for this sort of thing, I don't want it.' She was annoyed with herself for apologising. 'You shouldn't have done that,' she said, with some heat in her voice. 'You shouldn't just think … you shouldn't assume you can—'

He nodded, raised his hands again and turned back to his desk. 'Apologies, apologies, my fault entirely. Got a bit carried away, what with you coming over and our session this morning going so well and now this new business. All quite exciting. You did well, by the way. You did very well. Thank you, I hope you have a good trip back.'

His expression was one of frank sincerity, open and straightforward as if concluding a successful business discussion. Before she could stop herself she thanked him too, the automatic unthinking reciprocity of conventional politeness. She closed the door firmly behind her and headed across the landing for the stairs, angry with herself and him, and incipiently tearful.

CHAPTER SEVEN

'Something for you,' said Frank Stagg, waving a brown envelope from behind his desk . 'Your pay.'

Emily slipped it into her handbag. She had no idea how much she was getting; no one discussed pay.

'Rotterdam went well, the Old Man says,' said Frank.

'I haven't seen him yet. He must have heard from the station?'

'Nigel Nisbet briefed him this morning.'

'Oh, did he?' She had gone home to change before reporting to the office in the afternoon. Nigel hadn't said he was going straight in. 'But he doesn't know it all, he wasn't there for all of it.'

'So we gathered, after a while. He summarised what you said and we've had a preliminary report from Henry Landau via the bag. More to follow. Busy man, Henry. Seems to have something else going on too, apart from your business with TR/16.'

'Yes – yes, he was busy.'

'Straightforward chap, didn't you find? No messing around, gets on with things. Mining engineer. Comes straight out with it, whatever it is. They tend to, engineers. Same in the navy.'

'Indeed he does, yes.'

'The Old Man still wants to see you, though. He's got a meeting at the moment but I'll give you a shout when he's free.'

Having no office or desk, she wasn't sure where to go next. Dorothy and Miriam were busy typing, not quite ignoring her – they had welcomed her back and asked if she'd been seasick – but getting on with their work.

'I think I should write my report now, while it's still fresh. Is there a desk I can borrow?'

Frank pointed up the stairs. 'Go and grab any you find. Don't ask, just occupy. There's rarely a day when everyone's in. You might even find one with a typewriter. Need any paper?'

She found an empty office with three desks and a type-writer. She was still writing when, much later, she heard people in the corridor going home. Later still, Miriam came up to find her. 'Oh good, you're still here. Dorothy thought you might have gone. Frank's disappeared somewhere. The Chief wants to see you.'

Emily gathered her papers.

'Not in his office, in his flat. You're invited to dinner.' She smiled. 'Very honoured.'

'Oh – am I? My parents are expecting me at home.'

'Do they have a telephone? I thought you might, your father being a doctor. I'll telephone them from our office. But first I'd better show you the way. You'd never find it on your own.'

She led the way along the corridor, up more stairs and along another corridor. Emily wondered if the Chief had secretly occupied most of Whitehall Court apart from the hotel and the National Liberal Club. Miriam left her outside a polished unnumbered door. Her knock was answered by a maid in a white apron, who showed her through a hall into a high drawing room with double windows overlooking the Embankment. It had light wood panelling, a patterned carpet and few but expensive furnishings. The walls, however, were festooned with photographs and paintings of warships, motorboats, yachts and an unusually large houseboat. A small woman with short grey hair and glasses arose from the sofa, holding a copy of *Country Life*. She wore a pale cream woollen suit with matching blouse and a pearl necklace.

They shook hands. 'I'm May, May Cumming. Welcome back. I hope you're not too tired for dinner but at least we eat early. Mansfield – Manny, I think Manny for this evening, don't you? – will be with us in a moment.' She smiled. 'I understand you're Blinker's goddaughter? Typically generous of him to share you with us. Manny is sure you'll be most useful. You have been already, he says. Do sit down.'

They chatted for less than two minutes before she heard steps in the hall, unmistakable because every other step was louder than its predecessor. 'Miss Grey, Miss Grey, you bring us some sparkle,' the Chief declaimed, grinning. 'Tell us all about it over dinner. You're allowed to speak with your mouth full and May is as discreet as the grave so our secrets are safe with her.'

Dinner was in another panelled room, served by the maid who had apparently doubled up as cook for the evening. There was no nautical theme to the dining room but it was dominated by a large oil painting of a young man in army uniform. Assuming it must be their dead son, Emily could not help glancing as she sat. Clearly, they were not hiding from his death.

May noticed her glance. 'Manny tells me that you too have suffered loss. Quite recently?'

'Yes, Hans. He was killed at Dogger Bank. We were going to be married. At least, before the war we were. He was German.'

'So we understood from Blinker. How dreadful for you. British, German, French, Belgian, Russian, Austrian, Italian – it's the same for everyone. His family must feel it just as we would. You haven't heard from them?'

'No. I never actually met them.'

'Our son, Alastair – Ally – was killed very early on, in France but in an accident. With Manny.'

'Hence I'm half a leg lighter,' said the Chief. His tone was matter-of-fact. 'The only official visit on which I lost weight. I was visiting GHQ, to which Ally was attached, and we borrowed a car to do a spot of private recce-ing, trying to find the enemy. That was the nature of the war in those first few months, much more mobile than now. Trench system not established. So you've heard nothing at all from his family?'

'No.'

'Nor from anyone else? No one's tried to get in touch with you, directly or indirectly?'

'No.' She hesitated over whether to mention TR/16 since he obviously hadn't tried to get in touch with her. But she had included her knowing him in her unfinished report and it might look odd if she didn't mention him now.

The Chief was unperturbed. 'That makes you one of very, very few who know his real name. There's a list in the secret annex to the file. I'll see you're added to it.'

'Extraordinary, the role of coincidence in life,' said May. 'One never knows, never.'

She was tempted to mention her suspicions of the man in the brown bowler, but there again, coincidence was an obvious explanation. She hadn't seen him that day and didn't want to sound silly or alarmist.

Dinner was celery soup followed by beef with boiled potatoes and vegetables. The Chief ate rapidly, washing it down with two glasses of red wine, while May ate frugally, daintily sipping her wine. Pudding was stewed apple and custard followed by cheddar cheese and some tough dry biscuits.

'Ship's biscuit,' said the Chief, holding one up. 'I daresay your father has made you familiar with these, eh? Good for the jaw muscle.'

'I'm certainly no stranger to them.' In fact, her father hated them and used them as target practice when pistol shooting. She broke off a corner and nibbled it.

They were served tea. The Chief swallowed his almost at once. 'Now, let's get back to the office and finish off. Don't want to keep you too late, Miss Grey, you must be tired and you've got to get home. Barnes, isn't it? We'll get you a cab.'

'Don't be too late yourself, Manny,' said May. 'You've been burning rather too much midnight oil recently.'

Using both sticks, he hobbled with surprising speed along the corridors, managing the stairs with a sound like rapid fire musketry.

Once in his office, he leant across his desk, elbows apart, hands clasped. 'Thing is, this Heifer business.' He had lost his earlier joviality and stared hard, as if in argument with her. 'What do you make of it?'

'Well, I don't think I can make anything of it. No more than what I've said, anyway. It's all in the report I'm writing.'

'TR/16 was sure it was code-name for a person rather than a bit of kit or an operation or technique?'

'I think he assumed it from the phrasing of it. "We have to wait to hear from Heifer that they're all in", was what he said. The same in Danish and German.'

'Could be a piece of kit, early warning stuff, something like that. But I doubt it.' He took out his cigarettes. 'Don't mind if I—?'

'Please. I love the smell of that sort.'

'And it must be Rosyth they're talking about. It's the only

place that fits. Home of the Grand Fleet, waiting until "they're all in". They are every so often, all the capital ships, anyway. Re-supply, maintenance, that sort of thing. Can't stay at sea all the time.' His lighter flared. 'Sounds to me as if they've got a source in the fleet they've code-named Heifer Or in Rosyth, in the dockyard. I'm talking to Kell about it. My opposite number – d'you know who I mean? Colonel Kell, head of Military Intelligence Department 5 – MI5, they call themselves. It's their business, catching spies, but TR/16 is our agent and it's our information. Thing is, what you said – what TR/16 said – points to something else that's already worrying Kell. You're sure – quite sure – he said Heifer not something else that sounded like it?'

'Quite sure, the word for cattle. TR/16 made it very clear to Henry Landau and to me.'

The Chief made a note in his diary. 'And then this other business that Landau has written about, this offer of service from the Belgian gentleman. You met the man.'

'Yes, along with Lieutenant Nisbet. He actually saw him first but he didn't—'

'Understand a word of what was going on. No French. Admitted when I saw him this morning. But he's a trier, isn't he, Nisbet? Means well? Looked after you and all the arrangements, that sort of thing? No problems?'

'No problems, no.'

'Landau doesn't seem to have much time for him.'

'They might not get on if they were together for a long time.'

He looked at her as he smoked. 'Thing about Nisbet is that, although he holds a commission in the marines, he never fully completed his training. I was asked to take him on as a favour.'

Conscious that she too owed her job to personal favour, she didn't want to be drawn in to commenting on the lieutenant's competence. 'Yes, he injured his knee. He told me.'

'Not just that, or not so much that. He had a breakdown of some sort, a nervous thing. Over-worrying, perhaps. Do you think he'll do? Is he up to the job?'

She chose her words carefully. 'I think he's very keen and probably very loyal, but as a newcomer I don't feel quali-fied to—'

'Judgement? Lacks judgement, would you say? My impres-sion anyway. Thing is, whether judgement's an innate quality or whether it can be developed. Time will tell.' He flicked ash into the capacious glass ashtray. 'Now tell me about the Belgian. What did you make of him?'

Emily told all she knew apart from Henry Landau's promise of army ranks, pay and pensions. She felt dishonest. Remaining silent about Nigel Nisbet's inadequacies was one thing, but Henry's withholding of the Belgian's significant condition was of a different order, a professional deception. 'The essence of a lie is the intent to deceive,' her father had once admonished her. By that criterion her omission was a lie. But she said no more.

'You look tired. Let me drive you home.'

'I can get a cab, you said—'

He smiled again. 'I want to drive, you see. I miss it. Sent my driver home hours ago. Perfect excuse.'

Being told she looked tired made her feel she was. It would have been quicker to get a cab, because even with the lift now working it took some time for the Chief to hobble out of the building to his car parked on the Embankment. It took more time for him to lever himself in.

'Driver will be annoyed when he sees I've moved it,' he said. 'Thinks it's his job to drive and mine to ride. Just like May. She says I shouldn't drive with this new leg. Cork, you see. Not much feeling.'

May was right, Emily concluded, as they stuttered onto Whitehall, crossing it on the wrong side of the traffic island, through Horse Guards and across the parade ground. The blackout meant there were no streetlights anywhere, though vehicle and building lights were permitted. The Chief drove as if it were daylight and there were no laws of the road and no other traffic. He noticed her tension and grinned. 'Fear not, Miss Grey, I'm not a law-breaker. Not in this country, anyway. Chief Constable's number plates, you see. Means I can ignore all the rules. Now, you'd better navigate for me.'

At Hyde Park corner he sped without slowing through the Victoria Arch. 'I'm happy to drive if you like, if it's awkward with your leg,' she said.

'You can drive, can you? How did that come about?' He roared between two startled hackney cabs as she explained. 'Good for you, good for you. You enjoy it? '

'Yes. But, seriously, if it hurts I'm happy to—'

'Only hurts if I have to press hard and suddenly. Feel it on the stump where it joins. All right most of the time.'

However, they reached Barnes without incident. 'That business, that Heifer business,' he said as she clambered down, feeling she was shaking and hoping it didn't show. 'There's more to be said about it. Come and chat tomorrow.'

Emily overslept the following morning, something she hadn't done since leaving Cambridge. Her mother had not roused her because she assumed she was allowed a day off to recover from her travels. When eventually she hurried downstairs, she found a letter from Zara saying that she and Sean were meeting in the Charing Cross Hotel that evening and that Emily was welcome to join them.

It was almost lunchtime when she reached Whitehall Court, ready to apologise for her absence. No one remarked on it, although Dorothy said, 'The Chief was looking for you. He's out at lunch now. He's asked me to book you onto a course at Pitman's.'

'Pitman's? Aren't they the—'

'Where you learn shorthand and typing, that's right. Pitman's Metropolitan School in Southampton Row, just off Covent Garden. Very handy. It's the system we use.'

There was a note of satisfaction in her tone. Emily felt she was being brought down a peg or two, no longer the university lady, the officer equivalent. 'Oh, what a surprise. I didn't know,' she said, trying to sound pleased.

113

'Lieutenant Nisbet was asking after you, too. He's upstairs now, probably in the canteen.'

The canteen was in the attic, along the corridor beyond the workshops. There was a queue at the counter, but she found Nigel Nisbet at a table by himself. 'At last – I've been looking for you,' he said. 'Better order before you sit. Leave your hat and coat here. It's lamb chops today. Very tasty. Freddie Browning's done us proud, really transformed this place. Getting that Savoy cook was a masterstroke. Knows everyone worth knowing, Freddie. You still haven't met him, have you? Never mind, you will, you will. I don't think it's broken, by the way.'

'What isn't?'

'My knee. Managed without the stick today. Felt a bit awkward about bringing it in, to be frank. People might have thought I was trying to imitate the Old Man, getting ideas above my station.' He laughed. 'Better join the queue in case they run out.'

'I'm not hungry. I don't need lunch.' She sat.

'Don't mind if I tuck in, then? Seems to have gone down well, our trip. Had a session with the Old Man about it. He says he's got something else up his sleeve for us both. Working as a team again.' He smiled. 'Hope that suits you as well as it suits me.'

'That's odd. Dorothy just told me I'm being sent on a short-hand and typing course.'

'Really? Sounds a bit unnecessary. Don't suppose they taught you that at the university, did they? I don't usually . . .

I mean, I've never dictated to anyone before, no call for it. You'll probably find me exasperatingly slow. Typing could be useful, though, so long as we don't have to lug one of those heavy Underwoods or Remingtons around. Have you ever used one?'

'Perhaps you'll be sent on a course, too.'

He laughed.

Emily spent the first half of the afternoon at a desk in the SW – secret writing – room improving her account of the Rotterdam trip. The other occupant was Hugh, a tall, bespectacled bald man with an amiable expression who asked if she'd ever used SW. On hearing she hadn't, but was instead to learn shorthand and typing, he shook his head. 'All very well, these commonplace skills, but not if it means neglecting the basics of the trade. If you're going into the field you're more likely to want to conceal what you're communicating than make it plain to all. Would you like me to show you round, so you can see what's available?'

Over the next hour she was shown chemical combinations and techniques devised by professors of chemistry, along with examples of German SW and the means for revealing it. It turned out that Hugh was himself a professor of chemistry from Nottingham who had volunteered for war work. 'Always best if you can use some naturally occurring substance, saves carting various hard-to-explain chemicals about with you,' he said. 'Lemon juice at the most basic level, been used for centuries and is easily developed. Iodine vapour develops most of the commonly used chemicals, although there's one recent innovation that's resistant to it. Not sure I should tell you about that, though.' He looked at her with raised eyebrows.

She gave the smile he was waiting for. 'I think you should.'

'Well, I daresay the other ladies in the office have heard about it, so no reason why you shouldn't. It's semen, human semen.' He held up his hand. 'Don't laugh, it's serious. Well, almost. But it does actually work. Up to a point. The Chief Censor, Worthington, came up with the idea. You know they examine thousands of letters every day. Well, he said one of his staff had found semen did not respond to iodine vapour. We didn't ask how they knew, but the discoverer had to be moved to another office because the other chaps were making life intolerable by ragging him about masturbation. Anyway, the Old Man was tickled pink by the idea ... do stop me if I'm embarrassing you?'

'Not at all. I'm intrigued. Please go on.'

'Well, in no time at all the slogan "Every man his own stylo" went round the world. Station after station seemed to hear about. Then our man in Copenhagen, Major Holme, took it a bit too seriously and evidently stocked it in a bottle, because his letters stank to high heaven. Some wag told him a fresh operation was required for each letter. Eventually the Old Man had to put a stop to it.' He smiled and shook his head. 'At least it added something to the gaiety of nations in these sad times, you could say that for it.'

When Emily went downstairs to hand in her report, Dorothy said, 'Ah, you are here after all. We weren't sure where you were. The Chief was asking for you. He's got someone with him now. I doubt he wants to be disturbed. But hang on, let me see if he still ...'

She knocked, waited, knocked again. This time there was an answering bellow, 'Come!' She opened the door just enough to poke her head round, then turned to Emily and nodded.

The Chief was at his desk, smoking. Before him, also smoking, was a younger man in army uniform, with neat dark hair and a clipped moustache. He stood and held out his hand.

'Miss Grey, Colonel Kell. Colonel Kell, Miss Grey,' said the Chief. 'Pull up a chair, Emily.'

Colonel Kell reached it before she could, swinging it across with one hand and a smile. Emily sat.

'Colonel Kell is my opposite number,' said the Chief. 'He runs MI5. They deal with counter-espionage, catching spies, whereas we do the spying, of course. Chalk and cheese, you might think, but actually there's a big overlap. Except that he has to sit in the War Office for his sins. Which must therefore be many.' He laughed and coughed. 'He's going to explain why we're sending you to learn shorthand and typing.'

The colonel had prominent cheekbones which gave him, to her eyes, a slightly Slavic look. 'I must assure you, Miss Grey, that this is not a demotion, though it may feel like one and for a while must appear so to the outside world. I can also assure you that after the mission you will be restored to officer status – as C will confirm?' He glanced at the Chief, who nodded. 'The mission is for you to be posted to another

117

part of the country as a secretary in order to report on one of the people you'll be working for, someone we suspect may be a German spy. Are you content to do this?'

The idea of pretending to be something she wasn't was novel . It might even be liberating, she thought. 'Yes, of course. So long as I can manage it. I don't know how good I'll be at shorthand and—'

'You just need to be good enough to pass muster as someone with basic secretarial training,' said the Chief. 'Doesn't matter if you're not actually *good* at it so long as you show willing. Smile and be pleasant and they'll be tickled pink to have a nice girl like you with them. You won't be doing the whole course at Pitman's, just the first bit, enough to give you the essentials. We're in a bit of a rush on, you see. Need to get up steam before anything happens.'

'This mission arises partly from your own recent trip to Rotterdam,' said the colonel, 'on which C has kindly briefed us. It coincides with an investigation we were already running in the same area. But before I go into detail I'd like you to answer one question, if you wouldn't mind.' He stubbed out his cigarette and turned towards her, his polished Sam Browne belt and cross-strap creaking slightly. 'Have any of your late fiancé's family or friends, or anyone claiming association with him, contacted you in any way since you returned home?'

'No.'

'Have you had any personal contact with anyone from Germany?'

'No.' She glanced at the Chief. 'Except this week in Rotterdam, with an agent. Only I'm not sure I should—'

The Chief nodded. 'Colonel Kell is aware of the case.'

The colonel continued. 'Think hard, Miss Grey. No contact with any other foreigners, or anyone purporting to come from neutral countries, since you returned from Germany?'

'No.' His insistence made her feel under suspicion, which in turn made her feel guilty, prompting her to go on. 'Since I got back I've not seen very many people at all, of any sort. I've been at home most of the time. I had tea recently with a friend from Cambridge and I'm seeing her again tonight. But she's English.'

'You've not noticed anything suspicious? No unwanted attention, strangers hanging around outside your house or anything like that?'

'No – well, not really.' She hadn't seen Brown Bowler again, but neither had she thought to look out that morning. However, she worried about failing to report something that later turned out to be significant. 'There was one thing, probably nothing at all.' As she described the sightings, their significance seemed to diminish the harder she tried to convey it.

The two men heard her out, impassively. When she finished, Colonel Kell said, 'It may be coincidence. Don't let it worry you, just keep your eyes peeled and let us know if you see him again. Meanwhile, there is something else, some context to my questions, which I can tell you in strict confidence.' He looked at the Chief, who nodded. 'There is reporting

119

from Germany, which C has again shared with us, that the Germans have a programme to re-establish discreet contacts with people like yourself who had formed close connections with German nationals but had to leave Germany when war came. Some of these people, they reason – being mostly German speakers – might have jobs or move in circles giving them access to official secrets. They hope that one or two – that's all they need, one or two in the right places – might be sympathetic to the German cause and might be persuaded by their German sweethearts or friends to provide information.

'In your case, of course, with your former fiancé missing presumed dead, it's less likely that they would try to contact you. But not necessarily – they might hope to work on your grief and sympathy. That is why it's very important that you don't hesitate to report anything that strikes you as at all suspicious or unusual, as you just have. Meanwhile, we're keeping a close eye on you and others in your position, for your own protection, and will let you know if we spot anything.'

'But nothing for you to worry about,' the Chief intervened. 'You're not under threat, no one's going to kidnap you on the streets of London or anything like that. Nothing at all for you to worry about. Just watch and report. As you have just now.'

Emily nodded.

'Your mission,' he continued, 'is to proceed to the dockyard at Rosyth, near Edinburgh, there to work as an Admiralty secretary in the dockyard security office. They don't know they're getting a secretary yet. They've been clamouring for one so they're in for a nice surprise. They'll be pleased to see you. As for what you're to do there, remember TR/16's mention of – insistence on – the word Heifer? Some sort of source of intelligence, probably human but not necessarily. Puzzled us all, as you know, but Colonel Kell's people have come up with an answer.'

'Possible answer,' said the colonel. 'Do you think that what TR/16 heard as Heifer might in fact have been Hueffer, pronounced Hoofer?'

'I doubt it. He seemed sure it was Heifer, as in cattle. He might of course have misheard. However, I met an officer called—'

'Hueffer is a German name, nothing to do with cattle,' continued the colonel, as if she hadn't spoken. 'The Times had a music critic called Hueffer. German, married to an Englishwoman. One of his sons is a writer or poet, that sort of thing. Fluent German speaker. He joined up, unlike some of his kind, and is now a subaltern in the army, Lieutenant Hueffer, Royal Welch. Old for the job and the rank – in his forties – and his regiment probably doesn't know what to do with him because he's on loan to the Admiralty and was posted to the security office in Rosyth. He's number two to the officer in charge there, Lieutenant Commander Cooden—'

'Yes, I've met them both,' she said, determined to interrupt in turn. 'On my Admiralty Induction Course.'

'Oh. So they know what you're doing?' The Colonel looked concerned.

'I don't think so. I don't see how they could since I didn't know myself when I was there.'

'Shouldn't be a problem,' said the Chief. 'So far as they're concerned you're an Admiralty secretary recruited for the duration and liable to be posted to anywhere their Lordships of the Admiralty choose to send you. They'll be too pleased to have you to be curious about how you come to be there.'

The Colonel nodded. 'This Lieutenant Hueffer has German relatives with whom he sometimes stayed before the war. In a similar case we know about, the Boche intelligence services approached the man and persuaded him to spy. Fortunately, we found out about it and he's now serving time at His Majesty's pleasure. We don't know that anything like that has happened to Hueffer, of course. In fact, we've no reason to doubt his loyalty, but the possibility has to be taken into account when a chap is half-Hun. We already had indications of possible leaks from Rosyth and were separately investigating Hueffer when your reporting from TR/16 came in with its mention of Rosyth as a target and Heifer as a source. This obviously strengthened our suspicions.'

'Doesn't the fact that Lieutenant Hueffer volunteered despite his age suggest he's loyal?' said Emily.

'On the one hand, yes; on the other, it could be just what they've asked him to do. To get access to official information. So your job – assuming you're happy to do it?' He raised his eyebrows. Emily nodded. 'Your job is to watch Hueffer for signs of anything clandestine, sound out his attitudes, get to know him as well as you can and report back. Also, bearing in mind what I was saying about German interest in people with German connections, look out for any attempt to approach you through him. Assuming, that is, that he really is a spy and reports your arrival.'

This made learning shorthand and typing far more palatable, albeit useful skills in themselves, Emily told herself. 'Where will I . . . will there be somewhere for me to live?'

'Frank Stagg will sort something out for you,' said the Chief. 'We don't know how long you'll be there, of course, so best thing for family and friends is to tell them you're on detached duty to Rosyth where there's a desperate shortage of admin staff. Not that the Admiralty ever lacks administrators from what I can see. They'll administer themselves into the seabed before this war's over. And you'll take Nisbet with you as your communicator, the go-between with us. Wouldn't do to have you communicating directly from the security office. Does that sound all right?'

'Yes, thank you, sir.' She hesitated. 'I'm not sure that I'll need Lieutenant Nisbet if it's just a question of me going to work every day and reporting back. I can do that in my private time. Lieutenant Nisbet might get horribly bored.'

The Chief shook his head. 'I think you'll find it useful to have someone on hand to talk to and to keep an eye on this Hueffer creature when he's off duty. In fact, Nisbet should do your shorthand and typing course too. Useful for a communicator and skills we all ought to have, anyway. I'll tell Dorothy to book him on. Of course, he'll have to keep below deck out of sight in Rosyth and you'll have to take care how and when you meet. But he can spend his time getting to know the ground and being on hand if you need to confide or need another pair of eyes. Belt and braces always a good idea, don't you think? Both men nodded.

'Thank you, sir,' said Emily.

Teas were still – just – being served when Emily reached the Charing Cross Hotel after work. Breathless from hurrying up the stairs to the first floor tearoom, she immediately spotted Zara in a vivid green dress at a table overlooking the Strand. She was with a man of about thirty with tanned, open features and dark hair. His good looks were accentuated by the uniform of a naval petty officer. He stood, tall and smiling, as Emily approached. 'I see what you mean,' Emily wanted to say to Zara. Instead, she kept to conventional greetings and handshake as Zara introduced him as Sean Jephson.

'Sean's from Dublin,' she said.

'More recently from Portsmouth,' he said. His accent was soft Irish, his hand warm and firm. 'Pleased to meet you.'

'Emily's from Sussex,' said Zara, making it sound like an achievement. 'But she's in London looking for a job.'

'No longer,' said Emily, taking her seat. Over tea and a hard piece of rock cake she told them she had been taken on by the Admiralty as a trainee secretary. They told her they were going to a music hall at Shepherd's Bush that evening, Zara naming two performers whom Emily pretended to have heard of. She had never been to a musical.

Zara had an enamel Votes For Women brooch pinned

above her dress. She tapped it, laughing. 'I'm going to get another of these for Sean to pin on his uniform when he's off duty.'

'More than my life's worth, I'm afraid to say,' said Sean, smiling. 'Tampering with His Britannic Majesty's uniforms won't do, you know.'

'And in return I've promised to campaign for Home Rule for Ireland. In fact, I've started already – what do think of it?' She raised one shoulder provocatively, indicating her dress. 'The colour of Ireland, made from lovely Irish cotton. Feel it.'

Emily stroked her. 'It's lovely. Suits you too. You can't be missed in it. I saw you as soon as I was through the door.'

Zara clasped Emily's hand in both hers. 'Now, the thing is, Emily, we have to convert you to Home Rule too. Then we can both work on Sean and make a suffragette of him.' She lowered her voice. 'He's already a secret Fenian so it's easy for him to become a secret one of us too.'

'Zara, you're not supposed to say that sort of thing. You'll get me into trouble.' He was still smiling but had also lowered his voice.

'It's all right with Emily, secrets are safe with Emily, she never blabs about anyone, do you, my dear?' She laughed again and let go of Emily's hand. 'It's the most exasperating thing about her. She never gossips, never gets angry. I don't know how she does it.'

'That's why I see you,' said Emily. You're the half I lack.'

They laughed. There was no further talk of Home Rule or the suffrage. Sean, it turned out, was an engineer artificer, a specialist in the new diesel engines. He had served nearly ten years in the navy, more at shore bases than at sea. He had two cousins serving but knew neither well, having rarely met them. One was in the Mediterranean and the other, he thought, in Rosyth. He hoped to set up his own engineering business when eventually he left the navy.

He was charming, well-mannered and considerate. When they left for their music hall Emily hugged Zara, whispering, 'He's lovely,' in her ear.

On the way home that evening she counted no fewer than five brown bowlers.

CHAPTER EIGHT

The course was hard. Emily had worked conscientiously at school and quite hard at Cambridge, but at the latter, no matter how many hours she put in at the college library or University Library, she could come and go as she pleased, rest when she wanted, take longer over something or be diverted if she allowed herself. Pitman's, just off the noisy Covent Garden with its constant loading, unloading and shouting, was regimented work. She was in a class of eight women and four men, crammed with desks almost touching into a small room overlooking Southampton Row. The room was so stuffy that the window was permanently open, which made the market noises worse. There was one lavatory, shared with other classes, two floors up.

Their instructor – called so, rather than teacher – was a tall, thin woman from Lancashire who ran what Emily imagined the Chief would call a tight ship, with no concessions to time off, humour or repeated mistakes. They worked for eight hours a day, plus thirty minutes for lunch and a

fifteen-minute break morning and afternoon. Before starting the course Emily had imagined she might occasionally
meet friends in central London during the evenings, but the
first day, after which she returned to Barnes feeling near to
collapse, put paid to that. She felt an upsurge of respect for
women like Dorothy and Miriam, who had not only endured
three months of this but who now did it daily.

There were moments of light relief, the more welcome for
being unexpected. Nigel Nisbet was also doing the course,
as the Chief had indicated, although fortunately in another
class so he was unable to witness Emily's inadequacies. His
own he broadcast himself, repeatedly, during lunch breaks.

'Doesn't make sense to me, all these sounds and squiggles.
Typing, yes, I can hit the keys all right, maybe not always in
the right order, but I do understand it and will get better. But
relating sounds to squiggles ... I can't ... I mean, I'm not sure
what the sound is half the time. Maybe it's my ears. Wax or
something.'

His male instructor was always picking on him, he said,
and the girl he sat next to was the best and quickest in class,
which showed him up. She was also disinclined to help.
Above all, he resented having to do the course at all. 'Of
course one can't argue with the Chief. Orders are orders. But
no other officers have to do this and with my background
there must be many more useful things I could be doing,
especially as there's no shortage of people like Dorothy and
Miriam. And now you, too. I tried to point this out to the
Chief, but he got quite short with me. Said he could easily

find some decks for me to swab if I wanted to be really useful. Stress of his job and age, I suppose. He's getting on a bit and this is a young man's war. Not that I could swab decks, my knee being what it is.'

'Charles Dickens learned it, our instructor said.'

'Deck swabbing?'

'Shorthand. He got a job doing it in the Houses of Parliament.'

Nigel shrugged. 'You might be right. I'm not saying he didn't. Quite possibly he did. Probably easier if you're a writer, comes naturally. But I'm an officer of the Royal Marines. Doesn't come naturally.'

'What does come naturally, then?' He looked so troubled at this that she softened it with a smile. 'Lots of other things, I'm sure.' They were summoned back to class.

At the end of the second day, crossing the Strand, she thought she spotted Brown Bowler buying a paper outside Charing Cross station. She couldn't be sure because it was coming on to rain and umbrellas were springing up like mushrooms. But he was the right height and his coat looked familiar. However, on looking left as she crossed the road, she saw two more brown bowlers. Perhaps there was a secret society, a guild or an undercover army of brown bowlers, dedicated to following her. Her speculation would have remained playful had she not glimpsed another who looked very like the original – similar build and coat – ahead of her as she left the station at Barnes. By the time she reached the corner he had disappeared. The possibility that she really was being followed made her stomach feel empty and her heart beat faster, although it was reassuring that this time she was following him. Nevertheless, she walked rapidly home.

She might have left it at that had he not appeared again the following lunchtime when she left Pitman's in search of apples. She was looking forward to being alone after the close proximity of the class, but had run into Nigel on the stairs.

'Popping out for a sandwich or bun?' He put on his own bowler, which was black. 'Mind if I join you? There's a good stall on the Strand.'

'Actually, I'm going the other way, I'm after apples.'

'Good idea. Hadn't thought of apples. They help keep you awake in the afternoons. Only trouble is, it's hard to eat them quietly. People complain. D'you find that?'

As they walked up the Row she distinctly saw Brown Bowler ahead, disappearing round the corner into Maiden Lane. As he turned he glanced back. She was sure it was at her. When they reached Maiden Lane she saw him in the entrance to a shop just before Rules restaurant, looking back at her. Certain now, she felt her heart beat faster again. For once she felt grateful for Nigel's presence. He was describing a problem he'd had with a typewriter ribbon.

'There's a man back there in Maiden Lane,' she said in an undertone. 'He's wearing a brown bowler and a long dark coat. I think he's following me. I keep seeing him, it started before we went to Rotterdam and now he's come back. I hope I'm not imagining it but I'm a bit worried. D'you think I should tell the Chief? Or Frank Stagg or someone? I don't want to make a fuss about nothing, but it's a bit much for coincidence. Don't look round now in case he's watching us.'

Lieutenant Nisbet looked round. 'Which man, where?'

Emily couldn't help glancing back. 'The man approaching the post box. Don't stare, he'll think we're suspicious. Let's just keep going and see if he follows us.'

Lieutenant Nisbet stared. 'He can think what he likes but he's no right to follow people on British streets. Wait here while I go and see what he's up to.'

Before she could stop him, he was striding back down the Row. She missed the start of the fracas, distracted by the shout of a flower stall-holder into whose trolley she had backed. 'Mind where you're going, miss! Tread on 'em and you'll have to buy 'em!'

She recovered, apologized and moved away. Nigel and Brown Bowler now appeared to be locked in a swaying embrace. Both had lost their hats, Brown Bowler's upside down in the road beside the post box, Nigel's rolling along the pavement. Brown Bowler, his coat flapping, broke away, took a whistle from his pocket and blew a piercing blast. Nigel grabbed his arm and tripped on the kerb, clinging to the man's sleeve. A crowd of market porters and small boys wearing men's caps gathered, shouting encouragement. A boy picked up Nigel's hat and ran off towards the Strand. Two policemen ran out of the market behind Emily, jeered by the crowd. One grabbed Nigel's arm, breaking his hold on the coat, while the other embraced Brown Bowler from behind in a bear hug.

Emily started across the road towards them. Nigel was arguing with the policeman while Brown Bowler, one arm held by the other policeman, reached for something in his coat pocket. One of the porters picked up his hat and handed it to him. The policeman released him and joined the other in restraining Nigel, who was arguing and panting, his hair ruffled. Brown Bowler put on his hat and straightened his coat. The crowd began to drift away. A few remained to stare at Nigel, whom one of the policemen handcuffed.

Nigel spotted Emily. 'Miss Grey – that lady there, Miss Grey, she can vouch for me.'

Emily approached the policeman who had applied the handcuffs. 'It's all right, officer, I do know this man.'

'You do, do you, miss? And who might he be?'

'He's Lieutenant Nigel Nisbet, Royal Marines.'

'And you are, miss?'

'I'm Emily Grey.'

'We work together,' said Nigel.

'And where might that be?'

'The Admiralty,' said Emily.

'The War Office,' said Nigel.

The policeman looked from one to the other. 'Bow Street, you can tell your generals and admirals. That's where they'll find him.' They moved off, holding Nigel between them.

Emily pointed at Brown Bowler. 'But this man . . . this man has been following me. That's what . . . that's what Lieutenant Nisbet was trying to—'

'So you say, miss, so you say,' said the policeman over his

shoulder. 'Nothing for you to worry about now. He's on his way. You won't see 'im no more.'

Brown Bowler turned and walked away. Nigel twisted between his captors as they marched him off. 'My hat! Lost my hat!'

She felt she should follow Brown Bowler and accost him, also that she should follow Nigel to the police station. In neither case did she know what she would say or what use she might be. The street was already back to normal, Nigel's hat had vanished. There was no longer time for lunch before the afternoon class, but it felt wrong to go back and carry on as normal while Nigel was under arrest. Apart from waiting outside Bow Street police station, though, there was nothing she could do. She returned to class.

When they finished she hurried to Nigel's class to see if he'd returned, but he hadn't. She headed through the market to Bow Street police station. The waiting room was full, with all the benches occupied and people standing in the doorway. It smelt powerfully of old clothes and unwashed bodies. A woman was shouting at the young policeman at the desk, who was writing something in a ledger, ignoring her.

Emily didn't wait, but walked through Trafalgar Square to Whitehall Court. There was bound to be someone there to whom she could report Nigel's misadventure. Then she could go home. She was hungry.

Her heart sank slightly when she found Dorothy alone, who immediately asked how she was getting on at Pitman's.

She pretended she was enjoying it. 'It will be very useful, I'm sure,' she concluded.

Dorothy nodded approvingly. 'Essential. How's Lieutenant Nisbet coping? I understand he had a spot of bother today.'

'Oh, you know already?'

'So funny, his getting arrested like that. Made everyone's day here.'

It turned out that Brown Bowler was a police Special Branch officer assigned by Colonel Kell of MI5 to mount occasional surveillance on Emily – to watch over her, the Colonel had put it. Not because she was under suspicion, Dorothy explained with a smile, but because her time in Germany made her a possible subject of interest to German spies. The Chief had agreed. If Special Branch had detected anyone following her, they would have arrested him as a possible German spy. When Brown Bowler was accosted by Lieutenant Nisbet he had blown his police whistle and shown his warrant card to the officers. They had arrested Nisbet while they checked his identity. He had been released and had gone home.

'He was terribly upset about it, called it a gross indignity, an insult to His Majesty's commission, wanted to complain to the Chief Constable and goodness knows who else. The Chief laughed so much he had hiccoughs for the rest of the afternoon.'

Emily remembered the conversation with Colonel Kell, specifically his remark to the effect that they were keeping a close eye on her and others who had spent time in Germany. For her own protection, he had said. 'But why on earth didn't they tell me? If I'd known I could have made it easier for everyone. And I wouldn't have had the worry of thinking there was someone after me.'

'Perhaps they thought you wouldn't act naturally if you'd known you were being watched. It was all MI5's idea, apparently. The Chief had told Colonel Kell we were getting a new German speaker who had been to university in Germany and the colonel was terribly keen to see if the Germans would try to recruit you. They are doing a bit of that, it seems. There's one case they know of and a new one they suspect. The new one is somewhere awfully sensitive, apparently. Perhaps he didn't tell you because they like having secrets. There's relish for secrecy among some of our colleagues, I'm afraid. Secrecy for its own sake, some of it, if you ask me.' She shook her head, smiling. 'But we didn't know you'd nearly been involved in the fight. Was it frightening?'

Frank Stagg joined them, wanting to hear about it. The episode had evidently given pleasure to everyone except Nisbet and Emily. 'Not often we intervene in an MI5 operation, even by accident,' said Frank. 'Serves them right for not telling you. They didn't know Nisbet's our secret weapon.'

'But the Chief definitely knew?' Emily tried not to sound irritated.

'Sworn to secrecy, I suppose. I take it you haven't seen anyone else following you apart from the detective?'

'Not that I'm aware of.'

'Those two cases I mentioned,' said Dorothy, 'one's an old one dating from before the war and the new one is someone with a German background whom they suspect might have become a spy. Don't know where, as I said. It's all very hush-hush. But the Chief knows about it.'

Emily assumed this must be Lieutenant Hueffer in Rosyth. The fact that she had been entrusted with the secret while Dorothy and Frank hadn't took the edge off her irritation.

Nigel Nisbet was at Pitman's the next morning. He stopped her on the first landing, forcing others to squeeze past. 'That business yesterday. More to it than meets the eye. Can't say anything now. Meet me at lunchtime. Did you find my hat?'

'I'm afraid not, I saw a boy run away with it towards the Strand.'

'I think I should be compensated.'

'By whom?'

'Not sure yet. I'll think about it.'

At lunchtime they headed for the same stall, this time unwatched. 'Just as well I realised he was a policeman,' said Nigel. 'I'd have knocked him down otherwise. Ordered to follow us to make sure we were all right, I'm told.'

'Both of us?'

'You mainly. Worried about German spies following you around. Only followed me because I was with you. Silly, they should have known I can take care of myself.'

'How long did they keep you?'

'Nearly all afternoon. I was put in a cell for common criminals, then I was interviewed by a sergeant. Naturally I demanded an officer.'

'Did you get one?'

'No. Two hours later they told me I could go, no apologies. Would have been common courtesy to say something. Said I was lucky not to be charged with assaulting a police officer and preventing him going about his duty. I shall make a formal complaint, of course. I've told the Chief.'

'You saw the Chief?'

'I reported to the office on release. Seemed the responsible thing to do. I'm afraid to say, though, that he didn't seem to take it terribly seriously. But he assured me later that there's a reason behind what we're – what I'm – doing on this course. I'm being sent on a mission.'

'Did he say where?'

'Of course not, it's secret. But it's why I'm doing the course.'

She resisted the temptation to tell him, though not the temptation to tease. 'Perhaps you're going to be someone's secretary?'

'Wouldn't be anything like that, at my rank. Couldn't be. Probably cover for something.'

'So you'll be a pretend secretary?'

'Not at all, no. Not with my rank.' He turned to her. 'Has he said anything about where you're going? Some office somewhere, I suppose?'

'I suppose so. If I'm good enough.'

He nodded. 'Not sure I'll be up to it, either, to be honest, even as cover. Pitman's are back-squadding me. You know, sending me down a class.'

'Oh dear. Perhaps because you missed yesterday afternoon?'

That cheered him. 'You think so? Could be, yes. I felt I was keeping my head above water. Pretty well. More or less, anyway.'

The stall-holder recognised them. 'Got yourself into a right bundle yesterday,' he said cheerily to Nigel. 'They let you go, then?'

'They acknowledged it wasn't my fault.'

'Just as well they come along when they did, them rozzers. I could see you was goin' to get a proper pasting.'

'Impudent fellow,' said Nigel as they walked back. 'I was exercising self-restraint. I did boxing at school.'

CHAPTER NINE

Emily had a sleeper to herself on the overnight journey to Edinburgh but the train was slow, with long unexplained stops and jerking, clanking restarts. The kitchen was out of service, breakfast a stale current bun with a glass of milk. She had to wait at Edinburgh Waverley for a change of train to cross the Forth, followed by an uncomfortable motorbus journey to the port of Rosyth. The bus was packed with sailors returning from leave, but at least that meant eager hands to help with her luggage.

More sailors at the guardroom ticked off her name and directed her to the Port Security Office, a detached two-storey redbrick building at the end of a row of six huge warehouses. As it was a fifteen-minute walk to the PSO they suggested she leave her luggage in the guardroom for someone from the PSO to collect. She was tired and her shoes were pinching. She also felt increasingly conspicuous under the gazes and whistles of distant dockyard workers and sailors. Men on bicycles, of whom there were many, waved or gave mock salutes. She reached the PSO without having seen another woman.

The building was locked. She looked about, clutching her handbag with both hands, no idea where to go or what to do. Except that she increasingly needed the lavatory. Eventually she saw a man in a suit and hat carrying a briefcase and walking briskly. She waited, hoping he would let her in, but he headed past, apparently oblivious. She had to call out.

He pulled out a pocket watch from his waistcoat pocket. 'They'll all be at lunch now. Officers in the wardroom, staff in the canteen. Who is it you want to see?'

'Lieutenant Commander Cooden. He's in charge, I believe.'

He directed her to the wardroom, another fifteen-minute walk. The port was so large that she hadn't yet seen any water or docks, just superstructures of warships in the distance. Unseen vessels hooted, clouds of smoke rose and dispersed. From somewhere came a regular thump and hiss of steam. The lowering sky looked like rain.

The wardroom was another two-storey building, this time built of stone. It fronted onto a well-tended lawn with flower beds and two flagpoles bearing the Union Jack and the navy's Red Ensign. Steps flanked by two ancient cannon led up to a wide central door. Inside was a parquet-floored hall dominated by pictures of the King and Queen and a polished round table, on which sat an intricate model of an old sailing ship of the line. Despite the time of year, a coal fire smouldered within a large stone surround. A corridor led off left and right, carpeted in blue and lined with photographs of warships. From the left came sounds of men's voices and laughter. Emily ventured along it, hoping for a lavatory. A door opened and closed near the far end, briefly heightening the sounds of voices. A tall, overweight, middle-aged army officer emerged. His cheeks drooped like a spaniel's, his complexion was florid, his fair moustache stained yellow, his hair receding. He held a cigarette in one hand and approached with ponderous stateliness, raising his eyebrows. His eyes were china blue and kindly. Recognition was mutual.

'Ah, Miss Grey, saviour of the PSO, long-desired, only recently anticipated. How was your journey?'

There was pleasure in alighting so soon upon Lieutenant Hueffer, a friendly presence; but also consternation because he was, in Colonel Kell's words, her target. To be manipulated, worked upon, spied upon.

'Your sins in another life must have been grave for you to be posted to us. But we at least are unjustly rewarded.'

'I was ordered to report to Lieutenant Commander Cooden,' she said. 'But first of all I'd like to find a ladies'.'

'Follow me. Heads – they call them heads here, even though we're on dry land. The navy likes to pretend everything is a ship.' He led her back the way she had come.

'It's very kind of you. I hope I'm not taking you out of your way?'

'Not at all, I'm going there myself.'

They crossed the hall into the far side of the corridor, at the end of which a door with a brass plaque proclaimed Heads.

She was alarmed by the prospect of sharing, but her need was urgent. He stopped before the door.

'We're not set up for ladies here, no ladies' lavatories as such. The navy can't bring itself to acknowledge them. They know all about navigation here, not much about imagination. You go in and I'll stand guard, finish my cigarette.'

By the time she emerged he had stubbed out his cigarette in a silvered ashtray on a waist-high stand and was in the At Ease position, legs apart, hands clasped behind his back, facing down the corridor. 'No boarders to repel. My turn now. If you don't mind waiting I'll show you around.'

'The commander wasn't in the bar just now,' he said when he came out. 'We call him commander, by the way, promoting him by one rank. He never objects. Nor do most of these military and naval types, in my experience. Didn't see him at lunch. Keeps himself to himself rather, might be there now. Come with me and we'll see. You must be in need of sustenance yourself after that journey.'

The dining room was at the far end of the first corridor. During their stately perambulation she was struck again by how ancient and portly he was for a subaltern. She couldn't imagine him leading a platoon of young men at the Front. Perhaps he been injured, or perhaps he had never been near it, judged too old for active service. If he was a spy, he was quite unlike the popular archetype. But so were TR/16 and the Belgian lawyer. Spies, she was beginning to think, were ordinary – ordinary people who spied.

Lieutenant Hueffer asked about her journey, hoped she

had plenty of warm clothes, told her Commander Cooden had arranged a cabin for her in the wardroom. 'You'll be the only lady here and guaranteed a great deal of attention from eager young naval officers.' He grinned. His teeth, like his moustache, were stained yellow by nicotine.

A woman wearing a white shirt and dark tie sat at a desk at the entrance to the dining room. 'This is Miss Grey,' said Lieutenant Hueffer. 'She has just arrived from London and will be accommodated here in the wardroom on PSO ration strength. Commander Cooden should have put her on your list.'

The woman looked down a typed list of names, some of them ticked. 'No Miss Grey here. No misses at all.' Her accent was Scots and she sounded disapproving.

'In that case put her on my bill. She can be my guest for the time being.' His pendulous cheeks wobbled when he shook his head at Emily's tentative protests. 'I'm sure we'll find ways for you to pay me back once you start work. Anything to relieve the tedium and pressures of boom defence. Now I must leave you, I'm afraid. Someone has to man the office – or bridge, as the navy would have it – but eat your fill and sort yourself out here until sent for. Don't rush, there's no hurry. Just settle yourself in.'

There was one long polished table with places laid and gaps where lunchers had come and gone. About half a dozen officers clustered around the far end. The woman at the desk nodded towards the nearer end. 'Sit yourself down there. Someone will serve you.'

Aware that the officers were commenting on her, Emily

pretended to be engrossed in pouring water. Next she gazed out of the window, watching a steam engine chug slowly from one of the huge sheds, puffing neat gouts of stream. An elderly male waiter served her brown soup without a word. She picked up her spoon, but before she could use it one of the officers approached.

'Madam, would you care to join us? We are starved of good company and need civilising.' He smiled and gestured with his napkin at his colleagues.

Lunch passed in a haze. They were junior officers, older than her but not by much, openly delighted by female company. She was plied with so many questions that it was difficult to finish her unidentifiable soup. The same mute waiter then served shepherd's pie. One of the officers offered wine, which she refused, another warned that the PSO was a deadly place, more tomb than office, a third invited her to drinks on his ship as soon as it was ready. They took her account of her secretarial role at face value and seemed reassured that she was of a naval family.

'Don't take any nonsense from old Coody,' said one. 'He's terribly pernickety, pokes his nose into everything.'

'Coody? Is that what you call him?'

'Not to his face but it's what he does, Coody about everywhere. Hasn't been to sea since Nelson's day but gives the impression he's a real old salt. He's an engineer officer really, that's his trade. They didn't used to be officers but they are now. He's not a bad old stick so long as you don't let him push you around.'

'I've met him already in London, on the Admiralty Induction Course. And his deputy, Lieutenant Hueffer, an army—'

'Old Hoofs, yes. He's all right, decent enough fellow, for a brown job, anyway. That's what we call them here, 'scuse my French. Old as Methuselah. He must be passed over or very newly joined.'

'How does he come to be here, as an army officer?'

'No idea. Don't know whether he does. Temporary posting, apparently. Maybe his regiment didn't know what to do with him, given his age.'

'He's a writer,' said another. 'Writes. Writes books.'

'Really? What kind of books?'

'Haven't the faintest.' He glanced at the others but there was a general shrugging of shoulders. 'Maybe they want him to do one on boom defences. That's what he does here, all that stuff in the outer harbour. Assessing it and planning it.'

'He mentioned that to me. I wasn't quite sure what he meant, though.'

'Underwater nets and surface chains and obstacles, that sort of thing. To stop enemy ships or torpedoes disturbing our beauty sleep.'

Emily felt she mustn't appear too interested in Lieutenant Hueffer but wanted to make the most of their willingness to talk. 'It's a funny name, Hueffer. How is it spelt?'

One of them spelt it. 'German, he's half Hun. Father was a Hun, dead now. But Hoof was brought up and educated in London. Quite open about it. Speaks German. You'd think they'd use him in War Office Intelligence.'

'Strange they should send him here, then.'

'Wanted to get him out of the way, perhaps. As far from Germans as possible. Maybe he's not trusted.'

'Decent enough fellow, though,' said one of the earlier speakers. 'As I said. Helped me out with my mess bill when I'd overdone it. Not bad for a brown job.'

As they left for the afternoon session of the course they were on, one of them nervously invited Emily to be his partner at a forthcoming dance called the Rosyth Meeting. Another immediately urged her to take no notice but to be his partner, then a third – the best-looking – did the same. Finally, one of the others proposed she should be the official group partner for Advanced Night Navigation Course 57. She smilingly accepted all without knowing when or where the dance was to be, assuming none of the invitations could be serious. She had nothing to wear for a dance anyway.

She sat for a while after they had gone. It was young men such as these whom Hans had sailed out to kill. And young men such as these had killed Hans. They were so much alike.

She was roused by the woman from the desk. 'You are ordered to report to Lieutenant Commander Cooden in the Port Security Office.'

Her shoes pinched painfully by the time she reached the PSO building, but at least the rain held off. A notice pointed up stairs to the second floor where a half-glazed door forbade entry. Inside it a large young seaman sat at a desk, her two suitcases on the floor before him.

'Miss Grey? Commander's expecting you. Your gear's here,

sent over by the guardroom. I'll get it sent to the wardroom if you know your cabin number.'

'Twenty-two,' a loud male voice called from an office opening off. 'She's in twenty-two. Lucky girl. Send her in, Jackson.'

It was a large office with a conference table and chairs, a coal fire and a view of distant warships, quaysides, moorings and the river. Lieutenant Commander Cooden sat at a desk to one side. He seemed shorter and plumper than she remembered, his physique contrasting with his sharp, almost rodent-like, features. He stood and held out his hand. 'Miss Grey, the supernumerary from the AIC. Who would have thought they'd find a perch for you here? Delighted to have you aboard. Cup of tea? Two cups, Jackson.' He shouted the instruction without waiting for her reply. 'Sit down, do. How was your journey?' He held up his hand, grinning. 'No, say nothing, let me guess – late, crowded, uncomfortable, but could have been worse. That it, eh? Now, tell me, what happened to you? You and that other chap – academic clever-clogs, mathematical type, Edward something. You both disappeared, missed the final bit of the course. What happened?'

For a moment she could think of only what she mustn't say. 'I don't know about him,' she said, clearly recalling glimpsing him in Room 40. 'I was sent on temporary attachment to the War Office to help with casualty lists.' She thought that sounded plausible, unlikely to provoke further questions. 'And then I was recalled to the Admiralty and told to report here.'

'Glad to have you. Been pestering the Admiralty for admin assistance since the day I arrived. Then they sent Hueffer who's no help at all where that sort of thing is concerned. Not his fault, not his job, anyway. You must remember him from the course, don't you? Army chap on secondment. He has the other office here. Got knocked about a bit on the Front. They probably sent him here for a rest. Which is what he does, a lot of the time.' Jackson served tea and plain biscuits from a wooden tray. The tea was very strong. 'You'll share the other office with Hueffer. He's half German, by the way. Speaks it, I believe. Not that there's much use for that here. You'd think the powers-that-be would find a better use for him, but there's no fathoming the Admiralty mind. The same logic dictated that I needed to go on the AIC despite having spent my entire career in the navy. Reckoned I needed refreshment on Admiralty shore establishments and structures, as if anyone could find that refreshing.' He barked a laugh and she watched as he helped himself to six teaspoons of sugar. 'A great language, though, German. Don't you think? Great culture, so much in common with our own. Tragic that we should be at war with them. Must be awful for the Royal Family, the King and the Kaiser being cousins and all that.'

Emily agreed it must be awful.

'And him – the Kaiser – an Admiral of the Royal Navy – honorary, of course – until this nonsense started. People have forgotten that.'

Emily agreed they had.

He described her duties, the first of which was to begin

typing up his review of port security. It was currently hand-written in draft. Jackson had typed the first few paragraphs but he was ham-fisted, better suited to heaving ropes than fiddling with the keys of Underwoods or Remingtons or whatever they were. He laughed again.

'Do I work for Lieutenant Hueffer as well?' she asked.

'Yes, yes, of course. It's all PSO work. Not that he produces much. Nerves, you know, shell-shock.' He shook his head. 'Nothing much to be done, if you ask me, although he has treatment for it. That's where he'll be this afternoon, one of his sessions with the sawbones – you know, medical chaps. Also, he doesn't cover the full range of port security, just does our boom defence work, designing and planning. The Admiralty in their wisdom want boom defences right across the Firth of Forth, out beyond the new railway bridge you came over. Don't ask me why. The army has enough artillery pieces on shore and on the islands in the estuary to sink half the German High Seas Fleet, so I'm not pushing him to get on with it. Letting him take his own time. Best thing for him. Let me show you round.'

He took her into a smaller office with two desks. The one nearer the door had a typewriter on it. 'That's yours, your very own. Jackson will see you have plenty of paper and anything else you need. You don't work for him, by the way. Just me and Hueffer.' He paused. He had a small mouth and his puckered lips worked for a few seconds before he spoke. He turned and shouted, 'Jackson, get onto the guardroom for transport, something to take us out on a boom recce.'

'Right away, sir.'

He turned back to Emily. 'Talking of boom defence reminds me it's time I had another look at it. Useful for you so you can see what Hueffer is talking about when you're typing stuff for him. Have you any warm gear? Gets pretty sharp out in the firth in an open launch.'

'I have warmer clothes than these, yes.' She tried to sound positive as she ran through mental images of the clothes she had brought. There was nothing she would have chosen for nautical exposure.

'If Jackson gets a vehicle it can run you back to the wardroom, you can get changed and I'll pick you up and we'll take the launch out. How about that, eh?' He looked at her with raised eyebrow as if offering a child a treat.

Ordinary Seaman Jackson returned with car and driver from the guardroom. It was one of the new Morrises, painted the same dark blue as sailors' uniforms but with a white stripe running round its middle.

'Bored to tears, the men in that guardroom,' said the commander. 'Nothing to do most of the time. Kill each other for a distraction like this. Off you go.'

Her wardroom cabin was on the second floor at the end of a corridor next to a bathroom shared with three other cabins. It was what her father would have called Admiralty issue, plain and clean with its own washbasin and a view across the dockyard to a maze of cranes and a dozen or more warships. These ranged from stubby minesweepers through sleek destroyers and grim purposeful cruisers to two huge battleships, bristling with armament. Her father would be bound to ask their names, but even if she did find out it wasn't, she now knew, the sort of thing that should be written in a wartime letter. Which ships were where was one of the navy's closely guarded secrets, just as which German ships were where was what it most wanted to know.

But her mind was on what to wear for a trip across choppy water. There was no time for indecision, but even so she paused in almost tearful despair – brought on by tiredness, she told herself – as she sorted through her two suitcases. Eventually she chose thick wool stockings that made her feel like her grandmother, a heavy old tweed skirt she resolved to throw away every time she wore it, two light jumpers, the brown beneath the green, her raincoat and her brown floppy hat. She wore the heavy shoes she had bought in Germany for walking with Hans. It seemed unlikely that anyone would notice German shoes.

The commander wore his naval greatcoat, gloves and officer's cap. He told the driver which wharf to make for and settled close beside her, apparently unaware of their bodies touching. More than touching; he was pressing against her. Perhaps he couldn't feel it through his thick coat, she thought; she moved anyway, squashing herself against the side. He occupied the journey by naming and identifying everything they passed. His knowledge was impressive, his desire to impart it unrelenting. She imagined he might indeed be a stickler to work for, fussing over every detail, as one of the wardroom officers implied.

'Been on a boat before?' he asked.

She told him about her family's naval background, prolonging it in the hope that it would divert him from asking how else she had occupied herself since leaving school. She didn't want to mention university, still less her year in Heidelberg. Fortunately, he was more interested in her father's career, the ships he had been on and whether he kept up with his old shipmates.

'Who does he still see? Tell me who his friends are, give me a picture of him. Can't recall him now but it's possible we met.' He nodded as she named half a dozen officers, picking up on one. 'Captain Hall – now Admiral Hall, otherwise known as Blinker?'

'He's my godfather.' She guessed his knowing that would do no harm to her standing in his eyes.

'Really? Really? Extraordinary coincidence. Captained the battle-cruiser *Queen Mary*, didn't he? That's how I knew him. Quite a ball of fire, force of nature.'

She thought her father had also served under Hall on the *Queen Mary* but didn't mention it. He continued in communicative mood, as people often did, she'd observed, when driven in cars or carriages. She took advantage of it. 'Strange that you should have an army officer as your assistant rather than a naval officer or a marine.'

'Probably didn't know what to do with him, as I said.' He laughed abruptly again, shaking his head. 'No, but the ways of the Lord are strange and the ways of the Admiralty even stranger. I put in for an assistant and a secretary at the same time. Got approval for both. Then nothing. Then one day they tell me I've got a Hun – half-Hun – arriving the next morning. He had no idea about the navy, never served in a port, never had anything to do with security, never heard of boom defence. And has a touch of shell-shock from the Front. Perfect, just what we need. Apparently he – or we – are victims of some exchange scheme between the War Office and the Admiralty in which each posts men they don't know what to do with on temporary attachments to the other. They go back and forth like shuttlecocks, I'm told. Same chaps often as not, time and time again.'

'He was very helpful to me when I ran into him in the wardroom.'

'Well, yes, he's helpful enough, no doubt about that. Agreeable all round, really, despite being half-Hun.'

She feigned ignorance of that. 'If he's really half-German I'm surprised they posted him to a job in security.'

'Nothing surprises me about the Admiralty, nothing. He could be the Kaiser's son and they'd still send him. Promote him too, probably. They're good enough at doing the opposite, not promoting people when they should. I could give you plenty of examples of that. Oh yes.'

He fell silent until they reached the quay. Tied up alongside was a launch flying the harbour master's flag. Two crewmen on deck surreptitiously flicked their cigarettes overboard, one went to the wheelhouse and the other came smartly up the gangplank, saluting. The commander gave instructions while Emily settled herself on the cushioned stern seat. It was wide enough for them both, but she positioned herself so that she sat at an angle which created a gap between them, her back half against the stern and half against the port side. There was sun and breeze and the water was only moderately choppy.

Not for the first time she noticed how distances across water were usually greater than appeared from land. The famous railway bridge was well in view, but it took a while before it was obviously closer. Despite the exhilaration of being afloat and in the open, tiredness was stealing over her like an incoming tide. She desperately wanted to close her eyes and was about to say something to keep herself awake when the commander, who had been staring at the water rushing past, turned to her.

'Wonderful things, these heavy oil engines, diesels.' He nodded at the covered rectangular bulk between them and the half-cabin. 'Hun invention, of course, all thanks to Herr Diesel.'

'Bavarian, I think. Born in Paris and partly educated in London.'

'Was he, by God? I didn't know that. Take an interest in engines, do you, Miss Grey? Or just in matters German?'

'I hear a lot about engines from my father, who takes them very seriously indeed. Herr Diesel's fate was sad, wasn't it? Still a bit of a mystery.' The commander didn't know the story and so she kept herself awake by recounting Herr Diesel's overnight disappearance in 1913 from the SS *Dresden* en route to Britain from Amsterdam. She surprised herself by how much she had unconsciously imbibed, mostly from her father's conversations with others such as her godfather.

'If you don't mind my asking, how d'you know all this? Not normally a ladylike subject.' The commander barked his laugh again and when she explained, said, 'Of course, the navy is taking to oil, isn't it? In preference to steam. Not sure what portion of our ships are now oil-fired. Did he say anything about that, old Blinker? He would know, of course.'

She couldn't remember that he had, except that he, like her father, favoured oil.

'And British – our – submarines, all oil now, are they?'

'I don't know. Presumably.' She flinched against the spray.

'Slide along here if you like, it's drier.'

'No, I'm fine, thank you. It's quite refreshing.'

'Seasickness doesn't bother you?'

'Not usually, no.'

'Bothers Hueffer. Daresay that's why he doesn't get out as often as he should. Prefers to draw up plans on land rather than climb aboard and feel how the seas run. Probably the Hun in him. Essentially landlocked people, no real nautical tradition despite having a fine navy. That's why I've had to do so some of the boom defence stuff myself, as you'll see from my report. Not that anyone in the Admiralty will appreciate that. Too much to expect, eh?'

The size and scale of the Forth railway bridge awed her as they approached, its towers embedded in massive supports, themselves embedded in the river. The railway track looked far higher than it had felt from the carriage window. They passed beneath the great structure without slowing.

'Inchkeith, that's where we're heading,' said the commander, pointing to the still-distant island in the mouth of the firth. 'It's to be the linchpin of the boom defences, provided Hueffer gets his designs right. You'll soon see why.'

'Lieutenant Hueffer's designing the whole thing, is he?'

'Supposedly, yes, provided he cracks on with it. Trouble is – between you, me and the gatepost, Miss Grey – I can't be sure that he is. Cracking on, I mean. Can't trust him. That's why I have to intervene, keep an eye on things, make sure everything's recorded.'

His frankness surprised her, but that was no reason not to make use of it. 'You can't trust him? That must make things very awkward for you. Why not?'

'No wind in his sails. Maybe there never was or maybe it's shell-shock. Used to be a writer in civilian life. Novels and poetry, that sort of thing. Mind away with the fairies, probably. I doubt it's the Hun in him. Huns are usually hard-working, aren't they? Industrious, methodical people. Though you've probably never known any.'

'They do have that reputation.'

'Have you ever met any? Germans, that is?'

'Yes, some. A few. Not recently.' She tried to sound as if she were having to search her memory,

'What did you think of them?'

'Well, they seemed ... seemed normal, like us.'

'Exactly, exactly what I think. Despite all we hear about them or read in the newspapers, they can't be all bad. That's not to deny, of course ... I mean, we all get things wrong sometimes. Many people still think we did over the Boer War. The Germans were against us over that, very much so. But of course one has to be careful what one says nowadays, button one's lip. All very well in private but different matter in public. Where did you meet your Germans?'

She was spared a reply by a shout from one of the crewmen. 'Starboard gun battery coming up, sir. Shall we take her in closer?'

'Yes, do, close as you can,' the commander shouted back. He stood and went over to the wheelhouse, steadying himself against the rail.

The launch veered towards the right-hand shore. As they closed, the commander pointed to three artillery guns mounted on the rocky bank, about halfway between the shoreline and the level of the bridge. 'Number four battery. Twelve-pounders. They and the other battery on Inchgarvie on the other side there cover the gap between the island and this bank and a bit beyond. Should be enough to deal with anything trying to slip through this side. Army, though, not our own gunners, so we have to keep them on their toes. Fall asleep on the job, otherwise. Another reason why I have to inspect regularly.'

They slowed about a hundred yards out, wallowing with a motion that could, Emily felt, soon become sick-making. The three dull green guns were obvious when pointed out but otherwise easily overlooked. They were sited on ledges, surrounded by concrete and brickwork and aimed to the starboard side of the island.

'There – see what I mean?' the commander exclaimed. 'Not a soul in sight. Where are the lookouts? Probably in their bunkers brewing up. Half the German fleet could slip through here unnoticed.' He took a notebook from his pocket. 'I'll report this. Daresay we'll find the same at the next one. If we had a gun on board I'd be tempted to give them a blast, wake them up a bit.'

They turned and headed for Inchkeith island, a rocky outcrop in mid-channel half-covered by trees and vegetation. There were three gun emplacements pointing out to sea.

'Several batteries here, six-inch and nine-point-two. I've suggested to Hueffer there should be more. Depending on how far out the boom defences are – they can't be much farther, given the way the estuary widens – any vessel trying ram the defences would be a sitting duck. But the island's the obvious target for a battleship that could sit out to sea beyond range of these and give them a real pasting. We couldn't risk them being silenced, which is why we need more and bigger guns here with longer ranges. Not so worried about the shore batteries, harder to spot and hit from the sea because protected by the coasts. Must make sure Hueffer takes that on board.' He made another note.

There were signs of life around these guns. Soldiers waved, crewmen waved back. One soldier shouted what sounded like a plea for beer. 'Now the north shore,' ordered the commander. 'More twelve-pounders,' he added for Emily's benefit.

The gun positions mirrored those on the southern shore, again with no crew to be seen. 'Typical, what did I tell you?' said the commander.

'There's someone there, down on the foreshore, not near the guns.' Emily stood as a wave struck the launch side-on, forcing her to steady herself by clutching the commander's shoulder. She let go as soon as she could and pointed. 'There, see. A man in army uniform.'

The figure was standing below the lowest gun position, staring at the launch. The commander stared. 'Bless me if it isn't Hueffer. What on earth's the fellow doing here?' He called out and waved. Lieutenant Hueffer, whom Emily now recognised, waved back.

'Can you take her in closer?'

'Worried about them rocks, sir.' The launch edged forward, engine muted. One crewman took an oar and stepped nimbly around the wheelhouse to the bow, the oar held ready to prod them away from the rocks.

'What are you doing here?' shouted the commander.

'Inspecting gun positions, sir,' Lieutenant Hueffer shouted back.

'Want a lift back?'

'Most kind of you.'

The commander turned to the helmsman. 'Can we get close enough to get him aboard?'

'Maybe if we go the lee side of the rocks, sir.'

The launch reversed into open water, then edged forward again to the other side of rocks which projected from the shore like an incomplete natural jetty. Hueffer, who had a walking stick, teetered uncertainly from rock to rock until he reached the farthest point. There was a gust of wind and he almost lost balance while reaching for his hat. He laughed.

'Better take her back out and come in again port side on,' said the crewman. They reversed again and this time, heading into the run of the sea parallel with the shore, crept alongside the end rock on which Hueffer now stood like an incongruous memorial. 'Can't get closer, sir, can you jump?' shouted the helmsman.

'So long as I don't sink you.'

He jumped as a wave lifted the boat. One leg slipped into the water, but the waiting crewman caught and heaved him into the well of the boat. His hat came off, his stick was lost to the sea and he lay sprawling on his back beside the engine, grinning. He was a heavy man and the boat rocked alarmingly. The helmsman opened the throttle, trusting forward motion to overcome lateral. Emily was embarrassed for him but couldn't help laughing.

The commander was less amused. 'Have a care, man, you'll capsize us! What are you doing here anyway? How did you get here? I thought you were talking shell-shock with sawbones?'

The lieutenant heaved himself to his feet, leaning on the engine cover and puffing with the exertion. 'I did, sir. He recommended solitary walking in the country, so I took a bus part-way and walked the rest. Thought I'd combine the medical with the military and recce the coastline again. Didn't know you were coming out or I'd have asked to join you.' He straightened and almost toppled again, causing the launch to wobble.

'For God's sake sit down before you sink us. You've soaked Miss Grey, look.'

'It's all right, it's just spray.' Emily's coat and feet were wet, her hands and wrists cold. She tucked each hand in the opposite sleeve. 'I was already a bit wet before Lieutenant Hueffer joined us.'

Hueffer sat. He doffed his recovered cap with exaggerated ceremony. 'My apologies, Miss Grey. I must learn how to board more elegantly. Nelson would have hoofed out Hueffer. I fear I'm a dreadful landlubber.'

'You don't doff your cap in the navy, you salute,' said the commander. 'Same as in the army.'

'Correct, of course, sir, quite right. But you mustn't salute while seated, according to the army, and I fear to risk us all by standing again. Although I understand the navy are permitted to sit while drinking the loyal toast. Is that right, sir?'

The commander nodded and looked away. Emily suspected the lieutenant of teasing with elaborate politeness and lordly condescension. She also suspected that the commander felt the effect of it without knowing how to respond.

'Still don't see why you needed to be out here anyway,' the commander continued. 'You must have recce'd the shoreline enough times, judging by your plans and diagrams for the booms?'

'Indeed, sir, indeed I have. Recce'd it many times. But know your ground, sir, know every hoof and boot print, as the Iron Duke said.'

The commander turned away again. The southern headland was already shrouded in rain and as they got out into the firth the launch bucked and dipped. Lieutenant Hueffer smiled conspiratorially at Emily. 'Or might have said,' he added softly.

Emily smiled back. Like the commander, but for different reasons, she wasn't sure how to take the lieutenant. On the one hand, everything he said sounded contrived and artificial, as if he was speaking in inverted commas and assumed everyone knew he didn't mean it. On the other, his manner was insidiously confiding, making whoever he spoke to feel they were sharing secrets. He was not attractive physically – quite the opposite – but his speech and expressions suggested a potential for intimacy that she found worryingly appealing. If she were to fulfil her mission to cultivate, assess and investigate him, it would be impossible not to take advantage of it. But it would make her task more difficult. It would be easier if it were the commander she had to report on; he was certainly less likeable.

An intense rain squall put a stop to further conversation. One of the crew forsook the bench in the wheelhouse and offered it to Emily; she accepted only when the commander and Lieutenant Hueffer insisted. The car was waiting at the quay.

'We'll drop you two drowned rats at the wardroom,' said the commander. 'I'm going back to the office. Hueffer, join me there when you've changed and dried. You presumably have something to write up from your observations this afternoon? I know I have. Miss Grey, take the rest of the day off to unpack and sort yourself out. Report for work tomorrow at 0800.'

Four rows of letters were laid out on the round table in the entrance to the wardroom. A sailor was laying out a fifth alphabetically. Most were single items, but some addressees had three or even four. 'Well done, Watson,' said the lieutenant. 'Any for me? If it's from my bank put it in someone else's pile.'

'Just two, sir. Second column, over there.'

They were both handwritten white envelopes. Emily tried not to peer too obviously. One had been redirected from a Sussex address she couldn't make out, the other had a sender's London address on the back but she could make out no more than the word London as he turned it over. If either contained secret correspondence from Germany, he was acting in a convincingly relaxed manner, glancing at each and not at all concerned to conceal them.

'One for you too, ma'am,' said the sailor, pointing to a small lilac blue envelope.

'An admirer? So soon?' Lieutenant Hueffer raised his yellowing eyebrows and smiled.

'I very much doubt it.' Emily was irritated with herself for blushing. She did not recognise the flowery writing and could not think who could know where she was. Only Whitehall Court knew her address. She had promised it to her mother but hadn't had time to write. It was unstamped and there was no sender's address.

The lieutenant must have noticed the lack of stamp because he added, 'A local one too. Now if you'll excuse me I shall change and then go and humour our master. There's a bathroom on your corridor, by the way, plenty of hot water. Dinner at 7.30. See you there, I hope?'

She hurried to her cabin, leaving the letter unopened while she changed from her wet shoes, stockings, dress, cardigans, everything. She kept glancing at the letter. Eventually, still shivering and only partially wrapped in the small towel hanging by the washbasin, she opened it. It was a single paragraph from Nigel; he had tried to call on her but had been refused entry to the port, despite giving his name and rank. He gave the address of his lodging house in town, with directions. He had timed it at thirteen minutes' walk from the guardroom. Had she any messages for London?

She did, but the problem was when to get them to him. She was hungry and tired, was expected for dinner that evening, doubted there'd be time after to get into town, had to start work at eight the next morning and didn't know when she'd be free. She was longing for a bath and would have loved a hair-wash, but there was no time for that. A rapid bath might leave her time to get into town and back before dinner, provided the rain stopped. And provided she could get safely to the bathroom in a state of undress.

She put on her nightgown and cautiously opened the door. There was no one about and the bathroom was three doors farther down the corridor. She gathered dry clothes, put on her slippers and hurried out. The bathroom was empty and Spartan, but clean, with a large cork bathmat leant against the bath. She locked the door, checking it twice as she ran the bath. The water was indeed hot, as Lieutenant Hueffer had said, and it was blissful to sink into it. She would have loved to linger.

'A – er – a gentleman was here looking for you couple of hours ago, ma'am,' a marine at the guardroom told her. 'Said he was an officer and that you could vouch for him but he wouldn't give his name so we told him to . . . to . . . anyway, he left a note. Which was delivered to the wardroom.'

'Thank you, yes, I do know him. He is a serving officer and I'm going to call on him now. There shouldn't be any need for him to bother you again.' The marine and two listening sailors smiled, clearly thinking she was attending an assignation. She felt herself blushing again as she asked for directions. She would tell Nigel not to call again.

She calculated she would have ten minutes with him if she was to return in time for dinner. His street comprised facing terraces of modern two-storey stone houses with slate roofs and small curtained windows which, unlike those in Rotterdam, were very much not intended to facilitate internal inspection by passers-by. Number 17 was answered by a middle-aged woman with short brown hair, wearing a grubby patterned apron and holding a dishcloth.

'I'll get him,' was all she said. She pushed the door to.

Nigel appeared wearing his tweed suit and hat. He looked as if got up for a role with an amateur theatre company.

'We'll talk while we walk,' he said without a greeting, heading at pace down the street. 'She's taken against me. That woman, the landlady. Makes it obvious in everything she does. Her husband works in the dockyard. Wouldn't be surprised if they're both German spies.'

'Perhaps she thinks you are.'

'Treats me like a criminal, that's for sure. As did the sailors in the guardroom when I tried to get in and see you. Impudent lot. I've a mind to report them when we're finished here. Have you found out anything?'

'Yes ... well, no, nothing significant, just some circumstantial bits and pieces.' They walked through streets of stone houses, huddled as if to make themselves as small and humble as possible. She described Lieutenant Hueffer's boom defence responsibility and his appearance on the coast that afternoon when Lieutenant Commander Cooden thought he was seeing the doctor about his shell-shock.

'Recce-ing the gun positions, obviously,' said Nigel. 'We must find out how he reports back.'

'Presumably he knows where the guns are anyway as he's responsible for that area.'

'Checking for reinforcements. Do people know he's half-Hun?'

'Yes, he's quite open about it.'

'What does Cooden think of him?'

'Not much. He says he doesn't apply himself very energetically to his work, though allowance must be made for his shell-shock.'

'Probably just a ruse. They're cunning, these spies. We're still awaiting his army records from the War Office. They hadn't arrived by the time I left London. What do you make of Cooden? Sound enough chap? Would he help us, d'you think?'

'I wouldn't say he's naturally a helpful soul but he's quite a keen Hun-basher, rhetorically, anyway.' Using the term, like hearing it, caused her to wince inwardly but she felt she had to appear to fit in. 'Although he admires German culture and is prepared to allow that individual Germans may be just like us, more or less.'

'Some of them, anyway. Your late fiancé, for example – presumably you thought he was all right?'

'Yes, I did, yes. He was a good man. He never wanted to wage war.' She was taken aback by his casual directness but knew she would have to get used to it. The more people knew, the more she was going to hear it. She tried to respond with the same matter-of-factness, regardless of the inner tremors any mention of Hans still provoked.

'Anything else about Hueffer?'

She told him about Hueffer's two letters.

'No chance you could get another sight of them, go to his cabin on some pretext?'

'Not plausibly, no.'

'Any agent's clandestine communications are very important.

They're his most vulnerable point. If we can get across his comms we learn everything.'

'I'll bear it in mind.' They turned the corner back into his street. A few boys were noisily kicking a ball around.

'Don't see why they have to make such noise,' said Nigel.

Her allotted ten minutes were nearly up. 'Talking of communications,' she said, 'hadn't we better work out something that doesn't involve your calling at the guardroom? It does rather draw attention to us both.'

'Good point.' He stopped and looked down at his polished brown shoes. He looked up. 'Cold for the time of year. Are you cold?'

'I was, out in the launch. How will you transmit my reports to Whitehall Court?'

'That's easy enough. When I've written them up I take them to the police HQ in Edinburgh and they go by train to Scotland Yard as part of the Chief Constable's secure communications, then someone from Whitehall Court picks them up.'

She didn't like the thought of her oral reports subject to written interpretation by Nigel. 'Wouldn't it be better if I wrote them and handed them to you?'

'I know how they like reports to be written. Wouldn't have the same impact if you did it.'

'The Chief seemed happy enough with my Rotterdam reports. And it would be less work for you.'

'It might.' He contemplated his shoes again.

'I've got to get back. But we need to agree how and where we'll meet.'

He looked up at the footballing boys. 'Dead drop. DLB – dead letter box – whereby you signal when it's filled and I signal when I've emptied it. We'll have to go fully clandestine, never be seen together. I'll recce a site and leave a note for you with the guardroom.'

'I'd rather we didn't involve the guardroom, as I've just said.'

'I'll post it, then.'

'Is that safe?'

'Probably. Just once.'

'Look, I have to go. So I'll wait to hear, then? But if in the meantime there's anything urgent—?'

'Knock on my door. Only thing for it.'

As she turned at the end of the street she glanced back to see him outside number 17 surrounded by the boys. One held his hat and he held their football.

CHAPTER TEN

Emily was waiting outside the locked door of the PSO at five to eight the following morning when Lieutenant Commander Cooden arrived.

'Ah, good. Good start, Miss Grey. No sign of Hueffer?'

'He was at breakfast. I expect he'll be here soon.'

Her own appearance at breakfast had been brief, just enough for a cup of tea and half a slice of toast. It was all she felt she could take after the night before. Lieutenant Hueffer, however, had entered the dining room as she left, his round red face spruce and cheerful, looking the opposite of how she felt. She managed to smile and return his greeting before hurrying down the corridor.

The evening had begun well enough, the dining room thronged with officers. She wasn't sure whether she imagined it or whether the clamour of conversation did actually dip as she entered; she was the only woman and most of them turned to look at her. She was spared having to find a seat by hearing her name called from the far end and seeing the young officers she had met already waving her to a place they had saved.

There was immediate talk about the forthcoming ball and, despite her protests that she had no ball gown and no prospect of getting one, they insisted she was the official guest of three of them, that it was impossible to back out and that the right kit, as they put it, would be found for her. There followed questions about her background, especially her schooling, but nothing too probing and no one thought to ask what she had done in the years since school. Most of the talk was about the progress, or lack of it, in the war. Nothing seemed to be going well. There was doubt as to whether the new German policy of unrestricted submarine warfare would bring America into the war, talk of slow progress in implementing a naval blockade of Germany, of losses in the Dardanelles, of Turkish gains and Russian retreats and on the Western Front the costly failure of the Battle of Loos. Although depressed by the news, Emily was relieved that it shifted focus from her. At the same time she realised how out-of-date on the war she had become during the secretarial course, reading her father's *Times* for only a few minutes a day and not mixing with military people. Apart from Nigel, whom it was hard to feel really counted as military.

Lieutenant Hueffer joined them at the end of dinner. He stood with his hands resting proprietorially on the shoulders of the young officers sitting either side of Emily.

'Gentlemen,' he said, stressing the final syllable, 'may I

invite two or three of you to accompany Miss Grey and me to the bar, there to share a brace of celebratory bottles that stand open and waiting?'

Her three ball partners enthusiastically accepted, obliging Emily to do the same despite longing for an early night. There was, however, the consoling reflection that she might hear something reportable. In the bar the lieutenant led them to half a dozen leather armchairs around a table at the far end. On the table were glasses and two bottles of champagne in a silver ice bucket. Hueffer seated Emily next to himself. A waiter appeared and poured.

'What are we celebrating, Hoof?' asked one of the officers. 'Not your birthday, is it?'

Hueffer shook his head. 'I'm afraid I've passed the age at which birthdays are celebrated rather than mournfully counted. No, this is to mark my divorce. Well, not quite a divorce because we weren't quite married, but a divorce in all but name, as it were. An agreement, let us call it, a rec-ognition, an acknowledgement.' He smiled and raised his glass. 'May you all fare better in the marriage stakes than I did. Than I have. Doubtless ever shall.' He drained his glass.

They all drank. There was a pause. No one seemed to know how to react appropriately. 'You must have had quite a busy life, Hoof, what with all ... all that – and the books you've written,' said the officer on Emily's left. 'And you were an editor, too, weren't you?'

'Guilty as charged. But my editing was of a literary magazine. Mere literature.' He refilled his glass and passed the bottle. 'Now tell me what you've all done in your lives. Doubtless better organised than mine.'

Preparatory school followed by Dartmouth and the navy was their common story, with no time yet in their lives for anything else. There was talk of Lord Fisher's naval reforms and his detailed supervision of not only of the training at Dartmouth but of virtually every brick in the building of the college. This led to the discussion of the advantages and disadvantages of battle-cruisers compared with Dreadnought battleships, which in turn evolved into discussion of their own current ships, including rumours of future deployments. Hueffer said nothing more about his own life but showed sympathetic interest in theirs. Gossip about current ships and deployments must be, Emily thought, food and drink to a spy, although she noted that his direct questions mostly had an artistic or literary reference. He wanted to know what they thought of Marryat's evocations of warfare in the days of sail, the accuracy of painted depictions of Trafalgar, their opinions of Turner's nautical paintings. From their answers it was clear that, although possessed of lively intelligence, they had little cultural awareness or curiosity.

Emily was relieved not to have to contribute. Perhaps Hans was more like them than she had realised at the time. He had liked poetry, though, or said he did when they used to read Heine and Goethe together. But it was easy to imagine that any of these eager young men would take an interest in poetry if it appealed to a woman they wanted badly enough. She wondered whether she could take an interest in navigation if she wanted the man. Probably, she thought. In fact, definitely. Up to a point.

They were well into the second bottle. She was desperately tired, almost too tired to get up and go to bed, but felt she should stay as long as Lieutenant Hueffer was inclined to talk. And to hear what they might be telling him. He was holding forth now, answering questions about what it was like at the Front.

'Can't stand up,' he was saying, 'especially if you're on the tall side like me. Permanently stooping and bending to keep your head down, not only in the trenches but behind the lines, especially when there's shelling. Can't help it.'

'Same in submarines,' said one. 'I had to do a week in one. That was enough.'

'Dirty way of fighting, submarines,' said one of the others. 'Undersea, underhand.'

'Which boat were you on?' asked Lieutenant Hueffer.

He had the nomenclature right – the navy did not acknowledge submarines as ships, insisting they were boats. The ensuing casual chat about various naval vessels, their strengths and weaknesses, captains, tasks and deployments, would all be grist to the German mill, she thought. A waiter appeared with a bottle of red wine and more glasses. Lieutenant Hueffer handed her a glass, either ignoring or genuinely not hearing her protest. They toasted the navy, then the King and then Emily, which was embarrassing and forced her to sip the unwanted wine. The conversation moved on to the naval antecedents of the three young officers.

Feeling she ought to speak again, she turned to the lieutenant. 'What of your own family?'

He drank, shook his head and drank again. 'Nothing military or nautical, I'm afraid. Not a whiff of glory unless you consider music, art and literature fields of glory. Though my brother claims to be a general in the Mexican Army. Claims. No, I was brought up among painters and musicians on both English and German sides of the family. My father was music critic of *The Times*, my mother daughter of the artist Ford Madox Brown. The Pre-Raphaelite crowd, the middle-Victorian, tumultuously bearded great were heroes of my childhood.'

'You were educated here, then?'

'My education was as English as could be. Except that despite it all I somehow became a writer. That certainly wasn't planned for.' He offered to top up her glass and refilled his own.

'Did you have much contact with the German side of your family?'

'Quite a bit, holidays in Germany, some longer stays, that sort of thing. They were – are – mostly Münster-based. Ever been there?'

'Not to Münster, no.' She almost denied having been to Germany but thought it might encourage more disclosures if she admitted to some knowledge.

'Where, then?'

'I visited Munich and spent a little time in Heidelberg.'

'Sprechen sie Deutsch?' He lowered his voice and looked closely at her, his blue eyes watchful despite alcohol.

'Some,' she replied in German.

'I thought so from your pronunciation of place names.'

'They're the easy bits.' She pretended to take another sip. 'It's very generous of you to allow us to celebrate your – your divorce, or break-up. But it must also be an occasion for sadness, must it not?' Tiredness and drink made her feel she had to speak carefully, as if each word were a boulder she might trip over.

'Of course, yes, everyone is damaged in these things, everyone's burden becomes heavier. But to go through life with no baggage would mean one has not lived fully, would it not?' He was smoking now and leaned closer. She could smell tobacco and wine on his breath. 'You are too young, Miss Grey, to have acquired much baggage, but I suspect you have a sense of what it means, eh?'

His voice was soft, barely more than a whisper, his manner intimate, and inviting intimacy. She was torn again between not wanting to yield to it while wanting to exploit it. 'I have suffered loss, if that's what you mean.' She felt she could reasonably withhold details by saying she didn't want to talk about it.

But he merely nodded and looked past her. 'Always important to move on. Keep moving on. We may look back but we mustn't try to stay there. We can't live there anymore. Must move on.'

She took a chance. 'Are you very close to your German relatives?'

For a few moments his face was immobile. She thought

he wasn't going to answer. 'Culturally, yes; politically and personally, no.'

'The war must have made things very difficult for you.'

'Indeed. At the Front I may have been fighting my own family. That was constantly in my mind. Perhaps it was one of my cousins who fired the shell that blew me up? War is bad for families.' He ceased to look past and turned back to her. 'As perhaps you know, Miss Grey?'

He sounded as if he were seeking confirmation of something he knew already. He couldn't possibly, she thought. Unless by an extraordinary series of coincidences his family knew Hans's. Or he had reported her presence to his German secret service contacts and they had traced her and told him. Or unless he was unusually intuitive for middle-aged, overweight men in their cups. She nodded and said nothing.

When the party broke up she left the still-busy bar without, she hoped, betraying how drunk she felt. At least her cabin was not on the same corridor as the others, so there was no one to observe whether she walked it in a straight line. She had felt this drunk only once before, with Hans. She hadn't liked it then and didn't now. It was like being ill; how could anyone like it? Nevertheless, as soon as she reached her cabin and had accessed the toilet in relieved solitude, she made notes of Lieutenant Hueffer's conversation. Afterwards she sat motionless for what seemed a long time, too tired to undress. When eventually she got to bed she slept instantly.

CHAPTER ELEVEN

'This is extremely irritating,' Lieutenant Commander Cooden said. 'I told Jackson explicitly, told him myself – where is the damn fellow? – to get a new typewriter ribbon and paper and carbon and pencils and sharpeners and that sort of thing from the purser. We have a new secretary coming aboard, I told him, she must have all the tools for the job. And now you tell me the wretched typewriter has no ribbon at all, not even the old one. What can have happened to it? Can't just unreel themselves and roll away, can they?' He was silent for a few moments, gazing disconsolately at the papers heaped in his out-tray. 'Maybe they can. Ropes left on decks always seem to.'

Emily was relieved that she wasn't immediately able to get on with anything. Her head ached and she had dreaded an opening barrage of shorthand, likely to prove an embarrassing test of her competence. Jackson was nowhere to be seen and Lieutenant Hueffer had still to appear. She tidied a few things and worked out how to make tea with the tiny gas stove in Jackson's cubby-hole. There was a fresh pint of milk there, indicating that he must have been and gone.

Tea moderated the commander's irritation to a level at which he was able to take pleasure in it. 'Never ceases to surprise me, the amount of basic incompetence in the navy. Get the basics right and everything else will follow. Trouble is, we're run by too many over-bred English upper-class nincompoops covered in gold braid who owe their positions to family connections and have not the faintest idea how anything works or how to do things. Wouldn't know a spanner from a screwdriver most of them. What does your father think, eh?'

Emily's father had loved the navy and everything about it. 'Well, as a medical man he obviously has a practical bent ...'

'Quite so, quite so. Medicine's very much a practical profession. Like engineering, only with more guesswork. Your father never needed family connections to get on, I suppose? If I were to list you all the senior officers I know of who relied on connections for their promotions we'd be here all day.'

In fact, her father's father and grandfather had been regular naval officers and he made no secret of the fact that his family's naval tradition had helped him, despite his having broken the mould by becoming a doctor first. He saw nothing wrong with it and, challenged, would doubtless have argued that the navy benefitted by recruiting men from backgrounds of proven loyalty.

Cooden's peroration did indeed threaten to continue all day as he listed examples of family connections among senior ranks, either forgetting or tactfully ignoring her godfather, the admiral. Perhaps, she thought, it was only blood relations that constituted a crime in his eyes. Fortunately, he seemed to require only minimal responses from her. She nodded, sipped her tea and tried to look attentive. Her headache began to lessen. If only she could have remained quietly in her cabin, writing up her notes on Hueffer and getting them to Nigel, somehow. The day might then begin to feel tolerable.

Jackson appeared bearing a printed form, cheerfully unaware of his apparent failings. 'Requisition form for you to sign, sir,' he said, before the commander could fire off his reprimand. 'They've got all the kit for Miss Grey but won't release it until they have your signature.'

'But I sent them a list last week. In my own hand. You delivered it. Unless you didn't?'

'I did, sir, straight away, sharpish. They got all the gear ready but they won't release it without this.'

'What nonsense when they have it in my own hand. And what's happened to the old typewriter ribbon? Why has it disappeared?'

'They 'ave to 'ave it back, sir. Won't release a new one without the old one. Reckon they go walkabout, old typewriter ribbons. They use them again, they say. I 'ad to come back and get it. Third time I been over this morning, up and down like a yo-yo.'

The commander checked and signed the form, grumbling about how the dockyard organisation favoured the few while making life difficult for the many. Emily couldn't help wondering what it would be like to be married to him. If anyone was. It was hard to imagine why any woman would want the role. Everything about him – the way he moved, his tone, his wary expression – suggested a permanent state of incipient resentment, as if he suspected he was forever being imposed upon. She sensed he might also be mean, in her eyes one of the least appealing of many unappealing characteristics a man could have.

Jackson reappeared with a box of office supplies, Lieutenant Hueffer with him, as cheerful and fresh-faced as when she had seen him earlier. 'Morning everybody,' he said with a smile.

'I want a word with you,' said the commander. Lieutenant Hueffer followed him into his office. 'Close the door.'

Emily and Jackson exchanged glances, Jackson grinning and putting his fingers to his ears. 'Heavy shelling,' he said.

But there was no shouting, no raised voices, just a rumble of male conversation, after which both men emerged in apparent amity, with the commander saying to Hueffer, 'No, carry on as you were but let me have write-ups as soon as you can. Then I can just go out and inspect and confirm and we'll get the whole thing launched.' He turned to Emily. 'Miss Grey. Dictation, please.'

The day passed. The commander was unused to dictating, slow, hesitant, frequently losing track or contradicting himself and having to ask Emily where he'd got to. Fortunately, her approximations and guesswork were better than his recall and he accepted them without query. When typing them up, she found she could improve his English without his objecting, or probably noticing.

She spent most of the week drafting and re-drafting the first part of what he called the RPSR, the Rosyth Port Security Review. Part One, he explained, was a detailed description of existing security arrangements, Part Two would be recommendations for improvements and Part Three would comprise Lieutenant Hueffer's proposals for an outer ring of boom defences in the firth. 'He's done a draft version but will dictate the final version to you himself when he's ready. There's no hurry, I've told him. Parts One and Two are the priority.'

One day an Admiralty telegram was hand-delivered from the Port Admiral's office. Emily opened the brown envelope and read a request for an urgent progress report on the boom defences which the Admiralty – 'in the light of information recently received' – now regarded as high priority. The commander was out conducting one of what he called his surprise inspections, which involved a walk or cycle ride around the dockyard after lunch at the same time every day

She put the telegram on top of his in-tray and told Lieutenant Hueffer about it as they walked back from the wardroom after their own lunches. Emily had sat as usual with her navigation course admirers who were still talking about the ball a couple of weeks hence, though no formal invitations had been issued. Hueffer seemed happy to lunch with anyone he picked up in the bar over pre-prandial gins-and-tonic, followed by a glass or two of wine to help his meal down and, if there was time, a drop of port with his coffee after.

'Well, that's something,' he said, when she told him about the telegram. 'It might make up old Coody's mind for him. Seems to blow hot and cold on the whole thing. One day he says we must crack on with it, then when I ask if he's happy with my plans he says he's still making improvements. Submitted them ages ago, haven't seen them since.'

'He's actually got them, has he? I had the impression he was still waiting for the final version. They didn't come through me.'

'I gave them to him myself. Should have thought to tell you. Sorry.'

'That's all right, so long as I know. They must be in his cupboard somewhere. They're certainly not among the drafts he's been working on. He keeps updating his own and makes so many alterations I've had to retype the whole thing twice. '

'Not that I'm complaining, mind.' He smiled his toothy smile. 'Gives me an excuse for afternoon excursions along the coast to check that the existing defences are still defending. Which is what, despite appearances, they think they're doing.'

'You think they're not, then?'

'I think the troops there know they've got a cushy number and are determined to keep it. And they're right. Darn sight cushier than ... than where I was before ... before they sent me home.' He shook his head. 'The German High Seas Fleet probably assumes we're bristling with defences. Little do they

183

know they could creep in at night without anyone being any the wiser until they open fire.'

'But surely we'd spot them, wouldn't we? They couldn't get into the port without anyone knowing?'

'Oh, they'd be picked up soon enough. Once they got here. And fired upon. And no doubt badly mauled. They wouldn't all get out again, not all of them. But they'd have done the damage. Our ships in port are sitting ducks, not exactly cleared for action. All the Huns need is a few fast patrol boats, speed in, open fire, loose off a few torpedoes, then turn and run for the high seas. Imagine the damage to the navy's prestige, not to mention ships.'

Emily had never heard him refer to Germans as Huns before, as if he weren't half one. Presumably, if he were a spy, he would feel he ought to adopt the nomenclature of his colleagues, to fit in. He would doubtless also have reported to his German masters the vulnerability he had just described.

'You must come with me on one of my coastal excursions,' he said. 'Beautiful walks, especially at this time of year. So long as old Coody can be persuaded to let you out of his sight for a couple of hours.'

'Thank you, I'd like that very much.' Presumably the last thing a spy would want would be a witness to his reconnaissance of shore-based defences. On the other hand, inviting company would suggest he had nothing to hide, and if the company were a young woman it would also usefully suggest another motive.

Back in the office, she took advantage of the commander's absence to search his cupboard for Hueffer's boom defence paper. He locked the cupboard overnight but left it open during the day. She found the latest draft of Part One of his review of port security, though not the earlier draft, presumably disposed of by Jackson as confidential waste. Hueffer's draft paper was on the bottom shelf along with the previous year's accounts, old copies of the *Rosyth Review* – a port newsletter inaugurated by the previous harbour master, since discontinued – and a wad of blank forms for expenses claims. Hueffer's paper was badly typed and peppered with pencilled alterations in Hueffer's wandering hand. There were no alterations by Cooden, presumably because it was to be superseded by the finished version which Hueffer said he had already submitted. In which case it should have been there. She took the draft version, attached it to the telegram and put both in the commander's in-tray. She told Lieutenant Hueffer, who was at his desk lighting a cigar.

'Thank you,' he said, exhaling. 'As an author I am unfortunately all too well accustomed to the products of my pen going astray or being ignored.'

'Have you written very many books?'

'Too many in one sense, not enough in another. Do you read, Miss Grey?'

'I do, but not as much as I should like. Might I find one of your books in a local bookshop?'

'Miracles do occur, I'm told. If there are any bookshops in Rosyth. I've not seen one. I think you'd have to go to

Edinburgh, but even there you might merely confirm that I am invincibly unsaleable. I shall look one out for you.'

'You must let me pay for it.'

Jackson appeared with an envelope. 'Got this from the guardroom. Handed in by your gentleman friend, same one as previous.'

'Oh, not him again, thank you.' Irritated that Nigel had ignored her request to communicate by post, she took it to her desk and dropped it as if it were of little account, not wanting to open it until she was alone. When she did, she found a sheet of notepaper headed the Gothenburg Hotel, Rosyth. Nigel had been evicted from his lodgings, he said. But the hotel was better and she should contact him there as soon as possible as he had an urgent message from 'our mutual friend known by a capital letter' in London. She put it in her bag.

Lieutenant Commander Cooden was displeased by the Admiralty telegram. 'You took it upon yourself to open it without authorisation?'

'I'm sorry, sir. I thought it might be important, something we needed to act upon. As indeed it is, or seems to be. I'm sorry if that was wrong.'

He grunted, glanced at Hueffer's attached boom defence report and sat with a sigh. 'That will be all for the time being. You can close the door.'

There were gaps between rain clouds during the late afternoon, but Emily took her umbrella for the walk into town after work. She couldn't be sure whether there were leers as she passed the guardroom or whether she had imagined them. She twice had to ask the way to the Gothenburg Hotel, the second time because she couldn't understand what the first man said. It was a modern steep-roofed building in the Scandinavian style that stood out from everything else in Rosyth. Reception was cool and dark, redolent of furniture polish and pipe tobacco. The dark-suited young man at the desk said he hadn't seen Lieutenant Nisbet since breakfast but would send to his room.

She took a window seat and picked up the local newspaper. Prominent was a list of local men recently killed. They were several soldiers at the Front, one airman but no sailors. Given it was Rosyth, it seemed likely that more would have joined the navy than the army. So presumably there had been no sea actions, she thought. When Nigel appeared he was still wearing his tweed suit.

'Just been for a walk,' he said. 'Saw you from outside and waved but you didn't notice.'

'I was reading.' She resented the implication that she was to blame for not seeing him. 'Perhaps we should be more specific about meeting arrangements in future.'

He took off his hat and sat. 'Shouldn't be seen together, really, but now we're here we may as well have tea. Would you like tea?'

'I would, thank you.'

'I've been thirsty all day. Hope I'm not coming down with something.'

'That wouldn't be very convenient.'

'I've an inherited weakness where colds are concerned. My grandfather died of one.'

'Oh dear.'

'As did his grandfather. It seems to skip generations so I have to be careful.'

'Indeed. Is that why you're wearing all that tweed?'

He looked down at himself, as if to check. 'No, this is to fit in, to blend, you know. It's Scottish. Harris tweed.'

'I haven't seen anyone else wearing it. Must be rather warm, this weather.'

'Good in the rain but takes a long time to dry out.' He ordered tea, refusing without asking her the offer of cakes or biscuits, then leant forward, confidentially. She did the same. 'Much better here than the last place. More expensive, of course, but I hope C won't refuse my claim. If he does we might ... no, don't worry. Tea is on me.'

'That's generous of you.'

'Last place was awful. You had to pay extra for a bath and the food was ... well, I'd rather be on rations. Quite a relief when she slung me out, really.'

'She slung you out? Why?'

'Misunderstanding.' He looked down, shaking his head. 'They do seem very intolerant here, quick to jump to conclusions.' He looked up again. 'I'm not saying it was your fault.'

'My fault?'

'No, no, not at all. I don't think it was, not really. You weren't to know. Thing is, your calling the other day didn't go down well with the landlady, Mrs Maclean. Her late husband was a minister, very strict. She thought ... she misinterpreted your – my – motives. She thought we were ... you know ... and then another woman called to complain, a local woman, another misunderstanding. I'd had words with some children who were causing a ruckus in the street, playing around, you know. Just had words with them, that's all, but she – this mother – seemed to think I was threatening them in some way and Mrs Maclean must have got the wrong end of the stick because she assumed the mother was on at me because I was somehow connected to the wretched child – the father, as it were – and was trying to evade my responsibilities. Anyway, we had words, Mrs Maclean and I, and ... well, you know how one thing leads to another. I had to leave that night. Fortunately, this place had a room. Rather nice room, in fact. Pity I can't show you.' He smiled. 'Don't want to give the wrong impression here, too.'

'No, we don't. Anyway, you had an urgent message for me.'

'I assume it's a message. I don't know. It's an envelope. They don't want me to open it. I was summoned to the police HQ in Edinburgh to pick it up first thing in the morning after I'd arrived here. The hotel people thought at first I was making a run for it. I'd only told Whitehall Court where I was the night before. Just as well I did. It must have come up on the night train.' He waited while their teas were served. The waiter laid out the blue and white china slowly and precisely. Nigel lifted the teapot lid, sniffed and replaced it. 'Better let it stew a while.'

'Have you got it? The envelope?'

He took it from his inside jacket pocket. It was white and addressed to her in green ink, which only the Chief used. Written along the top, heavily underlined, were the letters AO.

'AO – addressee only – means you. Only you can open it,' he said. 'Common service phrase. Like ASO – addressee section only – which means only someone in your section can open it.'

'Thank you, I did know that.' She was tempted just to drop it into her bag and open it later but thought it might contain something she had to ask him. She looked about to make sure there was no one near them. The letter was a single sheet, covered both sides by green ink in a compressed hand, written in haste, not easily legible. With no preliminaries, the Chief told her that TR/16 now reported that a raid against the fleet would be launched 'as soon as the chickens have roosted'. He had picked up further references to information from 'Heifer' and further indications that the locus of the operation must be Rosyth. Emily was to stand by to debrief him again, along with Henry Landau. She was to mention it to no one, but should act surprised if the Port Security Office was ordered to release her for urgent temporary duty in London. If that happened she could brief her 'assistant' as to why she was going. Meanwhile she was to prepare him to monitor the main Heifer suspect, so far as he could without access to the base. The letter was signed C.

The prospect of seeing TR/16 and Henry Landau against

caused an inner spasm, a muscular contraction located somewhere between her chest and her stomach. For different reasons in each case: a reluctance to reawaken the past in one, embarrassment in the other. Although it should be Henry Landau who felt embarrassed, she told herself. But she doubted he would. She folded the letter into her handbag and leant forward. 'Shall I pour?' Nigel nodded, looking, she thought, like a dog expecting a biscuit. It was an effort not to smile. 'Possible future deployment,' she said. 'That's all.'

'Nothing that affects what we're doing?'

'Not at the moment.'

'They could have told me to tell you that. I thought perhaps it was something personal arising from your ... you know, your relationship with the ... with your late fiancé. Something upsetting.'

'Fortunately nothing like that.' She felt she could smile now. 'Nice of you to be so concerned, Nigel. Thank you.'

'It must have been very upsetting even though he was on the other side.'

'Of course, yes, it still is. But there weren't any other sides then, when we knew each other. We thought we were all on the same side.' She worried that she sounded dismissively brisk whenever she had to speak of Hans. It wasn't how she felt so much as that she didn't want to risk giving way to how she felt. She changed the subject. 'We need better communications. Between you and me, I mean. The guardroom—'

'I was meant to post it, I know. But the covering letter said it was urgent and, given who it was from, I thought I'd better get it to you. However, this place has a telephone, unlike the last. Do you have access to one in the port?'

'There's one on the wall near my desk which I assume works, although it's not rung since I arrived and I've not seen anyone use it. So far they do everything by letter or telegram.'

'Does it have a number, or would I just ask the switchboard for the PSO?'

'I'll find out and telephone you here and tell you.'

'I suppose telephone calls are an allowable? Expense, I mean. They cost quite a bit in hotels.'

'They must be, surely, if used on official business.'

'Supposing I call and someone else answers? Who should I say I am?'

'Oh, I don't know. Say you're my doctor. No one would ask details and they wouldn't expect me to give any.'

She leant forward again, lowering her voice. 'Now, our main suspect, Heifer.'

'Heifer? I thought he was called Hueffer?' He spoke quite loudly and she had to sshh him.

'He is, but Heifer is the code-name the Germans use for him. I thought you knew that.'

'I do, did, yes. Bit of a giveaway, isn't it?'

'Apparently they like code-names that are similar to the real ones. Anyway, I think it would be a good idea – it would help me a lot – if you could be involved in surveillance of him.'

He brightened. 'I'd like that. Much better than mooching

around town every day. Especially with those wretched little urchins following me about.'

'It might be a good idea not to dress as – as smartly as you are in that lovely new suit.'

'I know that, I know that. Done this sort of thing before, you know. Doing it before you joined. I may need cape and hat but I can manage without the suit.'

'Of course you've done it before, yes. But I have a suggestion.'

She told him of Hueffer's afternoon walks along the firth. 'He's invited me to go with him sometime. If I find out where we're going in advance, you could position yourself some-where you can see us so you'll know what he looks like if you see him in the town. You could then follow him to see if he's meeting someone secretly, or doing something' – she struggled to think what – 'something nefarious. And follow him on future walks if I'm not here.'

'Not here? Are you leaving?'

'Not there, I mean. If I can't leave the office.'

Later that week Lieutenant Hueffer made good his sug-gestion that she accompany him on an afternoon recce. 'If the rain holds off,' he said, in little more than a whisper, 'we might walk out to the bridge, the Forth railway bridge. Shouldn't take too long and we should be back before old Coody returns from his ... his ... whatever he calls his after-noon absences.'

'Spontaneous inspections.'

'I haven't looked at the area immediately around the bridge

because my proposed boom defences are quite a bit farther out into the firth. It occurs to me that we could put in inner ring near the bridge itself, perhaps using its supports as hinges, as it were. But I'm not sure there'll be sufficient space. The river's quite a bit narrower there.'

'Thank you, I'd love to, but it would mean leaving the office unmanned and I don't think the commander would—'

'He needn't know, need he? So long as we're back before him. From what he said to me he might not be back today at all. Said I was to shut up shop if he wasn't back by c.o.p. Close of play. Unless you're too busy, that is.'

She should have said she was. She was retyping the revised appendices of the latest version of the security review. The commander had also asked her to go through a cupboard full of old files, many of them predating not only his appointment but the war itself. Those still relevant to the PSO's work were to have typed summaries of contents inside every cover, those that might be relevant to the Admiralty but no longer to the PSO were to be returned to the Admiralty, those relevant to nobody were to be burnt. 'Serves the Admiralty right to get some of their own useless bumf back,' he said.

But the chance to get closer to Hueffer was too good to miss. 'Nothing that won't wait,' she said brightly. 'So long as you're prepared to say you'd asked me to take notes for you or something like that if he comes back early and catches us out.'

Hueffer smiled his gentle, toothy smile. 'A little conspiracy is like garlic. Adds piquancy to everything.'

'You like garlic? My father won't have it in the house. Disgusting foreign habit, he calls it.'

'Very British of him. But then I might have been the same were it not for the continental side of my family.'

'But Germans don't . . . I mean, do Germans use garlic very much? I've always thought it was more French.'

'So it is, so it is, to the credit of the Gauls. But both sides of my family have always been promiscuously cosmopolitan, which is to their credit. In the arts, literature, food, everything. Except dress. Very English in dress.'

'So you're English on the outside, continental inside?'

He smiled again. 'Mixed ingredients, well mixed. I'll see you in the wardroom. We'd better lunch early.'

When he had gone she approached the wall-mounted telephone apparatus. Her father had had one installed at home, to great fanfare. She had spoken on it a number of times but had only twice initiated calls. She put the receiver to her ear. The auditory void lasted for what felt a long time, until a male voice, greeting her as caller, asked which number she wanted. When she gave him the hotel number there was a pause, before he came back saying it was an outside line; where was she calling from and did she have chargeable authority?

'PSO, Port Security Office,' she said, rather too loudly.

'Who is the authority for the call?'

'Lieutenant Commander Cooden.' She was beginning to wish she hadn't started.

'Official or personal?'

'Official.' The moment she said it, she thought she should have said it was personal, then she could have offered to pay if it came to Cooden's attention. It was of course official in that it was part of what she was there to do, just not official PSO business. She was still considering how she might explain it when the hotel answered. She asked for Lieutenant Nisbet and was told to wait while he was fetched from the bar.

'Hallo, Nisbet speaking.' He bellowed into the speaker, making her flinch. 'Who am I speaking to?'

'Nigel, it's me, Emily.' She spoke quietly, hoping he would do the same. 'I'm going for a walk with my friend this afternoon. We'll leave the port in about an hour.'

'Walking with a friend? That sounds good. Do I know her? May I join you?' He was still shouting.

'It's a male friend, the man I was telling you about. The one who goes walking, remember?' She lowered her voice further. 'The one you want to have a look at.'

'Have a look at? Why would I—'

'Nigel, are you drunk?'

'Drunk? No, 'course I'm not. Just a couple of glasses before lunch.'

She controlled herself and spoke with slow deliberation. 'Nigel, listen carefully and please stop shouting. I'm going for a walk along the firth with Lieutenant Hueffer, the man we discussed. We'll leave via the guardroom in about an hour and head east towards the railway bridge, keeping to footpaths along the shore so far as we can. And probably

196

come back the same way. If you would like to see us from a distance you should position yourself somewhere along the route. Do you understand me?'

'Ah yes, yes, understood.' He spoke now in an exaggerated stage whisper. 'Chap we were talking about the other day. Sorry, I was thinking of something else.'

'Don't come too close. Just close enough to get a good look.'

'Good look, yes.'

'I won't recognise you.'

'I'll wear my hat so you know it's me.'

'I mean, I won't acknowledge you. We must pretend we've never met.'

'Never met, no. Well, I haven't.'

'Haven't what?'

'Met him.'

'Not him, Nigel, me. You and I must pretend—'

'Sorry, got you now. Understood. Not too close.'

The operator asked if caller wanted another three minutes. Emily said no and rang off.

She and Hueffer lunched early in the wardroom, then set off. Emily changed shoes for a pair of boots. They were stout and reasonably waterproof and made her feel like her great aunt. Hueffer assured her that the walk was mostly on footpaths. 'There is a road and there are plans for more but it's nicer to walk footpaths. Shouldn't take too long. We might doff our hats to the ruins of Rosyth Castle on the way. There are plans to build all round that, too, which would be a great pity. And we can say a prayer for the slain at the site of the Battle of Inverkeithing.'

'I've never heard of that.'

'One of Cromwell's many victories. An underrated general. A relatively minor Civil War encounter but bloody enough, as most of them were. Not that we're short of reminders of bloodiness these days.'

'Indeed not. You must have seen more than enough.'

'Didn't see much at all, to be honest. It was all a kind of daze for me, a kaleidoscopic confusion. Looking back, it's hard to establish even the most basic chronology. Doesn't help that one lost consciousness for an unknown length of time, of course.'

'When you were brought back here, where did you—'

'They sent me to a place called Craiglockhart, not far from here, near Edinburgh. Very good man there who talked me back to normality. As close as I shall get to it, anyway. Lots of people there writing poetry. Resumed it myself but no good. Too close to the experience, couldn't handle the rawness. Someone will one day, I hope. Someone must do it, as a memorial to the voiceless.'

Once past the guardroom they turned right and were soon on a footpath running parallel with the Forth. Ahead of them loomed the railway bridge. Like distant mountains, it appeared within easy reach and, like mountains, seemed to get no closer as they approached it. She looked out for Nigel, anxious that he might shadow them too obviously and hoping he'd remembered not to wear his new tweeds.

Something ordinary, old corduroys and a shapeless jacket such as Hueffer had changed into would be ideal.

'Did you come straight here from Craiglockhart?' she asked.

'Good Lord no, that would be much too straightforward for the War Office. I was sent down to London, then had about a day and a half in Hampshire, then off to Swansea, then Chelsea barracks again, then here. Obviously couldn't decide what to do with me. One job after another, none of which I was in long enough to do. I suggested they sent me to War Office Intelligence, given that I speak German and know a bit about the country. But that went nowhere. Finally I was sent here to write about boom defences. Didn't know what they were, never been to sea apart from ferries, never sailed, can't even swim. All wonderfully typical of the War Office. Gratifying when institutions conform so perfectly to stereotype.'

It was easy to imagine why the possibility of divided loyalties might debar him from Intelligence work; yet it was hard to imagine a more convincing demonstration of loyalty than volunteering for the Front. 'It must have felt strange to be fighting Germans?'

'Not as much as you might think. Never met any, barely saw any apart from dead bodies and a few prisoners who looked about as dazed as I was. If anything, the experience increased fellow-feeling. We were all stuff to fill graveyards, whichever side of the line we were on. We killed them, they killed us. There was nothing personal about it. Contempt sometimes, but indifference mostly, just indifference. Not like old Coody. I get the impression he really hates them, don't you? The way he goes on.'

'He does go on a bit, yes.' She remembered the commander's more conciliatory remarks about German virtues. 'At other times he seems more – not quite sympathetic – regretful, more regretful.'

'When all this business is over I think we'll find soldiers on both sides feel more in common with each other than with their own civilians back home. Coody has never seen action, of course. Makes a difference. But he has a point. When you think of German culture – their music, their literature, their science – it's hard to reconcile it with what they're doing now, not to mention all those atrocities in Belgium at the start. Hard to hate them completely, can't write them off entirely. The good about them is as true as the bad. This also is true – doesn't Lear say that? Think it was Lear.' He stopped and pointed. 'Here we are, look, Rosyth Castle, remains of. Mind if we take a closer look?'

It was the usual sort of ruin, roofless, some incomplete walls, foundations of others. A pair of crows got up at their approach. Emily had never taken great interest in ruins and now couldn't help contrasting them with the spectacular romanticism of the Rhine castles that Hans had shown her. They at least were complete.

'Do you think we were wrong to declare war?' she ventured. 'Some people do. Mr Russell, for instance, the Cambridge philosopher.'

Hueffer shook his head. 'What was the alternative – allow

the invader to occupy Belgium and northern France? We could've, I suppose, but would that have been the end of it? Would he have stopped there? Could we be sure we wouldn't have been next?'

'So we're right to fight?'

'Absolutely.'

If he was Heifer he was a consummate actor. Which, presumably, was what spies were. TR/16 must be convincing to his colleagues.

They strolled among the ruins, Hueffer peering at bits of stone, nudging loose ones in the grass, looking up to see where they came from. 'Castles were in use much longer here than in most of England. Tribal wars, cross-border raiding, reiving and thieving and all that. Although many of them were really fortified houses of several storeys rather than proper castles with motte and bailey.'

She tried to look interested. There was still no sign of Nigel Nisbet. She hoped he wouldn't suddenly appear from behind a motte or bailey, whatever they were, tweed cape billowing in the breeze.

'Hadn't we better press on?' she said. 'If we're going to get right out to the bridge. It doesn't seem to be getting any nearer.'

As they dipped down towards the coast they saw an artist with easel propped up in the heather, sketching the ruin from the seaward side. 'Seen him several times,' said Hueffer. 'Tried chatting to him but he wasn't inclined. Downright morose. Probably sensed I couldn't approve his drawing.

Seems to have learned nothing from movements in art in the past half-century. It's all too rigid and literal, more like plans.'

'Are you very interested in art?'

'I was brought up among artists, my grandfather and all that. Sadly I'm no artist. I've written about them a bit.'

'I'd like to read something you've written.'

'You'd be lucky to find anything, as I said before. I've written plenty of books – too many, can't stop. But rare as hen's teeth if you want to find them. Now – look – see that stretch of heath.'

He pointed to a stretch of relatively flat land, saying it had played an important part in the Battle of Inverkeithing. Like many men she had met, he took pleasure in explaining, pointing out the approximate dispositions of the opposing forces. She wondered if he really had written many books. If there was a library in Rosyth she could try there, or perhaps write to her mother asking her to try London libraries. Or ask Nigel to seek them out.

'How did Cromwell and his army cross the river?' she asked, hoping he hadn't already told her.

Hueffer stopped. 'Good point, very good point. It's never occurred to me. They must have had boats, lots of them. Either that or they crossed far inland from where it would have taken much longer to get here. Yet there can't have been enough boats lying around to transport an army. They must have made them and how long would that take? Good question, very good question.' He went on, stepping out more briskly. 'Tell me, have you been able to keep in touch with any of your German friends from before the war? I imagine not really – like me and my family?'

'Sadly not, no.'

'Does that frustrate you?'

'It saddens me. And you?'

'The same.'

'Does that mean you have no contact with anyone in Germany at all now?'

'Not unless you call being on the receiving end of their bullets and shells a kind of contact.'

She wanted very much to tell him all about Hans, sensing he would be sympathetic and understanding, whatever else he was. She briefly thought she could justify it as a tactic, dangling a confidence in order to provoke one. But her old familiar, the blanket of caution, smothered her as usual.

'Wonderful things, bridges,' he said when at last they approached the massive structure. 'I never really understand how they stand up. An engineer once told me that if it looks right it probably is right.' He smiled. 'Pity it's not the same with people.'

'Indeed.'

'Especially in marriage.'

She thought this might lead on. 'Is that what you've found?'

'It's a bit more complicated than that, I'm afraid.'

He continued at pace almost down to the water's edge. The giant structure towered above them. 'Sometimes I sit here and think I can feel a train coming before I can hear or see it. But I may be imagining it.'

'It's hard to believe something as huge as this could shake.'

'Shellfire would bring it down, eventually. Enough of it. Consequences would be unimaginable.'

'Really? Isn't your gun battery somewhere near here, the one you were inspecting when we saw you from the boat?'

'Farther on, round the headland. There are others out on the islands We need more here really, although the existing four twelve-pounds would do if my boom defences were in place.'

He pointed across the estuary, describing which kind of boom was to go where, and where great sea mines would be tethered. She had seen the plans, but the stretches of water and wide horizon he pointed at, identifiable to him, looked all the same to her. He described it all with surprising enthusiasm. Such detail would be very useful to the enemy, she thought. There was still no sign of Nigel.

As they retraced their steps he began asking her more about herself, but she shifted the conversation onto her father's medical work in the navy, which led to the idiosyncrasies of the navy itself, then to a comparison of naval and army idiosyncrasies, which he was happy to enumerate. All the time she looked vainly for Nigel, hoping he might have managed to see them without being spotted, but fearing he had missed them altogether.

'Not wishing to be disloyal, but our dear lieutenant commander is a type you meet in both services,' Hueffer continued. 'In the army he'd be a passed-over major, red-faced and resentful of his juniors, his seniors and his peers, for none of whom you'd ever hear him say a good word. I suspect in the navy you find them hiding in obscure posts in shore bases, desperate to avoid going to sea. In the army they're in training camps preaching ferocious fighting doctrine which they never get within a country mile of putting into practice themselves. Never go near the front, most of them. Never will.' He shook his head, smiling. 'Sorry, this is truly disloyal. Subverting the chain of command, making you party to it by making you listen.'

She smiled back. 'I come from a naval family, remember. None of it's new to me.'

'I'm not saying he's a bad man in himself. Probably no worse than the rest of us, but the poison of thwarted ambition runs in his veins.' He lowered his voice. 'Lord, talk of the devil. What on earth can he be doing out here? Serves me damn well right.'

They were almost level with the castle and there, walking rapidly along the path away from the ruins, was Lieutenant Commander Cooden. He was uniformed and walked head down, hands clasped behind his back. He hadn't yet seen them but very soon would.

Hueffer managed a decent simulation of surprise and delight. The commander, genuinely surprised, was initially at a loss. 'You two – what ... what are you doing here?'

'Informal recce of the shoreline, sir, out by the battery. I thought it might help Miss Grey make sense of what she has to type if she knows the ground. Or water, in this case.'

The commander looked Hueffer up and down. Finding

something to disapprove of helped him recover himself. 'Very informal. Why aren't you in uniform?'

'I thought it might attract less attention if we look like an ordinary couple out for a stroll, sir. In case there are German spies in the area'

'German spies – what makes you think that?'

'Simply that if there were any and they saw uniformed people making repeat visits to a particular area they might put two and two together and assume we're planning something, such as boom defences. Sir.'

'Nonsense, Hueffer, this whole area is crawling with people in uniform. You stand out more if you're not. Good example just behind you. Don't look now.'

Emily was all too soon aware of the figure approaching from Rosyth, tweed suit and with a hat pulled well down over his eyes. She looked away, hoping he wouldn't attempt any sort of conversation. They fell silent as he passed, heading for the ruins.

The commander gazed after him. 'Historical type, d'you think? Archaeologist or something?'

'Very likely, sir.'

'Stands out a mile, that sort of gear. You can see that, can't you? Same with yours, only you're scruffier. Even more noticeable.'

'Point taken, sir.'

The lieutenant commander turned away. 'Just popping out to the batteries myself. Part of my programme of surprise visits, keep them on their toes. Then I'll be back to the office.

Miss Grey, prepare for dictation.' He strode off towards the bridge.

'That chap who passed us, covered in tweed,' said Hueffer as they moved off. 'The archaeologist, if that's what he is. Think I've seen him around the town. Maybe he's a German spy.' He laughed.

'Bit obvious, don't you think?' said Emily.

CHAPTER TWELVE

Two days later, in Rotterdam, Emily looked at her notebook. 'So the message from Heifer is that '*Uncle and Aunt and all the family are coming to stay on the 24th. Therefore it must be the night of the 25th before the new moon.*' And those were the Herr Kommandant's exact words?'

TR/16 nodded.

Emily repeated them in German. TR/16 nodded again. 'And he definitely said the message was from Heifer?'

'Definitely.'

'He said it not to you but in your hearing?'

'He said more which I could not hear. He did not mean me to hear and when he saw I was passing he lowered his voice and turned away. I do not think he realised I had heard.'

'And this was on Wednesday, in another meeting with the harbour master and the torpedo boat flotilla commander? To which you were invited.'

TR/16 shook his head. 'I was not invited but I had arrived early for a meeting with the harbour master about repairs to the two damaged cruisers, how long they would be in dock, when the quays would be free, that kind of thing. The Herr Kommandant turned up unexpectedly to confer with the flotilla commander, who happened to be with the harbour master. They know each other well, they are good friends, as I reported before. After I arrived the Herr Kommandant and the flotilla commander went off together.'

'And you still do not know the Herr Kommandant's name?'

'They assume I do, which is why I have never felt able to ask. When we were introduced at the lunch I told you of before, it was by his title only. I think his first name may be Paul.'

'And then you and the harbour master had your meeting about the two cruisers.'

'Of which I can give you a full report. I have notes. But it is not urgent, unlike this. It will wait for my regular meeting with Henry.'

Emily looked again at her notes. For a moment the letters danced before her eyes. She wanted to keep talking because she felt that if she stopped her eyelids would droop. She had hardly slept during the past forty-eight hours. Even as she tried to concentrate on TR/16, scenes from the recent past flashed unbidden across her mind, beginning with her return to the PSO from the walk with Lieutenant Hueffer. She was greeted by Jackson with a plain brown envelope stamped *Secret Urgent* in red letters.

'Admiralty signal for you, ma'am. Just in.'

'You're much in demand,' said Hueffer, loitering.

She moved to the other side of her desk to open it. It was from C and simply said: *Return London immediately. Signal train ETA.*

'Not bad news, I hope?' said the lieutenant.

'No – well, yes. They want me back in London immediately.'

'Oh dear. What for? How long for?'

'I don't know. Not for long, I imagine. The Admiralty must be short-staffed.' Conscious that that sounded lame, she added, 'They've got a lot on at the moment.' That sounded no less lame but she could think of nothing better.

She used the port administration to book a sleeper berth on the night train from Edinburgh and returned with Hueffer to the wardroom to pack. 'Better hoist myself back into my uniform,' he said. 'May help when I have to make excuses for you to old Coody.'

'I'll make them myself if he's back before I leave.'

'Can't see why he shouldn't be. Doesn't take that long to walk out to the headland and back.'

There was another letter for her on the wardroom table, this time the formal invitation from the three trainee navigators inviting her to the ball, now confirmed. She had no idea whether she'd be back, but a ball – well, she had not been to one since Cambridge and she wouldn't be denying another unattached female a place by accepting, even if it turned out she couldn't go. She scribbled a note accepting.

'Would you like more coffee?' asked TR/16.

She started, fearing he had noticed her fading. 'I'll get it.' She stood, almost too abruptly.

He smiled. 'I only asked because I would like some and I didn't want to appear greedy.'

They were in the safe house in Rotterdam, sitting at the table in the back room where they had been introduced by Henry. They were alone. Henry was tied up with another operation about which everyone was tight-lipped but which Emily suspected involved the Belgian she had met. TR/16 had used his emergency signal procedure to request an urgent meeting. He had never used it before and it was at first feared that he was in danger, but he had sent a second message saying he had something urgent to convey, something 'for the lady from London'.

He looked exactly as before, with his casual clothes, sketch pad and hat. He had courteously thanked her for coming, apologised for using the emergency contact and sent best wishes to Henry. Yet there was a tension in him she hadn't sensed before. When she asked on arrival how long he had – C repeatedly insisted that it should be the first question in any agent meeting – his reply was terse. 'An hour. Not more.' Even though alone, they behaved as if they had not known each other before. She wondered if she appeared tense, too.

He told her that for his regular meetings he always ensured he had an official reason – 'a reason of duty' – to cross the border, but this time he had not said he was going and though he had an invented reason prepared, he preferred not to have to give it and wanted to get back before anyone realised he had gone. 'It's because this is urgent,' he said. 'They are preparing an attack. *Uncle and Aunt and all the family* must mean your fleet with your capital ships and your Admiral Jellicoe. But they are not planning a fleet engagement, the High Seas Fleet is not putting to sea. It must be just a raid with the torpedo boats they mentioned before.'

'Still only six?'

'So far as I know.'

'But you also overheard something else, about the torpedoes?'

'That was later, not from the Herr Kommandant. When I inspected the two cruisers in dock, the officer of the watch on one was talking to another officer, a junior lieutenant whom I recognised from the torpedo boat flotilla. As I climbed onto the bridge this junior officer was saying something like ... *the 25th, all so hush-hush we don't know what it is ourselves yet except that three of the boats won't even have room for their torpedoes because of all this other kit and people we've got to take.* When they saw me coming up the stairs they fell quiet.'

'You're certain this officer was from the flotilla?'

'Yes, I've seen him on their quay. He's often there.'

Emily noted everything, not trusting herself to remember. She had had a wakeful night on the sleeper from Edinburgh, which diverted to Crewe in the early hours with the usual clanking, jolting and shouting. The next night, crossing to Rotterdam on a contrary sea, had been little better. She had spent the intervening day in Whitehall Court being briefed on arrangements for her solo meeting with TR/16 and debriefed on what she had found out about Lieutenant Hueffer. He now had a file of his own, code-named Heifer.

'Quite a history, your gallant lieutenant,' said Dorothy, who had the file on her desk. 'He had a marriage – pseudo-marriage – in Germany which would have been bigamous if it were real and still ended up in a court case here, which he lost. It was in all the papers. The alleged marriage was to another writer who insisted on calling herself his wife de-spite the real one still being around, although they separated years ago. Now he's estranged from the would-be successor. Before all that he spent quite a time in Germany at a spa being treated for neurasthenia. Don't suppose he mentioned any of this during your tête-à-têtes? Slipped his mind, perhaps.'

'Scope for you, Emily, if he's footloose and fancy-free,' said Miriam. 'Do your duty for King and country.' She laughed.

It wasn't easy to reconcile this with the kindly lieutenant she knew, or thought she knew. A man could smile and smile and be a villain, she remembered from a school production of *Hamlet*. Presumably he could also appear perceptive and sensitive and be an adulterer. In which case he might also appear loyal to his country while betraying it, assuming the capacity for betrayal extended from the private to the public realm. Yet she was reluctant to believe it of him; there was surely a difference between public and private, though she wasn't sure what.

'He's open enough about his German family,' she said. 'Doesn't try to hide it. And we still don't have any evidence that he's Heifer, do we? Other than the fact that he's half-German and his name sounds similar.'

'And the fact that he's in Rosyth and that the intelligence

TR/16 is picking up has come to light only since he was posted there,' said C, who had quietly joined them from his office.

Emily was startled by the voice behind her. 'I'm sorry, sir, I didn't realise—'

'Quite all right, my dear, quite all right. Well done for getting back so promptly. Come and tell me all about it.' He lit a cigarette with a flourish of his oversize lighter, waving away the smoke as he looked around the room. 'More coffee,' he said to no one in particular. 'Coffee for Miss Grey too. She must need it.'

Now, sitting across the table from TR/16 with more coffee she didn't want, hoping it wouldn't make her dizzy, she struggled to think of further questions which weren't repetitions. 'What do you think they're planning?' she asked. 'What is your guess?'

TR/16 sat back. 'I might be able to guess if I knew the British ports. All I can say is that it is to be quick, an in-and-out raid, not an occupation. It involves landing some things or some people but not a lot and not for long. Maybe they want to steal something. But it seems to be aimed at your Grand Fleet and I don't think they plan to steal a Dreadnought. Does the date, the 25th, mean anything? Is anything happening with the Grand Fleet then? Where will it be?'

The Chief had told her that the capital ships of the Grand Fleet, with Admiral Jellicoe in his flagship, were due to sail from Scapa Flow and dock in Rosyth on the 24th. The movements and locations of the Grand Fleet were among the most closely guarded secrets, known only to very few even in the Admiralty. They could not under any circumstances be revealed to a German, even if he was, as C put it, one of ours. She knew she must not answer.

'The 25th is the last moonless night of the month, as you heard them say. So it must be something happening at night.'

'But where will the fleet be then? Will it be in Rosyth?'

It was clear from his reporting that the Germans knew when the fleet was setting to sea and that they had a good idea where it was headed. Karl Krueger knew too. Denial was pointless. 'It may be,' was all she could bring herself to say.

'In that case you must strengthen the port's defences or send the fleet somewhere else. That is all I can say.' He sipped his coffee. 'We live in an uncertain world, Emily. May I call you Emily when we are alone, in memory of our mutual friend? I often think of him. All we can be certain of is that there will always be uncertainties. We must do the best we can. That is life.'

Are you married? she wanted to ask. *What has your life been since Heidelberg? Why – really why – are you doing this? What do you think Hans would have said to you about it?* There was no reference in TR/16's file to his personal or family circumstances. He seemed a nice man, a decent man, as he had always been when not drunk. If he were married, what he was doing could have desperate consequences for his wife and children. Had he thought about that, or didn't he care? She was reluctant to believe he wouldn't care, just as she was reluctant to think Lieutenant Hueffer was Heifer. She wanted to believe both men, and believe in them. Yet both – one certainly, one possibly – were spies. But if the movements of the fleet were as closely guarded as C had said, how would Hueffer – if he was Heifer – have known about them?

'I must leave,' he said. 'You are content to wait for my report on the repairs to the two cruisers? I can give you notes now if you want or wait for my next meeting with Henry.'

'If it's technical and not urgent it might be better to wait.'

He made to help clear the coffee things but she told him to go. She was not to leave until a good fifteen minutes after him. The clerk and one of the two secretaries from the Rotterdam station had acted as counter-surveillance for his arrival, as she and Nigel had before. They would also watch him out, following him to the train station. She was to join them at the legation later, where Henry would encode her report and send it to London. With luck, she would return across the North Sea that night.

She got back just before Henry returned from his own agent meeting. 'How was he?' he asked as soon as they were alone. 'Is he all right? Not under suspicion?'

She explained, then wrote a summary of her report for him to encode, a laborious process which involved tables of numbers in a small book he kept in his safe. 'How was your meeting?' she asked. 'Was it with the gentleman I met?'

'His representative. It's going very well, we're getting some really good tactical stuff at last. GHQ are delighted. No more talking, please, while I'm doing this. Otherwise I'll lose my place or get the sums wrong and send a lot of indecipherable nonsense.'

She sat looking at his bent head. He was thinning on top,

which she hadn't noticed before. Thankfully, he had shown no indication of renewing his advances. His manner was entirely businesslike, as if they were colleagues of long standing or had no personal relations at all. Was it possible that he had forgotten about what he'd done, or was it so casual or so frequent that it meant nothing to him? She wondered whether she could be married to a balding man. In the long run there was probably little choice. Hans had had a wonderful head of vigorous light brown hair, soft to the touch even when cut brutally short.

Henry looked up. 'Good stuff. What a good man he is, our Dane. Bless him. Sounds as if you're in for a big show in bonnie Scotland.'

'But what kind of show? Even he can't work out what they intend. He says they wouldn't take on the fleet with just six torpedo boats. Even with the fleet in harbour it would be suicidal. They'd never get to it. I've seen the harbour defences. There are guns out in the firth, too, beyond the bridge. They might not even get past that.'

'Well guarded, is it?'

'There seem to be plenty of guns. And the man suspected of being Heifer is planning boom defences farther out in the estuary.'

'I suppose if he is Heifer he'd know how to circumvent them.'

'Yes but the odd thing is he's the one who's pushing for them. The lieutenant commander I work for, who's doing this big review of port security, doesn't appear to be interested.'

'Ours not to reason why. We just report. Tell our masters

what is the case and what isn't. Up to them to work out the significance. Maybe the lie of the land or water isn't suitable for boom defences. Time for a drink before you go?'

'I'm not sure there is. I—'

'It's all right, we don't have to go anywhere. We can drink here. I'll run you down to the docks in the station car.' He opened his desk drawer and took out a bottle of whisky and two glasses. 'No water, I'm afraid. You'll have to nip next door if you want water.'

She didn't want to appear unfriendly and thought it might help her sleep on the ship. She worried that he might try to move the conversation onto a more personal level, but he embarked on a series of questions about who was doing what in Whitehall Court and who was posted where abroad, most of which she couldn't answer. But she was as determined to appear as businesslike and relaxed as him.

'You must think I'm very unobservant but I've hardly spent any time in Whitehall Court and don't know many people. As soon as I arrived I was sent on a shorthand and typing course in preparation for Rosyth. And then Rosyth, apart from my earlier visit here.'

'What about your marine? Has the Old Man sent him back to the marines yet?'

She described what Nigel was doing. 'And what about you?' she asked. 'What was your life before all this?'

'Brought up in South Africa, as you can hear. Came over to Cambridge, read natural sciences, qualified as a mining engineer, war came and I joined the British Army.'

'How did you end up in the Service?'

'By buying dinner for a charming young lady when I was on leave in London. Dorothy, who works for the Old Man – you must know her? Friend of a friend, I was at a loose end, asked her out to dinner, we got on, she told the Old Man about me and he offered me this job. How is she, Dorothy? Haven't been in touch since I was posted here, sadly.'

It was hard to imagine Dorothy being courted, or even of having a life outside work. Let alone being described as young – which was unfair because she was, at least, not old. Nor was there any reason why she shouldn't dine with men now and again. Perhaps she could be charming. Perhaps he had tried it with her too, with more success. She now remembered something Dorothy had said when she was leaving for her first trip to Rotterdam, something to the effect of remembering her to all at the station. 'Would you like me to take her a message?' she asked.

'Message?' He looked puzzled. 'You could say hello from me, I s'pose. I'll drop in anyway during my next leave.'

The whisky might have had an effect, because she slept better that night despite the North Sea. It also helped her button her lips during Henry's erratic drive to the docks.

CHAPTER THIRTEEN

Emily did not go home on landing but went straight to Whitehall Court to report. Frank Stagg said the Chief had read Henry's telegraphic summary of her meeting and wanted to hear from her about it in the afternoon. Meanwhile, she was to get on with her full written report.

When she saw him he was not in his usual expansive post-prandial mood but was serious and businesslike, almost curt. He reminded her of her father's description of a ship's captain interviewing defaulters. What was more, he was accompanied by Colonel Kell of MI5.

She handed him her typewritten report. He laid it on his desk unread. 'Thank you, Miss Grey, I've seen your summary. We'll go through your full report later. Before we do that, Colonel Kell here has some questions for you. Sit down, please.'

Colonel Kell was uniformed, as before, sitting with his legs crossed alongside the Chief's desk so that he faced the straight-backed office chair that had been pulled up for Emily.

As Emily sat, the rustle of her skirt was the only sound in the room.

Colonel Kell nodded at her and then said, without preliminaries, 'Are you a Fenian, Miss Grey?'

'A Fenian?' Emily was as surprised as if she had been asked whether she was a species of bird or Albanian. She reflected afterwards that she probably looked it, which would have helped. 'No, I don't think I am, no.'

'You don't believe that Home Rule for Ireland should be achieved through violence?'

'No.'

'Do you believe in Home Rule?'

'No ... well, I don't know. To be honest I've not thought much about it. I know it's an issue that's debated in Parliament ...'

'Do you know who I mean by Sir Roger Casement?'

'I know who you mean, yes. I've read about him. He was a diplomat who now campaigns for Home Rule. But I haven't seen much about him recently.'

'That's because he's in Germany plotting with the Germans to supply arms to the Fenian movement in Ireland in order to foment an uprising there. He is also trying to recruit Irish prisoners of war to fight for the Kaiser. Have you any friends who are supporters of his?'

'No, I don't think ... well, I have one friend, yes, someone I was at Cambridge with, who I think now supports Home Rule, but I've never heard her mention Sir Roger Casement. I don't think she'd support violence. She's a suffragette too but not a violent one.'

'Would you describe yourself as a suffragette, Miss Grey?'

'Me? Yes, I suppose – in the suffragist sense that I think we should be able to vote too, just like men. But while we're at war I don't think we should be doing too much about it.' She was aware of her heart beating.

'Would you like to tell us about your Home Rule friend?'

Emily hesitated. The meeting – or debrief, as she had anticipated – had not only taken an unexpected turn but made her feel pummelled. It was as if she had walked around a corner and found herself in a boxing match, with no idea against whom or what she was defending herself. Or why. Colonel Kell, whom she remembered as well-mannered and correct, had now added to those qualities the cold, measured hostility of a prosecuting counsel. She looked at the Chief, but he looked at her with the same impersonal seriousness and lack of expression as when she entered the room. Both men acted as if they were strangers.

'Do you mean Zara?' she said. Her mouth was suddenly dry. She had done nothing wrong, she felt, but Colonel Kell's questioning made her feel she had. She felt, too, the first stirrings of indignation.

'Zara Millett, your Cambridge friend. The one with the criminal record.'

So they already knew about her. She took a breath and began, describing how they met, the nature of their friendship, what she knew of Zara's family, Zara's political views, Zara's account of her arrest for chaining herself to railings in Whitehall and, lastly, her recent meeting with Zara and Sean

Jephson. As she spoke her confidence returned. There was no reason to feel defensive about her friendship, she had nothing to hide. They might not approve of Zara being a suffragette or a Home Ruler like her new beau, but there was nothing to be ashamed of in either. They were public causes espoused by many, not secret sins to be investigated. While still speaking, she resolved to go on the offensive when she finished, to ask them why they were asking, why it mattered.

But by the time she finished, the atmosphere in the room had changed. Colonel Kell sat back in his chair, nodding when she described their meeting as if checking off points of agreement. When she stopped and before she could say anything else, the Chief smiled. 'Thank you, Miss Grey. Admirably comprehensive and succinct. I think that tells us just what we needed to know.' He looked at Colonel Kell with raised eyebrows.

The colonel nodded again. 'Indeed. Thank you, Miss Grey, you've put our minds at rest.'

'I think we owe you an explanation,' said the Chief. He told her tea in the Charing Cross Hotel with Zara and Sean had been observed by MI5's Special Branch surveillance officers. Not, this time, because they were following her to see whether Germans were following her, nor because they had any interest in Zara. They were following Sean Jephson, hadn't at first known who Zara was, but recognised Emily from having followed her before. They were following Jephson because his messmates had reported him as expressing sympathy with Irish nationalist violence. He could apparently recite by heart and with approval Fenian bombings and other atrocities going back into the previous century – bombings which had led to the formation of the Special Irish Branch, as it was then called. He claimed he was a cousin of Sir Roger Casement and, when in drink, that the English colonialist oppressors wouldn't know what hit them when the Irish Republican Brotherhood rose in support of the Germans. That day was coming, he often said. And now he had gone AWOL. 'Absent Without Leave,' the Chief explained. 'Colonel Kell's people suspect he may have fled to Germany to join Casement. Or, if he's still here, that he may be planning an outrage.'

'Unless he's simply too much drink taken and gone on what his messmates call a bender,' said Colonel Kell, with a small patronising smile. 'That's the most common reason for going AWOL.'

'Whatever his reason, we need to know,' said the Chief. 'In fact, we need to find him and Colonel Kell wonders whether your friend Zara Millett might know where he is hiding. Or whether she's hiding him herself.'

Emily tried to reconcile what she was being told about Sean Jephson with the quiet charm, gentle smile and far-away blue eyes of the man she remembered. He had not seemed a violent man, quite the opposite. And she was sure Zara would not condone bombings and assassinations, still less alliance with the Kaiser. 'I've not seen or heard from Zara since we had tea,' she said. 'Mind you, I've been away some of the time.'

'You have indeed and to good effect,' said the Chief. 'But do you think you'd be able to get in touch with her and see her before you go back to Rosyth? If only to confirm that she's still living with her parents and not hiding with Jephson somewhere. If she isn't, she may know what's happened to him.'

'But things are coming to a head rather in Rosyth, aren't they? According to TR/16. Isn't it important that I'm there?' She hoped it wasn't obvious that she was stalling. She wanted time to digest the idea of spying on her friend, which was what this amounted to, even if it was in the national interest. She recalled Zara's obvious fondness for the man and didn't want to do anything that might hurt her.

'They are coming to a head and we must get you back on the trail of Heifer as soon as we can. In view of what Petty Officer Jephson said about his two naval cousins, one in Rosyth, we especially need to know whether your man Hueffer has Irish relatives. But if you can meet Zara Millett without delaying your return for too long – perhaps just another day – it's worth a try in case Jephson is up to something awful. You need only sit down with Zara and talk to her, see what she says. You don't have to question her as we questioned you just now. Just be gentle and receptive. As you are with TR/16, I understand.'

The Chief's own manner was gentle, his weathered face reassuringly sympathetic. His description of her questioning of TR/16 could only have come from Henry Landau, which was surprising and gratifying. 'I'm not sure I could contact her in time,' she said, although she could feel herself yielding.

'I don't know whether her parents have a telephone. We normally communicate by letter.'

'Telegraph her. Say you're free tomorrow, going back on the night train tomorrow – as you must – but have time for tea or lunch or whatever she's free for. Even if she says nothing interesting we'll at least know she's not hiding with him somewhere. He may of course have gone back to Ireland, hiding with his folks there?' The Chief looked at Colonel Kell, raising his eyebrows again.

The colonel nodded. 'That's what most AWOLs do. If he is, we can relax. It's just a matter for the naval police then.'

Emily looked around the dining room with its tall sash windows facing the street, its gilded ceiling motifs, heavy damask curtains and thick white cloths over every table. 'So this is the famous University Club for Ladies. It's rather – I was a bit surprised ...'

'A bit smart for me, you mean?' Zara smiled. 'It was a gift from my godmother. Life membership. I hardly ever use it but this time I thought – well, why not? It makes a change. Change is good. Or so we tell ourselves.' She sipped her white wine and shrugged. 'I'm surprised you don't know it. It was founded by an old Girtonian, Gertrude Jackson, twenty or thirty years ago.'

'I've heard of it but I've never been. It's lovely.' Most of the tables were occupied by lunching ladies. The only man was a waiter. Her telegram suggesting lunch the next day had been answered promptly but cryptically, simply naming

226

time and place. Zara had appeared dressed with none of her usual flamboyance, a dark blue dress relieved only by white lace around the neck and her enamel Suffragette brooch. Her hat had a single matching blue feather. 'Are men allowed?' Emily asked.

'As guests, not as members.'

Zara's manner was as subdued as her dress, pleasant and matter-of-fact with none of her usual fizz and sparkle. She smiled little and had not laughed once. At first Emily had blamed herself, thinking that Zara had not wanted to turn out at all and did so only because she didn't want to appear impolite or unfriendly. But when she had apologised for the short notice Zara shook her head firmly and said, 'Don't, it does me good to get out. I've not been up to much recently.' She appeared disinclined to expand.

'So you could bring Sean here?' Emily said. She hadn't intended to mention him but this seemed a natural follow-on. As she said it, however, she reflected that Sean, who was not a commissioned officer, might feel out of place in such a setting, or that Zara might be embarrassed for him. On the other hand, Zara was well capable of using him to make a point. 'If he wanted to come,' she added, feeling it was a weak compromise.

Zara shrugged again. 'Haven't seen him.'

'Oh, sorry.'

'It's all right.' She sipped more of her wine. 'Look, don't let me drink alone. It's a bad habit. Drink yours too.'

Emily drank. 'Sorry, I shouldn't have—'

'We had a wonderful time, that night after we had tea. And two more times after that and then … I don't know what happened. He just disappeared. We were to meet at a hotel in Petersfield, on the way to Portsmouth. I told my parents – hope you don't mind – that I was staying with you at Slivericks again.' She smiled, this time with something of her old impishness. 'Anyway, I got to the hotel expecting to find him there but he wasn't, nor was there a room booked in his name as he had promised. Nor were there any messages. It was awful. They obviously thought – the hotel thought – that I was, you know, a bought woman who'd been abandoned. In the end I had to take a room myself, which fortunately I had enough money with me to pay for. It was that or sleep on the station platform. Then the next day I went into Portsmouth to his shore establishment called HMS something – they're all called HMS, aren't they, even if they're buildings? – but they wouldn't let me in or even tell me if he's on their establishment, as they call it. That too was a bit embarrassing because they assumed I was a girl in trouble looking for the father who was probably half-way round the world. Which – fortunately – I wasn't.' She smiled again, this time resignedly. 'So that's it, haven't seen hide nor hair of him since. He won't ever have lunch here, that's for sure.'

Emily, though genuinely sympathetic, felt fraudulent. Seeking truth because it was true was one thing, seeking it to use it another. When both motives pulled together it was impossible to feel wholly justified or wholly wrong. She asked the predictable questions – when it had happened, whether there had been any prior indications, what was known of his past and background, whether he had made Zara any promises.

Zara scoffed at the last. 'He never promised me anything, I'll give him that. I can't even pretend I was led up the garden path, I was running up after him. The only thing he ever promised was to show me round Ireland when they've kicked the British out.'

'And when was that supposed to be – after the war?'

'No, sooner than that. Imminently, I think. With help from the Germans, he said once. When I asked what he meant, he just said when the war's over, which will be sooner than people think, he said. Perhaps he meant the Germans are going to give in or the Kaiser's going to die or something. One thing's for sure, though: no more Home Rule for me. It's Zara Rule from now on.' She raised her glass again. 'Come on, Emily, drink up, for God's sake. Don't leave it all for me.'

As she went on with her questions Emily lost the uncomfortable sense of moral compromise with which she had started. National interest must surely be more important than personal, if not always then certainly now. Especially as Zara would not suffer in any way; she had already lost her man. By the time she reported back to the Chief before catching the night train that evening, all sense of compromise had dissipated. Exploitation was becoming normal.

CHAPTER FOURTEEN

Lieutenant Nigel Nisbet, Royal Marines, approached his professional life with the solemnity of a child. He loved to prepare and took pleasure in anticipating the unexpected. Unfortunately, where any duty was concerned, detailed preparation did nothing to lessen his anxiety that there might still be something he had forgotten. This sometimes reduced him to a paralysis of indecision. Thus it was that, on the afternoon when, in Emily's absence, he was to mount surveillance on the man Hueffer – whom he had privately decided must be Heifer – he dithered too long over choosing what to wear and was late.

It was not an easy brief, anyway, since anyone loitering outside the dockyard gates was bound to attract attention not only from the guardroom but from the small boys who infested Rosyth like sparrows. He had had enough trouble with them already. Having put on his suit again he remembered he'd worn it when passing Emily and Hueffer and another man on the way to the ruined castle. He changed into corduroy trousers, a roll-necked jersey, a faded green jacket and an old checked cap, all of which he hoped would make him look like an everyday working man.

On the way to the dockyard he bought a newspaper; a man on a bench or at a bus stop reading a paper was less noticeable than a man who had nothing to do but stare at passers-by. The nearest bench was about a hundred yards from the dock-yard gates. It wouldn't attract attention, but the comings and goings around the gates and guardroom made it difficult to see clearly what was going on. Once he got to his feet and set off after a uniformed man carrying a large bag, only to see him mount a postman's bicycle. Another time he half-stood before realising that the man he was about to follow was too young to be the target. However, at twenty past two – he was careful to note the time – a cyclist he recognised as his quarry approached the guardroom from within the dockyard, left his bike round the far side and walked out through the gates towards the footpath leading to the castle and the firth. He was uniformed.

Nigel folded his newspaper and followed. It would have been useful to have a dog; a man with a dog had an obvious reason for being anywhere. Even a walking stick would have helped, though his quarry clearly felt no such need. As he strode to keep within sight, Nigel resolved to write a surveillance manual one day incorporating all his thoughts on the art. Internal publication only, of course, and intended for people new to the profession. People such as Emily, who would doubtless find it a useful guide throughout their careers. He imagined himself lecturing in Whitehall Court to an admiring group of newcomers, watched over by a benevolent C.

When he rounded the first bend in the footpath there was no longer anyone in sight, just miles of gorse and heather. The man must be walking rapidly. Nigel prided himself on his surveillance skills and had never yet lost a quarry, though he had once followed and housed the wrong person. That was on an exercise, however, when mistakes were acceptable. Indeed, that was what exercises were for, to make mistakes and learn from them. He hurried on.

He rounded the second bend in time to see the hurrying figure turn off the main footpath towards the castle. Nigel slowed, pretending to look the other way. If he followed him towards the castle, the man had only to glance round to see Nigel outlined against the hills behind. It wouldn't matter if there were other walkers, but that afternoon he would be the only visible human.

The land to the left sloped down before rising to a low ridge parallel with the path and concealing ground the other side. If he got behind the rise he could keep parallel his quarry until level with the castle, hidden from everywhere except from the tops of the ruined walls. He cut left across bog and heather, not daring to run in case the man looked round. Cresting the rise, he half-strode, half-slipped down the other side, safely out of sight now. The effort left him breathless and his left foot wet. Keeping low behind the rise, he hurried towards the castle, which the target should be nearing by now. His plan was to enter the ruin from the far side, concealing himself if possible but if not, pretending to be another interested visitor who happened to be there already.

By the time he'd scrambled up to the crumbling outer wall, both feet were sodden and he had to pause again for breath, crouching in the rubble of a fallen section with a view of the flat grass keep. There was no sign of anyone. The uneven tops of the walls looked as if giants had taken bites out of them. The corner tower to his right had had its top bitten off, but at the bottom was a low doorway showing the first few steps of a stone spiral staircase. The keep was still empty. He walked with affected casualness to the doorway and climbed the narrow steps until he came to a window or arrow slit from which he could view the keep unseen.

A gust of wind brought a sudden rain squall. The turns of the stone stairs kept him dry at first, though he could make out grey clouds above the open top of the tower. No one appeared in the keep. Perhaps Heifer or Hueffer or whatever he was known as was meeting his contact in the outer walls. If he was meeting anyone. He would be getting wet, a pleasing thought. Then the familiar figure appeared, coming through the entrance arch on the far side. The man paused in the middle of the arch, checked his watch – left wrist, Nigel noted for his report – then turned and relieved himself against the wall. He took a long time over it. Nigel wasn't sure whether that was a clandestine signal or whether it was even worth noting, given that Heifer had perhaps reached the age at which male urination slowed. By the time the man finished buttoning his flies, which also took a long time, the squall had stopped. He ambled across the wet grass of the keep, looking up and about like a tourist studying the castle's configuration. He headed towards Nigel's tower.

Nigel rapidly reviewed his options in what he believed was the correct military manner: he could continue up the stairs to the ruined top, where he might hide but from where there was no escape if Heifer followed; or he could remain where he was in the hope that Heifer wouldn't come that far; or he could step out into the keep and cheerily pretend he had been sheltering from the rain; or he could do what Heifer had just been doing. Emergency peeing – caught short, he would say with a laugh – was a universal explanation. Of course, his urine would run down the stairs and he would have to tread in it on his way out, but it would be irrefutable evidence of need. Then a refinement occurred: when he heard footsteps mounting the stairs he could descend while pretending to button his flies. True, there would be no urinary evidence, but he could pretend to have been peeing into the wind and rain from the top. Once again, he found it difficult to decide.

He was still reviewing his options when Heifer entered the stairway below. He heard one step, then another, then nothing. Had the man paused on the stairs, sensing his presence? The pause lengthened, until ended by another step. Nigel unbuttoned his flies, ready to button them again as he descended, but then saw Heifer walking back across the wet grass of the keep. He walked briskly now and soon disappeared through the arch. The thought that the man must have filled a DLB – dead letter box – made Nigel's heart race. He had never filled or emptied one himself except on exercise, when they had been told to beware the common behaviour of people filling or emptying DLBs – an unrealistically slow approach followed by a rapid, relief-fuelled departure. Convinced that this was what he had witnessed, Nigel waited a couple more minutes, then stepped quietly down the narrow stair.

Nothing had changed – just the same rough stonework and steps worn by countless feet over centuries. He peered into every gap between stones, felt with his fingers above the stone lintel, climbed back up the first few steps and felt between cracks on the way down again. Finally he knelt on the stone floor and reached with one hand into the gap beneath the curve of the first few steps. He felt gingerly in case there were rodents; he had always feared rodents, especially rats. His mother had told him one had once climbed onto his pram when she put him out in the garden. Luckily, she had seen it before it had a chance to nibble him, but the imagined image of the incident had haunted him since. However, his probing fingertips found no sharp little incisors; rather, they felt a roll of paper. It was wide enough to be wedged beneath the steps and he had to work it free from one end.

There were several sheets neatly tied with familiar government-issue white string. He carefully untied it and unrolled the sheets. Innermost was a smaller sheet of lined notepaper on which was pencilled in capital letters:

THIS IS THE PORT SECURITY REVIEW I TOLD YOU
OF MINUS THE BOOM DEFENCE PLANS YOU HAVE
ALREADY. I CANNOT MAKE COPIES WITHOUT
PEOPLE KNOWING AND MUST HAVE THEM BACK
BY MONDAY. AUNTIE AND FAMILY STILL DUE HERE
ON 24TH.

It was unsigned.

Nigel leafed through them. He had never seen the review
but knew from Emily that it was what the PSO was working
on. He also knew that boom defence was Lieutenant Hueffer's
responsibility. He did not understand the reference to auntie
and family but knew the Grand Fleet was due in on the 24th,
having heard it discussed in the hotel bar by three naval officers entertaining their visiting wives. Presumably everyone
on the base knew it, so perhaps the reference to auntie was to
something else, something special and different.

He rolled the sheets and retied the string with the same
thumb-knot and bow. He now had to decide what to do. It
must surely be prevented from falling into German hands, in
which case his duty was to secure it, report to C in London
and have Heifer/Hueffer arrested. But C might not want that.
C might prefer him to replace it and wait for Heifer's contact,
a second German agent, to empty the DLB so that he too
could be identified and arrested. Maybe this would lead to a
whole network of spies whom he would have identified. He
could not resist imagining the glory of such triumph, praise
falling upon his head as bountifully as the recent rain. But

how long would he have to stay watching the DLB? Would the second agent empty it within the hour, as soon as Heifer was well clear? Or would he wait for nightfall, or the next day? If he left to report it he might miss him.

He was spared another decision by the sound of someone scrambling over the rubble from which he had entered the keep. He hurriedly slid the papers beneath the steps and climbed back up the stairs to the slit window. He heard nothing more apart from the cawing of rooks. Perhaps he had imagined it, or perhaps a stone had been dislodged, or perhaps it was a squabble between rooks.

Then he saw a tall figure striding away from the tower across the keep towards the arch. He wore a crumpled dark jacket and black broad-brimmed hat and carried an easel, with a leather bag slung over one shoulder. Nigel recognised him as the artist he had seen sketching the castle when conducting his discreet recce of Heifer. The rain returned.

The man walked determinedly with long strides, like one accustomed to hill walking. When he reached the arch he paused briefly where Heifer had urinated, then strode on and was soon out of view. Nigel once again descended the stairs, knelt and felt beneath the bottom step. There was no roll of paper. He hated getting wetter than he was already but had no choice if he was to do his duty. Doing his duty, the satisfaction of knowing he had done his duty, had always been important to him. He pulled his cap down more firmly – above all, he hated getting his head wet – buttoned his jacket and set out across the keep. In the dry arch he could see where Heifer had urinated. Above the spot, at head height, was a faint chalk tick, with a stronger chalk line through it. The man he now had to follow was well on the way to the main footpath, striding vigorously. Heifer, who must have been ahead of him, was nowhere to be seen. There was nothing for it but to risk being spotted. He set out across the moor, his feet squelching. The rain was now almost horizontal, gusting in waves that stung his cheek and soon had his sodden left trouser clinging to his leg. He hoped C would regard laundry as an allowable expense.

CHAPTER FIFTEEN

Emily sighed, took a deep breath and turned away from the mirror. There was no dressing table in her cabin, just a small desk, and the only mirror was head-size and head-height. No matter how much she worked on her face she still looked pale and tired. The light green ball gown she had been so pleased to wear in that last term at Cambridge now seemed insipid, making her paler still. And her shoes pinched. She couldn't believe her feet had grown. Perhaps the exhaustion of the past few days had somehow made them swell.

She would normally have been excited by the prospect of a ball but now – after the rush to and from Rotterdam, the unexpected interview in London, the debrief of her meeting with TR/16, her unannounced night at home to pick up ball gown, dancing shoes and handbag from her startled mother, the next day's lunch with Zara, followed by the debrief of the lunch, then the uncomfortable overnight journey north, then all day in the PSO with a cantankerous Lieutenant

Commander Cooden – having to be on parade at a ball was the last thing she felt like.

Cooden had been particularly difficult, resentful at her being withdrawn to London so abruptly, dismissive of her invented role in typing up the backlog of Admiralty assessments of the capability of the German High Seas Fleet and now seemingly unmollified by her unscheduled reappearance.

'Does our work here count for nothing in their eyes?' he expostulated. 'Do they not care about the security of our own fleet? Or of its home base? Did anyone mention that, eh? Eh? Anyone at all? Tell me.'

'I don't think they realised the disruption they caused. People were withdrawn from all over the country to get rid of the backlog. There were six girls from Plymouth and masses – shoals – from Chatham. There was even someone supposed to be coming from Scapa Flow but of course she never got there in time. She had to turn round and travel straight back, poor girl.' She was finding that the more she invented, the more she enjoyed it, almost persuading herself of her alternative world.

'They didn't pinch anyone else from here. Only you for some reason. All those typists in the Harbour Master's and Port Admiral's offices and God knows where else. Not one of them, not one. They picked on us. Must have. I suppose they think we matter less. Typical.'

'That's probably because most of those girls are permanently here whereas I'm on temporary detached duty. All the other girls I spoke to were temporaries.' She was particularly pleased with that; it would have convinced her.

It seemed to calm him. He lingered beside her desk, nodding and staring at the floor. 'You may as well make a start on the inventory. Port Admiral suddenly wants an inventory of everything we've got. Don't ask me why. Orders came in while you were away. Jackson will help.'

'Hadn't I better finish typing up the port security review first? If the fleet is due in on the 24th—'

He looked up. 'Where d'you hear that?'

She knew as she said it she shouldn't have. 'In the Admiralty. It's common knowledge there.' She hoped she sounded confident. He wouldn't be able to check, anyway.

'Leave that for the time being and jump to it on the inventory. Start with everything in Hueffer's office. That's where we dump stuff we don't use very much.' He turned away, adding under his breath, 'Like the man himself.'

She pretended she hadn't heard. 'Where is Lieutenant Hueffer? Is he not in today?'

'Off sick. Another of his ... you know ... turns, breakdowns, shell-shock things. Recalled to the hospital at Craiglockhart the day after you left.'

'Oh dear, I hope he'll be all right.' Her concern was unfeigned; she couldn't help liking him despite the suspicions that swarmed like flies about him. She had hoped he'd be at the ball, if only as a safe refuge, someone she could talk to.

'As I said, don't worry about the security review for now.

241

It's in my cabinet. I've done more work on it while you were away.'

Emily stole a last look at herself in the mirror. Her hair was marginally less lifeless for having been washed at home but the night on the train hadn't helped. Other women at the ball – she knew none but they were bound to be wives of senior officers – would judge it flat and neglected. She took another deep breath. As she stepped into the corridor she could hear the band from the other end of the building.

The dining room, its furniture cleared, was festooned with all the flags of the Empire. The band at the far end and what she had taken to be a solid wall had been folded back to reveal a large sitting-out area with tables, chairs and a buffet. She entered with what she hoped was a look of confident unconcern, only to be confronted by a blockade of the backs of naval officers in uniform, drinks in hand, talking loudly to their wives or guests. Several of the women glanced at the young woman coming in by herself. Ever since her first days at Cambridge she had hated entering social functions alone, feeling she was the target of critical attention. It was worsened this time by the wall of sound that almost made her flinch and by the swift appraising glances of the other women. She was the only one without a partner.

But not for long. Within seconds her name was shouted by male voices and she saw her hosts, the three trainee naviga-tors, rising and waving from one of the tables. This attracted more attention to her, but she minded less now that she could advance, smiling, across the room. There was a seat reserved, champagne on the table and the offer of a dance as soon as the band struck up a waltz. They could all dance, she discovered. 'We were made to at Dartmouth,' the first explained. 'Last thing you expect when you volunteer for the King's Royal Navy. Part of Lord Fisher's reforms, they told us. Where did you learn?'

'School. I was lucky not to be taller. Tall girls only ever learned to dance as men.'

'Which was where – your school?'

'St Paul's in London, the girls' school. It was quite new when I went.'

'And what after that?'

It was usually a pleasure to surprise people by having been to the University of Cambridge, but this time she shrugged and pulled a face. 'Learned to type and things and got a job with the Admiralty and came here.'

'But your folks are naval, you said before? Your father served?'

'Yes, as ship's MO. Mainly on cruisers.' That seemed to satisfy him. Once a naval connection was established no further biographical *bona fides* were needed.

'Can't wait to get a ship myself,' her partner continued. 'We're all waiting to hear about our berths but don't suppose we'll be told anything until the fleet's in.'

'That shouldn't be long.'

'Twenty-fourth, everyone says.'

'What are you hoping for – what sort of ship?'

'Oh – anything that will take me to the action, get at the Hun. That's what we're all waiting for.'

She next danced the new foxtrot with one of the others. Neither was confident about it, fortunately more a matter for laughter than embarrassment. 'Pity old Hoof's not here, he might have shown us,' her new partner said. 'He's a good dancer. We had a bit of a ceilidh, an informal wardroom do, just after he arrived. He was surprisingly nimble. Big fat chaps sometimes are. Don't know why.'

'That's Irish dancing, isn't it?'

'Irish or Scottish, looks the same as Scottish country dancing to me. Lots of people do it. Good fun. Easier than this damn foxtrot.'

'I heard he's had to go back to hospital. What happened?'

'He should have been here. On our table. We'd booked a place for him. He was looking forward to dancing with you, he said.'

'That was nice of him. But what exactly—?

'Neurasthenia, they say. Whatever that is. He had a bout of it before the war, apparently, years ago. Sounds like shell-shock, which he also had a spot of in the trenches, when he was out there. That's what brought him back here, apparently. So they say.'

'But what happened? What form did it take? Did he collapse or what?'

'Don't know. We just heard he'd had another attack and had been sent back to that place near Edinburgh where they send people. Old Coody must know, it was he who told someone. Ask him. He's here somewhere.'

'Commander Cooden is here? He didn't mention he was coming.' It was hard to imagine him willingly attending a convivial social function, let alone dancing. 'Who – with his wife?'

'No idea. Don't know whether he has a wife, does he? Lives out, not in the wardroom. In a hiring in the town. Sort of mental paralysis, I believe. Can't bring himself to do anything.'

'Commander Cooden? He was all right today when I— '

'No, no. Old Hoof. Apparently it's all you can do to walk from one room to another when you've got neurasthenia. You're perfectly compos mentis, not mad or anything, just becalmed, no wind in your sails. Don't know how long he'll be there.'

She wasn't sorry when there was a pause for the buffet dinner. Much as she loved to dance, tiredness was creeping up within her like an evening mist. It wasn't so much moving to music as the mental effort of making conversation. That was so even when the conversation was sharpened by relevance to her investigation, as in the revelation of Lieutenant Hueffer's familiarity with Irish dancing. Unless it was Scottish. If she could simply have danced without speaking she felt she could have gone on and on, albeit ever more gently and slowly. Later, waiting in the buffet queue with her three partners, she was accosted by Lieutenant Commander Cooden.

'Miss Grey, what are you doing here?' He stood before her holding a plate piled high with chunks of salmon, potatoes

245

and salad. He was already chewing and it was not clear from his tone that he was pleased to see her.

Her first reaction was to ask the same of him, but she suppressed it. 'Having a lovely time being expertly navigated around the dance floor, sir.' She smiled as winsomely as she could. 'I didn't know you were coming?'

'Whose table are you on?'

'Advanced Navigation 57.' She indicated her companions. 'The navigation course has its own table and kindly invited me to join them.'

'We had to, sir. Otherwise we'd have had to dance with each other,' said one of them.

Cooden ignored him. 'We must have a dance.'

'That would be lovely, sir.'

She hoped he didn't mean it, or that she might be gone by the time he got round to asking her, but he reappeared beside her chair moments after the band struck up again. 'Here to claim my dance, Miss Grey,' he said, with unconvincing gallantry.

She pushed her unfinished plate away. 'Delighted, commander,' she said, with what felt like equally unconvincing gallantry. The dance was another waltz, at which he proved surprisingly adroit, better in fact than her younger companions. There was no reason she should be surprised, she told herself. Middle-aged, unappealing, podgy men shouldn't naturally be assumed to be bad dancers. He guided them around the floor fluently and effortlessly. She didn't need to think about where to put her feet because they fell naturally, unavoidably, into place with his. If only he were young and attractive, she thought, trying not to flinch as his belly pressed against hers. If only he were Hans. He had danced well, too.

'Are you here with a partner?' she asked. 'Is your wife—?'

'Not married, never have been.'

'Perhaps you've not met—'

'The right one, no.'

He spoke as if to close off the conversation. They continued another minute or two in silence. She suspected he was dancing with her out of a sense of duty, devoid of pleasure. In which case she might as well make some dutiful use of the occasion herself. 'Have you heard how Lieutenant Hueffer is?'

'Not a word. Don't expect to. Nervous conditions like that, people don't say much about them.'

'Where did it happen?'

'Where did what happen?'

'His breakdown.' She had never seen what people called a breakdown and couldn't imagine what happened. Presumably there was some sort of event.

'No idea. I was ... I was out on my rounds, inspecting. Don't know where he was. Not in our office, anyway. Must have reported himself to the doc, old sawbones, the MO, and they shipped him off to Craiglockhart.'

'Should we visit if he's not back soon?'

'Visits can do more harm than good, people in that condition.'

The band leader announced a Viennese waltz. It was a

more demanding dance and there was a mixed chorus of groans and cheers. A majority of couples left the floor but a few more joined. Emily turned, assuming they would leave too, but the commander remained. 'Haven't done a Viennese for years,' he said.

'Nor have I.' She had done it a few times with Hans, who had been properly taught, whereas she had merely picked it up from him. Done well, it was a beautiful, exhilarating dance, but she knew she couldn't do it as it should be done. She need not have worried. Cooden was again unexpectedly proficient. In fact, more than proficient; he whirled her around the floor with perfect timing and without a misstep, dancing as Hans had danced but if anything even better. She was aware of others looking at them and commenting and wished again that he was Hans. By the end they were both slightly breathless and she could feel the stretching of her thighs.

'Where did you learn that, sir?' she asked as they walked off the floor. 'They didn't teach it at Dartmouth, surely?'

'I was never at Dartmouth. Late entry, specialist grade. Engineer. Dartmouth too posh for us.'

'But in this post you don't engineer—?'

He shook his head. 'Thought I'd branch out a bit, see a bit more of the navy. I'll go back to real work after this posting. No thanks for branching out, of course, whatever you do. The navy can't spell gratitude.'

'Where did you learn Viennese?'

'Lessons. Where did you, I might ask? You didn't pick that up at school or secretarial college?'

'In so far as I can do it, I owe it to a cousin,' she lied. 'He spent time in Vienna before the war. His parents were at the British Mission there. Apparently everyone had to learn in order to be accepted in Viennese society.' She had heard that and hoped it was true.

The band leader announced that the next dance would be something different, an Irish jig. To get the blood moving, he said. 'Mine is moving enough already,' said the commander.

'Mine too,' said Emily, with some relief.

'Do you know Ireland?'

'I don't, I've never been.'

'Wonderful country.'

'So I've heard. Am I right in thinking Lieutenant Hueffer has Irish connections?'

'No idea. Soon will be, though.'

'Sorry, what soon will be?'

'Ireland, wonderful country that it is. Soon will be another country.'

'Oh, Home Rule, you mean?'

'If things go on as they are.'

He left abruptly after returning her to the table. Her navigators were impressed. 'Would never have believed old Coody could scoot around the deck like that,' said one. 'And you too, Miss Grey. You were easily the best couple there. Where did you learn?'

She repeated her lie and said that the commander had presumably had lessons somewhere. She had never known anyone execute a Viennese waltz like that outside Austria or Germany.

She was still drugged with tiredness when she got up the next morning and was almost late for work. The commander was there already, offering no small talk about the night before. 'Better crack on with that inventory. Port Admiral's pressing.'

She had heard nothing about it from the Port Admiral's office, but was relieved to discover the previous inventory in the filing cabinet. It had been compiled less than a year before and nothing much in the PSO seemed to have changed. The wall-mounted telephone was an addition and there was mention only of the desk and one chair in Lieutenant Hueffer's office, not two. Jackson could think of nothing else new, repeating defensively that he hadn't been there when the previous inventory was done and knew nothing about it. She asked the commander whether she could check his office and cupboard when he went out for his afternoon inspection.

'Of course, of course. Doubt you'll find much different. Shouldn't take long.'

When she embarked on it that afternoon, however, she found the cupboard locked. Jackson thought there was a spare key but didn't know where. 'Not much in that cupboard anyway,' he said. 'He was sorting through it when I took him his tea this morning. Just a couple of files and some papers.'

'No equipment of any sort?'

'No kit, no. Not even his revolver.'

'He has a revolver? I've never seen one when I've been putting things in there.'

'No more have I for some time now. Used to, though, before

you came. Service revolver, Webley. Must've had it out from the armoury for when he practises in the indoor range. Pretty handy with it, I heard.'

When Jackson disappeared on one of his mysterious errands, and with the commander still out, Emily used the telephone. After going through the usual checks that the call was official and had Lieutenant Commander Cooden's blessing – which she thought she could obtain retrospectively – she was eventually put through to Craiglockhart hospital. She asked after Lieutenant Hueffer. After further checks as to who she was and where she was calling from, and another pause lengthy enough for the operator to ask whether she was still there, a man in Craiglockhart said they had no Lieutenant Hueffer. 'Are you sure you've got the right place, lassie?' he asked, with a laugh. 'Sounds German to me.'

'He's not German, just his name. Are you quite sure? He'd have been admitted in the past few days.'

'No admittances in the past week. Several discharges but he's not one of those. Couldn't be staff, could he?'

Later, when the commander returned, she told him what she'd done, adding, 'I thought it would be useful to know when he might come back, assuming he's coming back. I hope that's all right?'

Puzzlement and alarm flickered across his features. 'Official call, was it? Logged to me? Well, yes, useful to know when he'll be back, I suppose. Let me know when you hear anything.'

'But they say he's not there, as I said. Where could he be?'

'Can't think. He was always a bit ... you know ... here today, gone tomorrow. Not on leave, by any chance?'

'He hasn't put in for any. Should I have a look in his cabin when I get back to the wardroom?'

'No harm in checking. Doubt he'll be there, though.'

'Should I check with the sick bay, assuming he went there first?'

'You could try.'

'It's rather worrying, isn't it, if he's simply disappeared? Especially with shell-shock.'

'Indeed, yes. Can't have fellows here one minute, gone the next.' He turned into his office and shut the door.

The sick bay said they hadn't seen him. As soon as she finished work that morning she hurried back to the wardroom. If Hueffer was a spy fearing discovery he might have fled to Germany, perhaps via overnight ferry to The Netherlands or Scandinavia. In which case he should appear on a passenger list and she should alert Whitehall Court as soon as possible. But why should he flee when he had no reason to fear imminent discovery? Unless his job was done, with the Grand Fleet due in the next day and the sabotage arrangements – whatever they were – complete.

Wardroom cabin doors had no locks. Lieutenant Hueffer's bed was made and the wastepaper basket was empty, presumably the work of the orderly. His shaving tackle, as her father called it, was aligned neatly on the shelf above the washbasin, the wardrobe door was ajar, showing his army service dress jacket, there was a novel by Henry James on the bedside table, and on the desk was a white envelope and a couple of sheets of letter paper, one blank, the other written on. The lid of the inkwell was off and there was a black fountain pen lying next to it, its top screwed on.

She closed the door softly, feeling like the thief she might be taken for if the lieutenant returned or if the orderly reappeared. She wasn't sure what she would say; the truth, prosaic as it was, sounded inadequate. She should have sought out the orderly and asked if Hueffer had said anything about going away, but it was too late now. As she advanced towards the desk, she saw her name on the envelope. The page of letter paper next to it was dated the day before and covered in a sprawling untidy hand. It read:

My dear Miss Grey, I hope you don't mind my communicating in this manner. I do so because I don't know when you'll be back nor whether I shall still be here. Coody told me he'd heard from the Admiralty that I'm deemed fit and am to be posted back to my old unit. Strange the War Office hasn't told me but they've done stranger things. Unless Coody himself is trying to get the Admiralty to recall me – doubt he'd be sorry to see the back of me.

I can't pretend I'm looking forward to the Front but at the same time can't say I'll be sorry to be back with old comrades (those that are still standing). At least it will be good to feel one is doing one's bit again. Not that I think what we're doing here is unimportant but since I've submitted my boom defence plans I've had nothing to do

except walk out every day to see if anything's changed.
Coody seems to have lost interest in my project. I can't even
get the plans back for minor amendments since he's been
sitting on them, Lord knows why.

    But really I'm bothering you with all this for another
reason. As I was saying not too coherently when we last
talked, I think there's something going on. Or, rather,
there's so much not going on that it makes me suspect that
something else is and I want to share my suspicions with
you in case Coody succeeds in hoofing me out (Hoof out
Hueffer – the old cry) before we have the chance to speak
again. They – my suspicions – centre around

It ended there. Emily stood holding the paper. He would not
have been posted without time to gather his possessions, so
would surely return for them. But if he didn't return and she
left the letter for someone else to find, he would not have
wanted it bruited abroad, still less be read by Lieutenant
Commander Cooden. On the other hand, if he were a spy it
might be a ruse to divert attention from himself.

At the sound of footsteps in the corridor she stuffed the
letter and envelope into her handbag and turned to face the
door. Then it occurred to her that it might be Hueffer himself,
in which case they'd be better left on the table. But the footsteps passed, fading as another door opened and closed. She
hurried back to her own cabin.

There were over two hours before dinner. She wanted to
discuss Hueffer, to talk through her inchoate thoughts, but

there was no one apart from Nigel, from whom she had heard nothing. He was supposed to report on his surveillance of Lieutenant Hueffer while she was away, assuming he'd conducted any. She thought of ringing his hotel, but that would have meant going back to the PSO and using the telephone there, which would require explanation if the commander returned unexpectedly. He would eventually come to know anyway because it would be logged to him. However, the evening was cool but fine and a walk might clear her head. She would call on Nigel in his hotel again. She put on her coat and her old brown felt hat and strode determinedly past the guardroom, this time without any embarrassing grins or comments about messages.

The hotel reception desk was unmanned, which meant she had to go into the bar and ask for Nigel, which in turn meant that the grizzled barman who'd seen her before had to go off to find the receptionist. He turned away with a knowing leer. Emily returned to reception, already irritated with Nigel. Almost everything to do with him, even the simplest things, became needlessly complicated, awkward or absurd. She sensed he was a loyal, perhaps even loving, soul at heart, but there was something about him that spawned difficulties, endless trivial, daily difficulties, something that denied him a straightforward relationship with the world.

The receptionist returned to say that Lieutenant Nisbet hadn't been seen for a couple of days and that the maids reported that his bed had not been slept in. But he was still booked in and his room paid for until the end of the month.

Her irritation dwindled as she walked back to the port. It was unlike him not to be in touch. He was a man who constantly wanted – needed – contact, even if to report that he had nothing to report. He'd have wanted to know what was going on and didn't like feeling left out, especially as he still thought of her as his junior.

Within sight of the guardroom she took a decision, turning left towards the firth along the path that both missing lieutenants knew. There was just time to get to the castle and back before dinner. Not, she admitted to herself, that the castle had any particular significance; she was no more likely to find either of them there than anywhere else, but it was a local focal point and it made her feel she was doing something rather than nothing. If she had no contact with either by tomorrow she would have to get in touch with London somehow. That would be difficult without Nigel. If all else failed, she would have to telegraph home to ask her father to ask her godfather, Admiral Hall, to ask C to get in touch.

The sun was still high enough to bathe the remnants of towers and battlements in a mellow glow. She stood in the entrance arch looking across the keep. There was no sign of life apart from the rooks or crows and she couldn't imagine either man pottering around ruins as dinner approached. But it was just conceivable that Nigel was lying in wait somewhere for a sight of Heifer. It would appeal to his relish for the clandestine, whether or not there was reason to believe Heifer was there.

She walked through the arch to the middle of the keep.

There was no breeze within the walls, the rooks and crows – or were they ravens? – flapped and croaked. She was tempted to call out, but that felt silly. If Nigel was watching he would have seen her by now. She ambled across the grass towards the collapsed stretch of wall which offered a view of the firth, with Edinburgh a murky smudge beyond. She paused by the low doorway into the nearby turret. Dark open doorways, like holes in the road dug by navvies, were an almost irresistible temptation, especially this one, because she could just make out the bottom step of the stone spiral staircase. It dipped in the middle, worn she imagined by centuries of cold, trudging watch-keepers. In such spots she had always fancifully hoped that, by keeping still and quiet, she might be susceptible to some vague flickering image or impression, some half-heard speech, some mysterious vibration from the past. It had never happened, of course, but that never stopped her waiting to see, to feel, to apprehend something of what had gone before.

She did see something this time, something very much of the present: a man's brown brogue shoe resting on its side a few steps up. On the next step she could see the sole of another shoe at an angle a few degrees off vertical. This shoe was attached to a leg encased in thick grey flannel trousers. Tentatively, she mounted the first two steps and peered around the bend. Above the trousers was a Norfolk jacket, one arm and shoulder jammed awkwardly against the wall, one white inert hand palm upwards. Above that was the face of Lieutenant Hueffer, and above that his other arm flung carelessly against the upper steps. He stank of urine.

His face was blotched red and white, misshapen as if in a seizure, the left eye and cheek a pulpy reddish mess. The other eye was closed. His lips were slightly parted, flecked by spittle, and there was dried blood on his smoke-stained moustache. Emily had never seen a dead body, as she took this to be until she saw – or thought she saw – a twitch of the single visible eyelid. But she could hear no breathing and the spittle on his lips didn't move. She felt she should do something, feel his pulse or turn him over to a less contorted position, but she didn't like to touch him. Or it, if that's what it was. Eventually she swallowed and spoke his name, twice, without response. Aware of her heart pounding and an empty feeling in her stomach, she retreated carefully, almost reverentially as if there were something not to be disturbed.

She half-walked, half-ran back to the guardroom where she reported breathlessly to the sailor on duty. A solemn, fresh-faced boy, younger than her, he seemed unable to take in what she was saying. She twice had to spell 'Hueffer' and 'lieutenant' before the officer of the watch stepped out of an inner room, grinning.

'Found a stiff, do I hear? We get them now and again, usually in the water. They're called soggies then. But yours is definitely a stiff, madam?'

'I'm not sure he's actually dead. I thought his eyelid—'

'They do twitch about a bit sometimes, especially if they're fairly recent. Not the soggies, of course, they've always been there some time. Drunks mostly. Where is yours?'

He shook his head and resumed before she had finished

explaining. 'Civil police matter if he died off base, unless killed in action. I'll telephone them. We'll send some men out to cordon off the area if you can show them where it is. Army, was he? In which case we can leave repatriation of the remains to the War Office. With the police handling the investigation and the army the rest, we'll have done our bit.' He grinned again. 'You're Miss Grey, are you not? Admiralty civilian working here? I've seen you in the wardroom. You were at the ball.'

'I was, yes. But I'm not sure he's dead, as I said. We should get an ambulance and stretcher-bearers—'

'You were dancing with old Coody. He's another oddball.'

She presumed the first oddball was meant to be Lieutenant Hueffer, though whether he was odd for being dead or for some other reason wasn't clear. 'Yes, he is a bit,' she said, thinking to elicit more. 'He dances well but I'm not sure—'

'Queer cove, isn't he? Takes all sorts but all right to crew with, perhaps? We've got an ambulance and crew on base. I'll shake them out and send them up with the police. I'll also get some men together for you now so you can set off and show them. No need to wait for the police.'

She didn't want to see poor Lieutenant Hueffer's body again, if that was all it was. Death was undignified and untidy, and it smelt. 'I could describe exactly where it is for them.'

'Better you lead them to it. You've no idea how at sea sailors are on land.' He laughed. 'And the police will want a statement from you.'

The sun had set by the time she and four sailors reached the castle. As she led them across the keep she momentarily feared that Lieutenant Hueffer might have somehow disappeared, that she had suffered a hallucination. But the faint possibility that he might still be alive kept her going.

The senior sailor, a burly red-bearded Westcountryman, went farther up the stairs than she had, peering closely. 'Been shot,' he pronounced. 'Exit wound through the top of his shoulder. Dead enough, anyway. You can see where it come out, look.'

The others were keen to look but Emily held back. She also held back the obvious question, which he answered for her. 'Didn't find no pistol with him, did you, ma'am? Nothing fallen down the steps? Can't 'ave done it hisself, then. Must be someone else. Someone done him in, if you ask me.'

'He ain't dead, he's breathing a bit,' said another sailor. A third said he wasn't, it was just that he'd leant on the body and pushed the air out. The second sailor thought he could feel a pulse, the others couldn't. This provoked discussion of an officer two of them had served under who had shot himself while they were lying off Jamaica. The top of his head has disappeared and had to be pieced together later. Emily stepped back into the courtyard, grateful for grass and air. 'You don't really need me, do you?' she said. 'You'll be here till the police and stretcher-bearers come?'

'We'll be here till the cows come home, they're such a dozy lot. They'll want a statement from you, ma'am, but so long as your details are logged in the guardroom they can catch up with you later. On the other hand they might not, might be happy enough to say we found him. Less writing for them. They don't like writing. No more do we.' They all laughed. Then the senior sailor came closer to her, his reddened face creased with concern. 'Sure you're all right, ma'am? If you want to sit down for a while one of the boys will sit with you and walk you back.'

She thought she must look pale. 'Perfectly all right, thank you. It's very kind. I know my way back.'

Light was fading but there was enough to make out the footpath. She had not gone far when she met four more sailors, two carrying a folded stretcher on their shoulders. They listened to her directions.

'No hurry if he's dead, is there?' asked one.

'There is because he may not be.'

'Can't no one tell, then?'

'It's not easy. Apparently.'

'We'll know soon enough once we start bouncing him around on this.'

The possibility that Lieutenant Hueffer had been murdered was hard to take in. She could think of no one who would want to murder him. In fact, she could think of no one who would want to murder anyone. But perhaps that was the point about murderers: they weren't until they were. It was easier to imagine suicide if he was badly shell-shocked. Or if he really was – had been – Heifer, through shame or fear of discovery.

Cold, hungry, late for dinner and feeling more upset than she had thought she was, she tried to slip unnoticed past the guardroom but was hailed by one of the sentries. 'Message for you, ma'am. Telephone.'

The officer of the watch had changed and was now a freckled fair young man whose face she knew from the wardroom. 'Telephone message for you, Miss Grey. Official call, gentleman, didn't leave a name, said you'd know him when you spoke to him. You're to telephone him at the Waverley Hotel, Edinburgh. You can use our instrument.' He smiled as he spoke.

Annoyingly, she felt herself blushing. They no doubt assumed it was Nigel, as did she. Reassuring as it would be to hear from him, her irritation increased when the Waverley receptionist told her there was no Lieutenant Nisbet in the hotel. Before she could respond, the receptionist asked if she was Rosyth. She said she was, was asked to wait, and was then startled by the brisk and abrupt tones of the Chief.

'Ah, Miss Grey. Tracked you down at last, eh? Where've you been? I've had everyone in the dockyard searching high and low for you. How soon can you get here?'

Flustered, she asked where. 'Here, of course, the Waverley which you've just telephoned.' She said she'd enquire about trains and buses but he cut her off. 'Port Admiral's car will bring you. I've spoken to him. There have been developments and it's important you get here as soon as possible. Doesn't matter how late. Have you eaten? Don't. I'll get them to rustle up something. There's a room reserved for you. Tell old what's-his-name – fellow you work for, Cooden – Admiralty's summoned you back again. Or tell him any damn thing you like. We're onto something and it's happening soon. Young Nisbet's come up trumps for once.'

'Nigel – you've heard from him? I've been—'

'Here now. Soon as you can. 'Bye.'

She replaced the receiver but stood with her hand resting on it. She was alone in the back room and it sounded as if there was some sort of good-natured ruckus in the outer office. She lifted the receiver again and waited for the operator. She asked for her home number, confirmed that the call was official and would be accepted as a charge on the PSO. Happily, it was her father who answered, which meant she didn't have to give her mother an account of the ball.

'Funnily enough, I was thinking about Cooden after you mentioned him,' he said, in answer to her second question. 'Pretty sure I never met him myself but the name stuck in my mind. Not just because it's unusual but I was sure there was something else about it. Anyway, I dined with Blinker in the club last week and asked him. He knew him in Portsmouth before the war when Cooden was under his command, doing something or other. Blinker wasn't very impressed and considered getting rid of him. Said he's an engineer officer and actually half-German, born in Ireland to an Irish girl and brought up there and in England. His father was a German shipping agent who died before he was born and his mother married an Englishman, Cooden, whose name she gave him and who was his father as far as the navy is concerned. Apparently he used to make a great thing about being Irish-German but not British.'

'He's never said anything like that to me.'

'Daresay he wouldn't these days. Probably wants to keep quiet about it.'

It was late evening by the time she reached the Waverley. The lengthy road journey was in the dark but the naval driver, a Rosythian of blessedly few words, was familiar with Edinburgh. She arrived tired, with her hastily packed bag and an empty stomach. As she approached the reception desk she realised she didn't know under which name the Chief would have booked in, but she was spared any awkwardness by a touch on her elbow.

'This way. He's asked me to show you up.'

She realised that her eye had rapidly passed over Nigel Nisbet. She had yet to appreciate that dirty-looking men in shabby clothes, men who were neither clean-shaven nor neatly bearded, were almost invisible to her. It wasn't that she consciously ignored them; it was more fundamental than that. As well as dirty, Nigel looked tired and damp and was limping slightly. His hair was a mess and his shoes were muddy. People in the foyer glanced at him and averted their eyes, as she had. She was surprised he was allowed in.

'We have news,' he said, his eyes excited despite his pallor. He spoke no more while they shared the lift with a silent elderly couple.

'Where have you been, what's happened?' she whispered as they walked along the carpeted corridor.

'Following and housing Heifer, that's what. Not bad, eh?

Tell you about it in a moment. Also, the Old Man has news from Rotterdam.'

The Chief received them in a panelled suite not unlike his apartment in Whitehall Court. The air was thick with Turkish tobacco and he was smiling, whisky in hand. He waved her to a low table on which was a half-bottle of champagne and a plate covered by a white cloth. 'Sandwiches for you, my dear. Best the kitchen could do at this time of night. And something to celebrate this evening's successes. We're almost there, I think.'

Over egg and cress sandwiches and two glasses of water, seasoned with sips of champagne, she listened to their accounts. The Chief's was crisp and concise: Rotterdam station reported another meeting with TR/16 who had learned that the torpedo boat flotilla was being readied for operation during the night of the 24th, by which time the fleet would be 'in' and the tides favourable. TR/16 had been asked to recommend someone with explosives expertise to join the raid and had been put on notice to go himself if they didn't find anyone in time. But he had not been briefed on the target or how they were to reach it. Details of Rosyth's new security measures, including the proposed boom defences, were 'in our hands'. It was known that the fleet would be in Rosyth for some days but the operation should not be delayed, since moon and tides were ideal and the new defences could be put in place at any time. Heifer had sent his last report and was to be withdrawn. It would be too risky to leave him in place. Given his position, he was bound to come under suspicion.

Despite her hunger, Emily paused, sandwich in hand. She imagined the little back room in the immaculate Rotterdam house, with TR/16 reporting slowly and carefully, checking Henry Landau's translations, patiently answering his questions. 'So we know when the operation is,' she said, 'but not what? What the target is.'

'The fleet,' said Mansfield Cumming. 'Has to be. They don't mention it by name but what else is there in Rosyth? What we don't know is how. How do they think a few torpedo boats could get through even the existing defences? Madness, even on a moonless night. Once upstream of the Forth Bridge they'll be heard and seen and once seen they'll be blasted out of the water before they reach the dockyard. And even if they did reach it they'll never get out again, as they seem to think they will.'

'But why would they – might they – want TR/16 or another explosives expert along with them? Is TR/16 an explosives expert?'

'Mine-laying, sir,' said Nigel confidently. 'That's what it will be. They'll be laying mines to lock the fleet in.'

The Chief shook his head. 'No time for hanging around outside the dockyard dropping things into the water. Suicidal. And even if they did, they must know we'd sweep up any mines pretty sharply. It's madness, as I say. But one thing we know about the Hun: he may be many things but he's not actually mad. He knows what he's about. There's something we're not getting.'

Emily's question remained unanswered. She was surprised

by how concerned she suddenly felt about TR/16, but she had no time to dwell on it because Nigel had begun his own, somewhat less concise, account. He described what he had witnessed at the castle and how he had followed the tall cloaked figure through gusting rain all the way to the railway station where the man boarded an Edinburgh train. He must have had a return ticket, because Nigel nearly missed the train while buying his own. Fortunately he had enough money on him, although when he had dressed for the operation he hadn't anticipated needing any, he said more than once. As it was, he had to stand all the way in the corridor in order to be sure of seeing where the man left the train.

'Never mind all that, tell Miss Grey what happened when you got here,' said the Chief.

In Edinburgh he followed the man on foot from Waverley station to a pub, the Sad Cow in the New Town. Or not in the New Town, a bit beyond it. Quite a walk. It was small, hardly more than a bar, and Nigel loitered outside before following the man in, not wanting to be obvious. When he did enter, he was just in time to see the back of the man being ushered through a door leading to stairs behind the bar. 'They know him there. I could tell from the way the barman was talking to him as he showed him upstairs. So I stood at the bar and ordered a drink and sat down to wait.'

'Did you see his face?' asked the Chief. 'Colour of hair, beard, clean-shaven, distinguishing features?'

'I only ever saw him from behind and he kept his hat on. I told you what he was wearing. He's tall, quite a bit taller than Heifer. Assuming it was Heifer I'd seen leaving the papers in the turret. Must have been, mustn't it? Couldn't have been anyone else. Anyway, I settled down by the fire in the pub. Felt a bit awkward, actually, clothes still so wet I started steaming. People were staring. After a while I realised it wasn't just that, that it was … you know … that kind of pub, the kind I was telling you about before, sir – before Miss Grey got here.' He glanced at Emily and then at the Chief.

The Chief turned to Emily. 'He means the kind of pub where only men go. They go to meet other men.'

Emily had been in hotels, cafes and restaurants but never in a public house, most of which seemed to be rough, noisy, male places smelling of beer and tobacco. Sometimes there were fights, she had heard. 'Of course, yes, I understand,' she said, but wasn't quite sure she did.

'Anyway, I stayed,' continued Nigel. 'Had another half pint. Couple of chaps came and spoke to me but I … I didn't encourage them. Actually, I was so cold and wet I just wanted to sit and get warm. Then before I'd finished my second half the door to the stairs opened and an arm appeared holding a large brown envelope, A4 size. I didn't see whose arm but I'm pretty sure it was the chap I'd followed. The barman took the envelope without saying anything and put it under the bar. Then a while later – I was just finishing my beer and … only halves, sir, in view of expenses.' He glanced at the Chief. 'The street door opened and in walked Heifer himself. Couldn't believe my eyes. He didn't spot me – not that he'd know me anyway. The only time he could've seen me was when

I passed you with him and the other chap on the footpath, Emily. I was wearing different gear this time, of course, and sitting the other side of the fire, away from the door. Not that he was looking around. He was wearing a civvy raincoat and dripping wet, like me. Breathless, too, and looked worried. He stood by the bar, the end near the door, not saying anything. The barman didn't say anything, either, when he saw him. Just took the brown envelope from beneath the bar and handed it to him. Then Heifer reached inside his coat and pulled out another brown envelope, smaller and a bit crumpled. He said something to the barman and gave it to him. The barman looked surprised at first but Heifer leant across the bar and whispered to him. He looked really worried, Heifer, and the barman did too. Then Heifer turned and left and the barman went through the door behind the bar and up the stairs with the envelope.

'Then, as you know, sir, I went to the police headquarters and asked to see the Chief Constable and ... well, as you know, sir, there was a bit of a misunderstanding, but the message got through eventually and it turned out you were here already.' He raised his glass and grinned, as if proposing a toast.

The Chief did not grin. 'Let's go back to what we know. We know they're planning a raid, we know it's aimed at Rosyth, and we know the target must be the fleet because they waited for the fleet to be in before launching it. We also know – thanks to your good work, Nisbet – they were getting their information from the traitor Heifer. What we don't know is

269

how they intend to go about it and where their agent – this Heifer/Hueffer fellow – is. First thing we must do is put a port stop on him.' He turned to Emily. 'You haven't seen him in the port today? No idea where he might be hiding?'

Emily looked from one to the other. 'Lieutenant Hueffer? You think he's Heifer? You saw him, here, in Edinburgh?'

Nigel nodded. 'The very man, the one you set up for me to see when you walked out to the castle with him. He was the man I saw hiding the report under the stairs in the turret, as I've just said. The same man came into the bar of the Sad Cow and picked up the envelope. It was definitely him. Sure of it.'

'When?' asked Emily.

'When what?'

'When did you see him in the Sad Cow?'

'This evening, between six and seven, as I said. Well, as I told you, sir, before Emily got here.' He looked as if he felt he was being unjustly accused.

Emily spoke with gentle deliberation. 'I don't doubt you saw someone, Nigel, but whoever it was, it wasn't Lieutenant Hueffer. It could not have been. I know that.' They looked at her. Neither spoke. 'Lieutenant Hueffer has been shot. He may be dead. I saw his body earlier this evening. He was lying on the stairs in the castle turret. He'll be in the hospital now. Or the morgue.' She described what had happened.

When she finished, the Chief lit a cigarette and exhaled towards the ceiling, saying nothing.

Nigel Nisbet shook his head. 'It was definitely him I saw, the man you were with that afternoon.'

'I was with two men when you saw me, Nigel.' She still spoke gently. 'The man you saw must have been the other one. It could only have been.'

'Who was that?' asked the Chief. When she told him he said, 'Oh, God,' and poured more whisky.

'Describe him,' she said to Nigel. 'Describe the man you saw.'

While Nigel talked, the Chief got awkwardly to his feet and, without his stick, limped over to the telephone on the wall. For the first time it struck Emily that he might be in permanent pain from his amputation. 'They promised me this thing always works,' he said, picking up the receiver. 'It had better.'

CHAPTER SIXTEEN

Despite her naval background and childhood years around Portsmouth, Plymouth and Chatham, nothing in Emily's life had prepared her for the awesome sight of the Grand Fleet entering the Firth of Forth the following day. What began as smoke and indistinct shapes on the horizon gradually materialised into a host of warships, grey and sinister, low in the water at first but looming larger and higher as they approached. Led by the Dreadnought, *Iron Duke*, Admiral Jellicoe's flagship, they re-formed precisely and silently from line abreast to line astern like well-drilled dancers. The day was clear and breezy, the sun turning the North Sea into sparkling, deceptively inviting blue.

They were watching from the southern headland of the firth. The Chief and Nigel were now uniformed, as was the Port Admiral's driver. Emily alone had had no time to go back and change. She had slept deeply and gratefully in the soft hotel bed until awoken early on instructions from the Chief in order to give a statement to Edinburgh police on her finding

Lieutenant Hueffer. They confirmed he had been shot though the shoulder and had injured his face and head when falling on the stone stairs, but was still alive. Loss of blood and hypothermia had seriously weakened him but the doctors said he should pull through. He was conscious but incoherent, his mind wandering. He had, however, managed a sentence in the hospital. 'Coody shot me,' he had said.

'He must have disturbed Cooden there,' said the Chief, 'while he was concealing another envelope of more stuff. Cooden panicked, shot Hueffer and, leaving him for dead, took the stuff to the Sad Cow and gave it to his contact there, whoever he is. Obviously must've told him via the barman what had happened and now they've both done a bunk, vanished into thin air. Only things Cooden took are the revolver he kept in his cupboard and a briefcase from his digs in the town. Left all the rest – clothes, possessions, uniforms, everything. At some point he must have gone back to the PSO because the plans, including Hueffer's boom defence stuff, were back in his cupboard again. Presumably they were in the big envelope and his contact had copied them. God knows what he took in his briefcase, probably other secret documents he'd purloined from Rosyth. Often hung around the Port Admiral's office, apparently. I spoke to Kell at MI5 and they've put on a port stop but it takes time for everyone to get the message and then act on it. Cooden could be on his way to The Netherlands or Scandinavia by now.'

Emily found it difficult to credit that a man she knew, a man she had touched, danced with, conversed with at length, could cold-bloodedly shoot their colleague. A colleague, what's more, who was so patently good-natured and considerate, who had done him no harm. Would he have shot her if she had discovered him concealing documents? Presumably. But at least Lieutenant Hueffer was cleared of suspicion; Hueffer was not Heifer. She was greatly relieved.

The Sad Cow had been searched by the police and the landlord – the barman – arrested. The bar was known to the police, she gathered, although she was not told why. But since it did not advertise itself, conformed to licensing laws and caused no trouble, it was quietly tolerated.

'Actually quite a nice place,' Nigel had volunteered, oblivious to the Chief's raised eyebrows. 'Nice crowd. Seemed to know each other, most of them, but they weren't hostile to strangers. Left me alone when I made it clear I didn't want company.'

Search of the accommodation upstairs had revealed signs of another occupant, along with a typewriter, quantities of banknotes, paper and ink, and an address in The Hague which Colonel Kell had confirmed was known to have been used by a German spy MI5 were investigating. There was no sign of the occupant, whom the landlord claimed was an Irish commercial traveller who had recently taken the room for a month but had used it infrequently. 'His name was Jepson,' he said, 'or Jephson. Paid his rent, came and went a bit, was never any trouble. That's all I know.' Delivery and collection of large brown envelopes occurred only when he was in residence, always by the same man, who never said anything apart from the occasional pleasantry and never identified himself. Except this last time when he had said to tell Mr Jepson or Jephson there had been a dramatic development and they should both take a holiday.

'Hence their choice of Heifer as a code-name,' the Chief had said. 'Because he was run out of the Sad Cow. They like code-names with connections. Seems to amuse them. And your friend's AWOL Petty Officer Jephson, her Fenian friend,' he said to Emily, 'turns out to be even more interesting than we thought. He told you he had a couple of cousins in the navy, didn't he? One at Rosyth, to which he did not know you were bound otherwise he might not have mentioned it. Turns out he did have a cousin here, according to Kell's people. Lieutenant Commander Cooden, no less. Related through Cooden's mother, knew each other for a few years as children near Dublin. And both related, a bit more distantly, to the traitor Casement. Jephson seems to have been Cooden's contact for getting stuff back to Germany. Gone to earth now, on his way to Germany, no doubt. Permanent AWOL. Good luck to him there. Latest news we have of Casement is that he was chased out of a POW camp when he tried to recruit Irish prisoners for the Kaiser. Kell's put a port stop on Jephson too but, like Cooden, he's one step ahead of us. No chance, I suppose, that your friend Zara was in on it with him?'

Emily shook her head. The suggestion shocked her into indignation. 'No. Absolutely not. She was baffled and upset, very upset. So far as she's concerned, he's just abandoned her. She's no idea why or where he is. As I told you and Colonel

Kell.' But she now began wondering whether Zara would feel better or worse for knowing the truth.

'Less said the better so far as she's concerned,' said the Chief, as if reading her thoughts.

'What about the other cousin Sean – Jephson – mentioned, the one with the Mediterranean fleet? Might there be a network of Fenian spies?'

'Kell's looking into it.'

From the top of the headland the leading Dreadnoughts of the Grand Fleet grew more imposing by the minute. They came on with slow, purposeful menace, grey monsters rolling with the swell, the sun glinting on their wet gun barrels. As the *Iron Duke* entered the Forth it was possible to make out figures on the bridge. Emily had to resist the temptation to wave; it seemed inappropriate, frivolous, yet the sight affected her. She felt a swelling in her breast and had to turn her head away, afraid she was about to weep. It was partly pride, pride in her country, and partly relief at beholding such towering creations. With these, the war would surely not be lost. Yet at the same time she knew it was those great guns, or the guns of others like them – and there were many, many such behemoths in the Royal Navy, spread across all the world's seas – that had done for Hans. For a moment her mind was filled with an involuntary image of his sodden body rotting on the seabed, fishes feeding off it.

She was recalled by something the commander was saying and turned back to him. 'Sorry, sir?'

He was staring at the *Iron Duke*, now abreast of them, and

at the countless lesser craft in regal procession behind the battleships.

'Cloudless the sky and calm and blue the sea,' he recited,
'As round Saint Margaret's cliff mysteriously
Those murderous queens walking in Sabbath sleep
Glided in line upon the windless deep.'

He turned to her with an uncharacteristically self-conscious smile. 'Read it years ago, always remembered it. Ships of the line in the days of sail. Always think of it when I see battleships but can never for the life of me remember who wrote it.'

'Robert Bridges, sir,' said Nigel.

'Ah. Read poetry, do you, Nisbet?'

'All the time, sir.'

The Chief nodded and turned back to the warships.

Nigel continued to surprise. As they watched the *Iron Duke* steam slowly in mid-stream beneath the Forth Bridge, he murmured, 'Fifty-seven feet.' They looked at him. 'Clearance,' he continued, 'at high tide between her topmost mast and the bridge. A lot of thought went into the building of that bridge. It had to take the tallest warships at the highest tide with plenty to spare in case of exceptional tides. Otherwise the fleet could be locked out – or, worse still, in – while waiting for the tide to drop. Not much good if you have Hun raiders shelling our North Sea shipping and you can't get out. And that's not to mention the construction of the bridge. After the Tay Bridge collapse, the design of this bridge was strengthened and then strengthened again. It's not built down to specification but way beyond it. Should be good for centuries.'

'Read about bridges too, do you, Nisbet?'

'Yes, sir. And tunnels. Always have. I was all set to study engineering until my father died and we – my mother – couldn't afford it and so I joined the marines. But I did a basic engineering course at Chatham and I read everything I could about this bridge. And others.'

The Chief stared. 'Very good.' He turned back to the fleet.

Below them, along the shoreline and among the rocks above it, soldiers worked on and around artillery pieces, hauling them into place, angling and sighting. There was shouting and calling. Lorries and horse teams pulling more and bigger guns were parked on the road behind. Two supply boats were moored against Cramond Island, unloading ammunition for the 4.5s. Two others were skirting the incoming fleet and heading out towards Inchkeith.

'Funny thing about the British Army,' said the Chief, 'they either do nothing, won't get off their backsides, or they do everything, more than anyone wants or needs. Until yesterday you couldn't get them to send a single extra .303 round to reinforce positions here. All they'd do is order more tea for the men. Now, as a result of our putting a bomb under the War Office in the middle of the night, we've got half a division digging themselves in, more than enough to deal with a few torpedo boats. Provided they can see them. That's the trouble, you see, no moon tonight, and if there's mist and we can hear but not see we'll have to put up flares, which will probably frighten them off and then we'll never know what the dickens they intended.'

The artillery reinforcements were supposed to be in place, camouflaged and manned by three in the afternoon. A self-styled Naval Observation Unit, which the Chief had declared would comprise himself, an armed naval officer with three armed ratings and Lieutenant Nisbet, was to insert itself on the shoreline beneath the bridge before nightfall, remaining all night. The defences around Rosyth dockyard were rein-forced and all leave cancelled. Most of the fleet would be at moorings but fully crewed and within a ring of destroyers at action stations, steam up, gun turrets manned.

Emily learned the details of all this at lunch in the Rosyth wardroom. They were there for meetings the Chief had with Admiral Jellicoe, the Port Admiral, the harbour master and a disconcertingly youthful and handsome army brigadier in charge of troop reinforcements. Recently returned from the Front, he wore a kilt, had a black eye patch and was keen to get back into action. It was by sitting next to him at lunch that Emily discovered she was not to be part of the Naval Observation Unit.

'I don't quite understand who your chief is or what he does but he seems pretty influential,' he said. 'Mind you, the ways of the navy are always a mystery to us. And that marine fellow – apparently he's some sort of engineer and your chief wants him to guard the bridge all night. Though what a few torpedo boats could do to it, I don't know. Couldn't bring it down. Even if they could, stopping trains from Edinburgh to Inverness and Aberdeen wouldn't be the end of the world. They'd just go round the long way round, as they used to before the bridge was here.'

'I'm afraid I'm not yet au fait with all the plans,' said Emily.

'Well, my job – apart from making sure our guns work and point the right way – is to see that your chief, your marine and four navy chaps are in position to watch the torpedo boats as they come under the bridge. Plan is to let them through so that the destroyers can deal with them when they approach the port and then for us to sink any survivors as they try to escape. Unless we're ordered to open fire on them when they're still in the firth on their way in, which would always be my preference. Hit 'em before they land their first punch. But it's your chief who's giving the orders to open fire. Or shoot, they say in the navy. Must remember that.' He smiled. 'Now tell me, Miss Grey, what are you doing here?'

He took a flattering interest in her and his kilt showed off his good legs. She was enjoying herself and wanted to ask about his eye, but the prospect that she was being excluded from the action was too distressing to permit dalliance. She left lunch as soon as she could and went in search of the Chief, who was still in meetings somewhere. She had already changed from yesterday's clothes in her cabin and on the way out looked in on Lieutenant Hueffer's. The door was ajar and all trace of him had been cleared. The navy dealt briskly with absence.

She walked across to the PSO and found it in turmoil, with

naval police, civilian police, port officials and two men she took to be plain-clothes detectives competing for possession of papers, equipment and furnishings. Jackson revelled in it. 'They all want the commander's revolver,' he said. 'I keep telling them it disappeared days ago and they need to ask the commander about that but they can't find him either. D'you reckon someone's taken a pot-shot at him, too, ma'am, like Lieutenant Hueffer? I reckon someone must've. Or he's done hisself in.'

She left before anyone else realised who she was and wanted to question her further. Back in the wardroom there was still no sign of the Chief. But in the entrance, beside the round table, was a pile of suitcases and bags with a tweed hat on top.. There was enough for a small party of arrivals or departures, but they were clearly all Nigel's. She was about to leave a note on them when he hurried out of the bar, uni-formed and looking pleased with himself.

'Wondering where you were,' he said. 'Presumably you'll hang on here, will you, while we go and do our stuff? The Old Man's in conflab with the high and mighty and I've got to wait here until his car comes to pick me up.' He pointed to one of his bags and whispered, 'Been told to bring my pistol.'

'Why aren't I coming?'

He looked puzzled. 'I don't know – no reason why not, I s'pose. Probably no one's thought. Probably assumed you wouldn't want to. Why, would you like to?'

'Very much.' Conscious of sounding sharp and cross, she made no effort this time to soften her tone. 'I mean, why not?

I've been involved in everything so far, it ... it would make sense, wouldn't it? I might be able to suggest things. How to find Commander Cooden, for example.' She had no idea how she would do that, but felt an example would help. 'I probably know him better than anyone else.'

'Well, yes, I suppose you do. But we'll be there all night. It will be cold and wet. I don't know what sort of kit you've got. '

'I've got wet weather clothing.'

'In that case, better cut along to your cabin and get it and wait here with me for the car. Don't know what the Old Man will say but I guess he can turf you out if necessary.'

She hastily changed into her boots, dress, jersey and jacket, gathered her floppy hat and leather gloves, dithered over her handbag but finally decided to bring it, and was back with Nigel within minutes.

'That was quick.'

'Yes, well, just one night, isn't it?' She tried to sound breezily indifferent. 'Why have you got all your things?'

'Couldn't leave them at the hotel because I won't be going back. Not allowed to leave them in the wardroom because I'm not booked in here. I'll be able to leave them in the car, I hope.'

The car arrived with the Chief in the front. He nodded to Emily as the driver and Nigel loaded Nigel's bags. When she got in the back and the car began to move off, he turned stiffly in his seat. 'Coming along for the ride, Miss Grey?'

'If I may, sir.'

'The car will return here after dropping us off.'

She swallowed. 'I'd sooner stay with you if I may, sir.'

'What – all night?'

'If I may, sir.'

He turned away. The back of his neck and his short bristly grey hair seemed eloquent with disapproval. She felt her heart beating. He remained silent as they drove out past the guardroom.

'It'll be cold, you know, even at this time of year,' he said eventually, without looking round. 'And no – er – no ladies lavatories. No lavatories at all, in fact.'

'I'm sure I'll manage, sir. Thank you, sir.' She had thought of that at the start, a small but irreducible nugget of anxiety. She would manage, she told herself. It might be uncomfortable but at least it would be dark.

It was not quite dark by the time they were in position. The fleet had long since passed beneath the bridge, the army gun positions were still and silent and there was little breeze, but the temperature was dropping. Their naval protection party, as the Chief styled them, had taken up fire positions on the hillside a few yards below the large overhanging rock which the officer in charge called their command post. They were almost directly beneath the bridge. Emily noted some waist-high rocks to their left which she thought she could find in the dark if necessary.

'No smoking, no talking, unless operational,' the Chief said.

They sat on rough grass with their backs against the rock. The Chief was uniformed, with his naval overcoat and cap,

Nigel in his marine equivalent. Emily had her floppy brown hat pulled well down, her coat buttoned to the neck and her legs tucked beneath her. The sun had gone down and already she could feel the dampness of the grass.

'Important to get our ears attuned to the natural sounds around us so we can distinguish anything different such as muffled engines or commands,' continued the Chief, in lowered voice. Less than a minute later a distant rumble became an all-enveloping roar as a train passed over the bridge. They could feel the vibrations. 'I'm afraid that will have to count as a natural sound,' he added.

'Stopping service to Inverness via Perth, sir, last one of the day,' whispered Nigel. 'Won't be another until it comes back at 0739 tomorrow.'

'Thank you, Nisbet.'

'Got my service revolver, sir. Just in case. Here in its holster.'

'Keep it there.'

Darkness intensified the damp cold and a mist came off the firth. Some sounds were permanent, such as the lapping of water; others intermittent, such as the brief calls and squawks of seabirds. There were occasional soft movements from the naval protection party below as they shifted position.

After a while the Chief whispered, 'If you'll forgive me, I have to stand and stretch, get the blood moving. Age, as you'll find one day. Even you, Miss Grey.'

He had difficulty getting to his feet, bracing himself against the rock behind and grunting. Emily got up to help him, glad of the chance to unbend her own legs. She put out her hand and he gripped it firmly while heaving himself upright. 'Thank you, thank you. Not so easy with a leg that doesn't always obey.'

'I'll stay here, shall I, sir?' whispered Nigel. Although only feet away he was invisible against the rock.

'Yes, Nisbet, you stay there.'

They walked a few yards up and down along the ledge, the Chief leaning heavily on her arm. She had almost offered it before when they scrambled down to the rock. His wooden – or was it cork? – leg was already troubling him, she had noticed, but he seemed stubbornly independent.

The river itself was invisible now, although it was unceasingly heard and felt. There was no moon, no stars, no lights out to sea, though there were two or three isolated pinpricks on either bank upstream. The unlit bridge was a massive looming presence overhead, more sensed than seen. Emily shivered.

'Are you cold, my dear?'

'No, I'm fine, thank you.'

When they settled down again the Chief sat with his legs stretched before him. He leaned across to Emily.

'You can borrow my coat if you get really cold.'

'Thank you, sir, I'm perfectly all right. Just a little shiver as I get used to it.'

As the hours passed she continued getting used to it, as she told herself, without getting warmer. Unable to read her watch, she could only guess the time. It must, she thought, be well past midnight, with luck perhaps even getting on for dawn. She hoped it was.

The first indication was a faint rumble, so faint that by the time they noticed it as something distinct from the background lapping of water, Emily realised she had heard it without registering it for a minute or two. She nudged the Chief who, after listening for a few moments, agreed. She wasn't convinced he really had heard it, but within less than a minute it became more distinct.

'Shall I go down to the shoreline, sir?' whispered Nigel. 'See if I can see something. I've got my revolver.'

'Stay where you are. No good getting mixed up with our escort and getting yourself shot.'

The rumble was definitely of approaching engines, and of more than one source. For a few minutes more it was impossible to see anything, but then Emily detected, or thought she detected, a mass of dark moving very slowly amid the background dark. She whispered to the others; Nigel thought he could see it too; the Chief shook his head.

Then there was another noise, this time to the side of them. It sounded like someone slipping and dislodging stones. Nigel reached for his revolver just as a crouching figure appeared on the ledge before them and a voice, low and urgent, said, 'Three craft, sir. One close in shore, the other two farther out and stationary, engines running. They don't seem to want to go beyond the bridge. Shall we give them more time or launch flares?' It was the officer in charge of the escort party.

'No indication what they're up to?'

'No, sir. Only that they're being very careful and haven't gone upstream of the bridge. Unless there's others we haven't heard.'

'Well, whatever they're up to we'd better stop them. Give them two more minutes and if they haven't moved, launch flares and prepare to engage.'

The escort officer slipped away. The dark mass Emily could see seemed to be stationary, which made it harder to make out, but from the sound of the engine it was closer in shore. They waited. 'Better get up and be ready for action,' whispered the Chief.

Again Emily had to help him to his feet. As they waited in silence she heard more scrabbling and slipping, this time off to their right. The escort party was below them and to the left. 'Did you hear that?' she whispered. 'There's someone else moving.'

The Chief had heard nothing but Nigel said he had. 'There it is again,' he said. 'Could be an animal.' He unholstered his revolver.

'Put it away,' said the Chief.

'My gun, sir?'

'Yes, put it away. If there's to be any fireworks I'll give the orders.'

With a startling bang and a tearing whoosh a flare streaked skywards, bathing everything in brilliant white light. It hovered way above the tops of the bridge, flickering on the giant dull red structure, bright enough to show up fields above the

287

far bank, with before it the great black mass of moving water. On the water were three stationary torpedo boats, with guns mounted fore and aft. Two were alongside huge granite piers supporting the vertical steel structures. The third was close to the shore immediately below them, the white faces of men on deck clearly visible.

Sudden exposure stimulated frantic activity on each craft, like a stick thrust into an ants' nest. Men ran to the guns while others jumped off the lower bridge girders onto the flat tops of the granite piers. Each pier had an iron ladder built into it with a torpedo boat hooked to the bottom rung, rising and falling on the water below. The flare floated lazily down, bathing everything in its merciless white glow as men shinned down the iron ladders. Before the first reached the decks their gun crews were training the guns. The forward guns were bigger and slower to manoeuvre, but the machine guns mounted aft swivelled to the source of the flare just as a second rocketed skywards, intensifying the light.

'Down! Get down!' shouted the Chief. 'Now! Roll away!'

Emily dropped to the ground and lay on her side, grazing her head against the rock behind them and clutching at her hat. At the same moment the machine gun on the nearest craft opened fire with a stunningly loud staccato, spurting flame. It was answered by a ripple of single-shot return fire from the escort party. As bullets smacked and ricocheted on the rocks Emily rolled off the ledge onto a steep slope of stones and rough grass, coming to a stop in a foetal position with her eyes closed and her head in her arms, still clutching her hat and handbag. The firing increased into a numbing, clattering crescendo, then abruptly stopped.

She opened her eyes. A few yards from her, clear in the harsh, merciless light, lay Lieutenant Commander Cooden, like her on his side, head in hand. He wore his officer's coat, like the Chief's, but no cap. For a moment or two they stared, blinking at each other, then of one accord they sat up.

'You!' she heard herself say. He got awkwardly to his feet, staring. 'You shot Lieutenant Hueffer,' she said.

He continued to stare, his mouth working.

'Sir! Look, he's here, it's Heifer!'

Nigel's shout from behind broke the spell. The commander looked beyond Emily, reached beneath his coat and produced a revolver which he pointed over her head. There was a spurt of red and the loud retort, then he got up and ran down to the shoreline, stumbling and tripping over small rocks.

'It's Heifer, sir!' Nigel shouted again. 'May I shoot him?'

Emily turned to see Nigel on his feet with his revolver in one hand pointing over her head down towards the in-shore torpedo boat. The Chief was struggling to his feet, bracing his back against the rock. Below them the squat dark figure was wading into the water towards the in-shore boat. A sailor threw a rope with a practised swing. Cooden grabbed it as the water reached his waist and two sailors began hauling him towards the boat.

'Go on, then, shoot the bugger!' shouted the Chief.

Nigel fired twice over Emily's head, causing her to flinch

and duck. There was no result. The two sailors manning the machine gun swivelled it towards them.

'Down!' shouted the Chief. 'Get down!'

She dropped and rolled again as the gun snarled and clattered, making repeated hammer strikes on the rock just above. It felt as if the noise alone was pinning her to the ground. There was more firing from one of the boats farther out, then more single shots from the escort party. Nigel, just behind her, slipped on the rock as he ducked down, kicking her in the lower back and dropping his revolver. It struck her painfully on the back of her left hand, which was holding her hat to her head. The firing stopped and she heard Nigel groan.

She opened her eyes and in the weakening light of the flare saw the commander being hauled aboard the boat. His head and shoulders were flat on the deck and the sailors were reaching for his torso. She picked up Nigel's gun and sat up. It was the standard issue Webley .32 service revolver, heavy, hard to use accurately, but the sort her father had taught her to shoot with. She held it in both hands, resting her elbows on her knees, and squeezed the trigger. As she knew it would, the gun bucked in her hands, kicking the barrel upwards towards the bridge. Always two shots – two taps – her father had taught her. Bring the barrel right down and aim low with the second. The commander was on deck now, almost upright, supported by the two sailors. The boat was rocking up and down. She fired at his feet and he fell forwards, taking one of the sailors with him.

With a loud revving of its engine and a great churning of water, the boat turned about and headed for the open sea. The two others did the same, leaving the granite piers and, in the dying light of the flare, throwing curving glittering wakes as they accelerated. The officer with the escort party shouted that they had no more flares.

'Any casualties?' shouted the Chief.

'No, sir!'

The sky was lightening, with a wide streak to the east. Another flare was launched from the gun positions on Inchkeith island out in the estuary. Receding rapidly, the three boats were clearly visible. The island's guns opened up with four very loud barks, followed after a pause by two more. Their shells fell beside and behind the speeding craft. TR/16, if he was aboard, was safe.

Thinking about it afterwards, as she did many times, Emily couldn't recall deciding to shoot at Lieutenant Commander Cooden. Whether with the intention to kill him or simply because he and the boat he was hauled aboard had become the focal point of their resistance, of return fire, she couldn't say. It seemed the natural thing to do at the time, a continuation of what Nigel had done when ordered by the Chief. She had never in her life imagined killing anyone and if asked whether she thought she could, would very probably have said no. Yet she had done it, or possibly had done it. He might have been wounded or she might have missed, as with her first shot, and his fall might have been due to the motion of the boat. But he was a traitor who had shot Lieutenant

291

Hueffer. He was armed and he had shot at them. She could well have persuaded herself that he deserved it, that it was legal and appropriate, had she had leisure to weigh motives and options. But the moment of decision was an almost unconscious moment, not a conscious process. There was no time for weighing pros and cons. Perhaps in action there never was.

Her companions had no such doubts. While she remained seated, shaking, the Chief shouted, 'Well done, Miss Grey, spot on! You got the bugger. Where did you learn to shoot like that?'

'I'm not sure I did. He might have fallen over.'

'You hit him full square. Went down like a sack of potatoes. Dead as a door nail. Who taught you?'

'My father. My brother and I were brought up to shoot. I don't know why.' She still did not trust herself to get up. She turned to see Nigel Nisbet crouching behind her holding his knee. He hadn't said anything. 'I'd better give you your gun back.'

'Landed on my knee. The one I injured in Rotterdam.'

'Oh dear, is it very bad?'

'That was a good shot.'

'Or a very lucky one. Except for him, I suppose..' She didn't like to dwell on it.

'I think my shot might have missed. Might have.'

Led by Nigel, who was limping, they made their way down to the water's edge beneath the bridge. Emily again gave her arm to the Chief, who leant heavily on it. She felt as if her whole body was trembling but he didn't appear to notice. Twice she had to pick up his stick for him. He grunted his thanks. 'Three of us and only four good legs between us. You'd think we could do better than that, wouldn't you? Watch your footing, Miss Grey.'

The naval protection party was already there, pleased with themselves for having fired their rifles. 'Whatever they intended to do, they didn't get very far with it before we drove them off,' said the officer. 'Not a foot upstream of the bridge. Nowhere near the fleet. Unless that wasn't their target. What do you think they intended, sir?'

The Chief stared at the massive bridge supports out in the firth. Ropes still dangled from each of the iron steps. 'Can't think what they hoped to achieve up there. They couldn't have got anywhere near the track in that time. Much too high.'

'And what would they have done if they had got there – lay mines on it? Blow up a train or two?'

They stared up at the rail tracks high above them. 'Wouldn't have had time to get all the way up there and down again, surely?' said the Chief. 'Unless there's one or two left up there.' He grinned. 'They'd be pretty damn cold by now.'

'Could they have fixed charges on those suspension arms to bring the whole thing down when the next train comes?'

'Wouldn't need to,' said Nigel. 'The way to bring a bridge down is to sever the pivot points – the horizontals joining the two towers right at the top. But it would take even longer to climb all the way up there and down again, as you say.' He pointed at the massive lower girders sprouting up from the granite piers. 'Next best thing are those. The weight of the structure is transmitted downwards through them. Take out one – ideally two, with the linking arms between them – and the weight of the structure will do the rest for you. Bring the lot down. It would need an awful lot more explosive than doing the pivot points, though.'

He spoke with such authority that everyone looked at him. The Chief held out his hand towards Nigel. 'Our resident engineer speaks. If he's right, would they have had time to lay all the charges he says they'd need before we threw a spanner in their works by launching our flares? And if they did, presumably it's timed to go off when the next train goes over. When did you say it was, Nisbet – 0739?'

'Shall I send a runner back to HQ to get it stopped, sir?' said the escort officer. 'Plenty of time, fortunately.'

'Do that. Do it now.'

'That's assuming the bridge and not the fleet was their target,' continued Nigel. 'They may have been intending a diversion here while other boats we didn't see carried on up to Rosyth. There were meant to be, weren't there?'

'They must be standing off in case of need. We'd have heard all about it by now if they'd reached the defences,' said the Chief. 'Not a peep from there until this, look. Come to see what our flares and firing were about.'

It was now almost daylight and they turned to watch a Royal Navy torpedo boat approaching downstream at high speed. Seeing them by the shoreline it slowed and executed a graceful turn, coming almost to rest more or less where the inshore German boat had been.

'That's another thing,' said the escort officer. 'What was that third boat doing, picking up that chap? Who was he?'

'He was their spy, damn him,' said the Chief. 'The Port Security Officer, of all people.'

'He got away with it, then.'

'Not with Miss Grey's sharpshooting. She nailed him good and proper, no doubt about it.'

They all turned to look at Emily. She felt suddenly self-conscious about the state of her hair and clothes. She shook her head. 'I wasn't even sure I'd hit him at first.'

'Oddly enough, I couldn't be sure about my shots, either,' said Nigel, as if announcing a surprise.

There were shouted conversations between the boat crew and the shore party, ending with agreement that the shore party would make its way back up to the road and wait to be picked up, while the boat would moor alongside the gun batteries out on the island and use their telephone link to call for an army bomb disposal squad to search the bridge.

'If they used timed charges they'd presumably consult the timetable and set them for later when it's busier and there are more trains,' said Nigel.

'Not if they knew anything about our trains and timeta-bles,' said the escort officer.

Emily, trying to conceal her shivers, took no part in the exchanges. She stood by the Chief, aware now that his wooden leg made walking or even standing on uneven ground hazardous and painful. He looked thoughtful, possibly troubled. Perhaps the cold, tiredness and age were getting to him. Sensing he wouldn't welcome a display of feminine concern, she ventured a thought she had so far hesitated to voice.

'I've been wondering, sir, whether it's possible that the fleet is the real target after all.'

He looked at her. 'How so? You mean they didn't intend to blow up the bridge? What were they doing on it, then?'

'No, I mean that they do – did – want to blow it up. But not just to stop the trains running. They'd blow it up to bring it down.'

'Bring it down? It would certainly do that if they did a proper job, knew the right places to blow it, as Nisbet said.'

'Yes, but ...' – she hesitated, afraid of making a fool of herself and wishing she hadn't started – 'but if you think about it, if they did bring it down, where would it be? Where would it end up?'

'In the river, of course. Nowhere else for it.'

'Exactly, sir.' She pointed upwards at the great structure. 'All these thousands of tons of steel, these huge girders, collapsed into the river. And where would the fleet be?' Saying it emboldened her; she felt more confident now.

'Well, it would be where it ... where it is, in port.' He broke off, his eyes on hers, nodding slowly. 'I see, I see what you mean. I think you've got it, Miss Grey. I really think you have. Another bull's eye. The fleet would be bottled up in port, neutered, couldn't get out. No need for the Germans to engage in battle since it would be out of action until the river was cleared. Their High Seas Fleet could run riot, they could even invade. My God, they could.' He looked up again at the girders. 'Hold on! Hold hard!' he shouted at the torpedo boat as it began its turn. It was the stentorian voice of command, the kind of shout she had heard only on naval ships. He turned back to her. 'If you're right – and I think you must be, it's the only explanation for what otherwise looks like a botched and pointless raid – if you're right, they'll want to bring the whole lot down as soon as possible rather than wait for trains or anything like that, especially as they know we caught them at it. We can't wait for army bomb disposal to traipse out here from wherever they hide. We must get up there and check for ourselves. And disarm it if necessary.'

After more shouting, the torpedo boat edged closer again. The Chief summoned Nigel and the escort officer. 'It'll have to be you two. Know anything about explosives and demolitions? Done any courses?'

'Had a week on them with the Sappers at Chatham, sir,' said Nigel. 'Part of my engineering course, but it was very basic and they didn't seem to have much patience with—'

'Well, you'll just have to manage. The boat will take you out to the piers, you shin up the ladders and dismantle anything you find. Without blowing yourselves and the bridge to Kingdom Come. And us, come to that. Any questions?'

Nigel, whom Emily thought looked as cold as she felt, stared at the yards of water between the rocky shoreline and the swaying craft. 'How do we board the boat, sir? Without a—'

'Wade out. Like Cooden. Get wet.'

The escort officer went first and was hauled aboard when waist-deep. Nigel followed, still limping. He tripped when he was thigh-deep and almost disappeared, to the unrestrained merriment of the sailors on the boat. When they eventually hauled him roughly onto the deck the boat edged out into the river.

The Chief turned to Emily. 'I'd go myself but for this dammed leg.'

'They'll get awfully cold now they're wet. I hope they'll be able to climb all right.'

'They'll have to. We don't want them to be all fingers and thumbs if it comes to disarming, either.'

The boat pulled alongside the first pier and hitched up to the dangling rope. Then the escort officer climbed steadily hand over hand up the iron ladder. Nigel followed, more slowly, almost hugging the ladder. After he had reached the top, two sailors swarmed up it like squirrels.

'See what difference being a seaman makes,' said the Chief.

They waited. The Chief was motionless, leaning on his stick and staring at the boat as it rose and fell. The escorting sailors sat on rocks and smoked, rifles between their legs. The sun rose, glinting on the water but bestowing no warmth. Emily shivered again.

A seaman reappeared at the top of the ladder and shouted down to the men on the deck below. There was a brief exchange and then the boat pulled slowly away, curving back round to its position just off the rocks. A young officer emerged from the cabin and leant upon the rail, gripping it with both hands. 'German speaker required, sir,' he shouted.

'What? What for?' shouted the Chief.

'Translation. They've found an explosive device with instructions for assembling it but they're in German. They want someone who can read them in reverse. They say you have a German speaker with you.'

The Chief turned to Emily. 'No good you wading out and climbing a ladder dressed like that. You'll die of cold if you don't drown. I'll tell them to send then instructions back.'

The young officer turned away to listen to more shouting from the top of the pier, then leant over the rail again. 'They report it's urgent, sir. There's a timer and they don't know how long it has left.'

Emily tried not to imagine wading out in her coat and long skirt and ruining her boots, then climbing the iron ladder with the weight of wet clothes and with hands that already felt cold and weak. There was also the thought that the sailors on the deck below might see up her skirt. 'I'd better go then,' she said.

'You can't, it's not safe. We can't afford to lose you. They can work it out themselves. It can't be that complicated. I'll tell them—'

'We can send the dinghy,' shouted the young officer. 'We'll have to pull away to launch. Tell whoever's coming to walk as far out on the rocks as he can.'

The torpedo boat revved gently and turned away. They watched as a small clinker-built rowing boat, stowed on the starboard deck, was lowered on ropes by two seamen. One clambered into it and rowed towards the shore.

'I'd better go then,' Emily repeated.

The Chief stared at her. 'Better had. I suppose. Nothing else for it.' He put his hand on her shoulder. 'Mind how you go, my dear.'

The dinghy rocked as she stepped into it, but she managed without mishap. Climbing up onto the torpedo boat was more difficult, until they were lifted by a wave high enough for two crewmen to get their hands under her arms and haul her over the railing onto the deck. As they approached it, the massive granite pier seemed much higher from sea level than from the shore. A seaman secured them with the rope that the Germans had obligingly left and pulled them fast to it. 'Up you go, ma'am,' he said with a grin. 'One hand, one foot at a time, take it steady and you'll be fine.'

The rungs were cold and wet and her hands felt weak, but she took him at his word and climbed slowly. She dared not look down, concentrating instead on the next rung, and only on that. As she climbed higher the wind buffeted her, causing her coat to flap, which in turn made her hug herself to the ladder, gripping harder still. She was glad she had put her hat in her coat pocket and left her handbag with the Chief, but realised she must have lost a hairpin, because strands of hair were whipping about her face. She no longer worried about whether anyone could see up her skirt. She concentrated on hanging on, keeping going and not looking down.

When she reached the top, her forearms were aching and her legs trembling. Getting off the ladder was easy because it continued for several feet above the flat surface and she had only to step off it. The protection party officer gripped her arm reassuringly. 'Well done, they'll want you in the navy now.'

The pier was wide enough to play netball on, she thought inconsequentially, but the wind would have blown the ball away. The struts that curved up from the centre were giant trees of steel, yards across, rather than the prongs or branches they appeared from the shore. Nigel was sitting against the base of one, a length of wire in one hand, a piece of paper in the other. As they walked towards him, a sudden gust whipped her hair across her face again and unsteadied her, forcing her to grab the escort officer's arm. They squatted down next to Nigel. He was drenched and pale with cold, but he smiled. 'Good of you to come. Hope you had a pleasant journey?'

'Lovely, thanks for inviting me.'

'Problem is this, look.' The wire he held stretched across his shoulder and up onto the strut above. Its bottom end was connected to a round brass box about the size of a small sweet tin, disappearing through a hole in the side. The box was on his lap. 'Put your ear to this and you can just about hear it ticking. Better when the wind drops. It's the timing mechanism, must be. I haven't tried to open it because I'm not sure how and don't want to set it off. Nor have I tried to disconnect it in case that sets it off. It's still ticking – here, listen.'

He let go of the wire and held up the box with both hands. She bent her head to it. It was difficult with the wind, but the tick was just audible. She nodded at the paper he still held. 'Are those instructions?'

He lowered the box to his lap. 'Don't know how many ticks we've got left. The other end of this' – he tapped the wire – 'goes right up this girder where it connects to a detonator and primer which in turn are buried in blocks of TNT, scores of them, more than we can see. TNT is a kind of explosive.'

'Tons of the stuff,' said the escort officer. 'Dozens, scores of blocks of it wedged and taped between and around the girders.'

'And those are the instructions?' she persisted.

Nigel handed her the damp sheet, which looked like plain letter paper. 'We found it beneath the timing box, folded. Almost as if someone left it there deliberately. If it is instructions I can't think why they'd need them. Shouldn't if they've been trained. Unless it's designed to trick us. But then they can't have expected us to be here to find it, can they?'

'Let me see.'

'I mean, I'm no explosive expert, but in the military component of my engineering studies we did enough to understand the basics. From what we've seen of this arrangement it looks pretty basic to me. We just need to disconnect it from the timer, which sounds like clockwork. But it's the box itself that worries me, whether there's some trickery in it that would set it off if we interfere with it.'

She held the paper in both hands, her back to the wind.

It was not formal instructions but pencilled notes in abbreviated German, written apparently as a reminder. It was densely written but in capital letters which were not hard to make it out. 'It gives the order of assembly,' she said. 'It says the cable is already attached to the timer which is to be armed by winding the top half of the box three full turns. Sounds like clockwork. No mention of how long it takes to run down.'

'Must be a battery in there,' said Nigel. 'That will make the connection. It's heavy enough.'

'It doesn't mention one. But it does say not to interfere with the timing mechanism in any way and that winding it is the last thing they had to do. The first step was securing the charges at correct cutting angles on the girders, then taping the – I'm not sure of the word, but you mentioned a primer and it's probably that – into position on one of the charges. Then they had to take the detonator from its secure box, holding it carefully at one end between thumb and forefinger and being careful not to heat it with the palm of the hand. Then they had to attach the two wires protruding from the cable to two similar wires protruding from the detonator. Then it says to place the detonator in the hole in the centre of the primer. Finally, they had to wind the timer and withdraw. It also says not to smoke.'

'If that's all there is to it and we can just break the circuit without it triggering anything, it's straightforward,' said Nigel. 'We don't have to touch the timer, just remove the detonator from the primer and disconnect it from the cable. Then we can drop the det in the water if we want.'

'Better get packing, hadn't we?' said the escort officer. 'We don't know how much time we've got. I'll shin up and do it if you can tell me what the det looks like.'

They looked up at the undersides of the girders. The cable Nigel held snaked up the girder and out of sight. 'Better I do it,' said Nigel, without enthusiasm. 'I've done it in training. In Chatham.' He got to stiffly to his feet, rubbing his knee. He looked at Emily. 'Still a bit dicky.'

'Oh dear.'

He climbed onto the strut and began a cautious monkey-crawl up it. The bottom part of his uniform jacket flapped in the wind. Twice he paused, holding on during stronger gusts. When the curve of the girder took him almost out of sight he lay full length, his arms stretched forward. 'More charges farther up on this side,' he called, 'beginning where the others leave off. Designed to ensure a clean cut.' There was a long pause while he reached to the far side of the strut with his left hand. 'Having to do this by feel so it's a bit ... ah, here we are. Done it, I think – yes. Coming back down.'

He descended backwards, partly on his stomach, clutching about a foot of cable with what looked like a short silver pencil dangling from it.

The escort officer took it from him. 'Should we leave the det on there or disconnect it?'

'Makes no difference. Just try not to handle it. They're highly unstable.'

'But it doesn't matter now if the timer runs down?'

'Timer's irrelevant now. Can't initiate anything when the

det's unconnected. But mind what you're doing with that det. If it blows it'll take your fingers off or blind or deafen you.'

The escort officer dropped it. 'Leave it there, eh?' Emily stepped back as smartly as he did.

'Don't do that. Worse thing you can do.' Nigel spoke with unusual sharpness. 'Sudden movement can set it off. Don't touch it.' He rubbed his knee and looked at Emily. 'Crawling didn't help.'

'I suppose not, no.'

He sighed, knelt on his other knee and carefully picked up the detonator, holding it by the cable end. 'Davy Jones's locker's the best place for this.' He limped to the edge of the pier and dropped it into the water far below.

'Will nothing blow up now? What about all the explosive?' asked Emily. 'You said there's lots of TNT.'

'It's inert. We could leave it there for years and it wouldn't go off. Even if we put a match to it, it would only burn. Needs another explosion to ignite it. That's what the det was for. The det ignites the primer, the primer ignites the TNT. No det, no bang.'

'That was very brave of you, Nigel.' She felt he was owed that, especially as the escort officer seemed phlegmatically unappreciative.

Embarrassed and pleased, Nigel shook his head. 'Very basic stuff. People doing it all the time in Flanders, with booby traps and things. So I'm told, anyway.'

'What about the other pier?' asked the escort officer. The third boat went there. Will they have rigged up that one too?'

'Most likely. You'd want to do both.'

'So that one's still ticking away?'

'Presumably.'

This time Emily and the escort officer did not leave the torpedo boat, Nigel insisting with weary finality that he might as well do it alone now that they knew what to expect. 'No point in us all getting blown up,' he said. Neither argued.

The Chief ordered champagne in the Waverley that afternoon. They had all changed and bathed but none had slept. Emily had reached the detached dream-like stage of tiredness, a pleasant but slightly worrying sense of unreality. Nigel looked exhausted, but the Chief beamed irrepressibly.

'You've done well, both of you. Very well. You've saved the nation from disaster and the fleet from humiliation. If it had been bottled up in Rosyth even for a few days, our merchant ships, our food, our oil, our coal, our seaside towns, our supplies to the Front, everything within reach of German guns – London itself maybe – would have been prey to the wolf pack. They might even have staged a landing somewhere, seized a chunk of Norfolk. And you did it by helping to ensure that nothing happens.' He raised his glass. 'Here's to you.'

They drank. Emily, longing for a cup of tea, took the smallest sip.

'Which means no one will ever know about it,' the Chief continued. 'No medals, no bouquets, no thanks, nothing. But that's the nature of our business, we do good in secret, we stop bad things happening. And if nothing happens, that means we're doing our job. But no one knows. However, I know and our masters know. They know already. They are grateful.' He turned to Emily. 'I understand it's still touch and go with your friend, Lieutenant Hueffer. A sad loss, from what you say, if he doesn't pull through. But this war is full of sad losses.' He inclined his glass towards her. 'On both sides. So thank you both.'

They drank again. 'But why?' said Emily. 'I don't understand why he did it.'

'Why who did what?' asked Nigel.

'Cooden?' said the Chief, ignoring him. 'Good question. Always is. Fenian sympathies from childhood, perhaps, knowing he was half-German but keeping it secret, making him feel he wasn't really one of us. Unlike Hueffer, who's open about it. Admiration of German culture? Not alone in that. Plenty do. Resentment, frustrated ambition as Hueffer remarked to you, feeling that as an engineer officer he was second class? Who knows? There are usually personal motives mixed with public concerns. Maybe even money. Maybe they paid him well.'

'But what about TR/16? He's doing the same thing in reverse. Why is he doing it?'

The Chief gazed at her with something of the impersonal, assessing interrogativeness she recalled from the interview with him and Colonel Kell. 'The devil alone knoweth the heart of man,' he said quietly. 'So wrote a medieval judge and nothing I've seen in this game makes me think that people are any different now to what they were then. It's what makes the business so fascinating.' His gaze softened and he smiled and limped over to her, placing a heavy hand on her shoulder. 'I hope you'll stay on with us, Miss Grey? At least for the duration?'

Surprised and pleased, more pleased than she would have expected, her tiredness dropped away. 'Yes, please, thank you, sir, I should like that very much.'

He turned to Nigel. 'As for you, Nisbet, you've not done badly for a marine. As long as Miss Grey stays, you can. Seems to me you make a good team. Don't you think?'

Nigel's weariness looked as if it too had fallen away. 'Thank you, sir. Thank you.' He smiled at Emily and raised his glass again.

Later in life, looking back on those times, Emily was struck anew by how few life-changing decisions were recognised at the time. The big ones were – marriage, for example, or deciding to live abroad – but others, occasioned by chance, mood, whim, convenience, exhaustion, optimism or social obligation, provoked chain reactions either impossible to predict or simply unconsidered.

On this occasion, unwilling to spoil Nigel's obvious delight, she raised her glass in turn and took a long sip of the champagne she didn't want.

ACKNOWLEDGEMENTS

With thanks to David Crane and Honor Clerk for the original idea and for introducing me to Hew Scot's 1907 novel, 'The Way of War'. Thanks too to Derek Hillier for essential advice, constructive and destructive.